# THE ROMAN'S WOMAN

## A SINGULAR OBSESSION BOOK FOUR

## LUCY LEROUX

PUBLISHED BY: Lucy Leroux
Copyright © 2016, Lucy Leroux
http://www.authorlucyleroux.com
ISBN: 978-1-942336-13-6

First Edition.

❀ Created with Vellum

# DISCLAIMER

This book is a work of fiction. All of the characters, names, and events portrayed in this novel are products of the author's imagination. Any resemblance to actual events or persons, living or dead, is entirely coincidental.

This eBook is licensed for your personal enjoyment only and may not be re-sold or given away to other people. If you would like to share this book with someone else, please send them to the author's website, where they can find out where to purchase a copy for themselves. Free content can be downloaded at the author's free reads page.

Thank you for respecting the author's work. Enjoy!

# TITLES BY LUCY LEROUX

Peyton's Price, A Singular Obsession,
Book Six
Coming Soon

Cursed, A Spellbound Regency Novel
Available Now
Black Widow, A Spellbound Regency Novel, Book Two
Available Now
Haunted, A Spellbound Regency Novel, Book Three
Coming Soon

Writing As L.B. Gilbert
Discordia, A Free Elementals Story,
Available Now
Fire: The Elementals Book One
Available Now
Air: The Elementals Book Two
Available Now
Water: The Elementals Book Three
Coming Soon

Kin Selection, A Shifter's Claim Book One
Available now
Forsaken, Cursed Angel Collection
Available now

# CREDITS

Cover Design: Robin Harper
   http://www.wickedbydesigncovers.com

Editor: Rainy Kaye
   http://www.rainyofthedark.com/

Thank you to all of my readers especially Karen Shoridge. Special thanks to Jennifer Bergans and Cynthia Shepp for their editorial suggestions. Extra special thanks to Alexandre Albore for his advice on life in Italy and help with translations. And finally thanks to my husband for all of his support even though he won't read my sex scenes!

# PROLOGUE

Gio Morgese was so eager to leave that he didn't see the toy lying forgotten on the leather seat in his private jet. When he sat down, he winced when the thick, plastic square dug into his back.

Fishing the cube out from behind him, he stopped and stared at it for a moment. Shoulders tight, he set it down on the table next to him, determinedly pretending it wasn't there.

The toy was one of those interactive things with dials and buttons everywhere. It was designed to stimulate and help develop cognitive skills. Gio had done a lot of research before buying it. It had been meant for his friend's daughter, but Calen and his family hadn't been able to attend the impromptu reunion of his university friends.

They had gathered at his best friend Alex's Greek island retreat for well over a week, but Calen missed it because his little girl had fallen sick. The illness was nothing serious, but because she wasn't there, Gio left it behind on the plane. He had plenty of other gifts for his other friend's children. Taking his duties as an honorary uncle seriously, he never arrived empty-handed when he saw them.

Without thinking about what he was doing, Gio stood and shoved the toy out of sight in one of the storage bins. Slamming the door closed with a little too much force, he grabbed his laptop. He started going over the latest reports from work, but his mind refused to focus. Giving up, he set his computer aside and poured himself a large glass of bitter Amaro before settling heavily back in the chair.

Gio hated to admit it, but it was getting harder to spend time with his best friends. And the reason why made him feel like shit. They were all so happy now. All three of his old university mates had found love with fantastic women.

After his divorce, Gio had started to doubt good women existed, but his friends had proved him wrong. Each of those former playboys had encountered a special woman and wasted no time to snap up their chance at happiness. They were even starting families—leaving him behind.

Gio rocked back further in his seat, ignoring the pang in his chest. He'd always wanted children. A lot of them. When he was younger, he believed he would have at least two or three by now. But his dream image of a big family had been shattered along with his marriage.

Everything he'd planned for had slipped away from him. In a giant, ironic twist, his friends now had the lives he wanted for himself. He'd never expected to see the day any of them would give up their hard-partying and womanizing ways for relationships. Or that they would stay monogamous after marriage.

Stop that. They were his best friends, and he loved them. He was the problem. *I'm turning into a cynical sonofabitch.*

Gio took a bracing sip of his drink and squeezed his eyes shut. But the image that had just popped into his head was burned into his brain. He hadn't meant to spy. Calen and his little fairy Maia had taken a break during their Italian honeymoon to stop at Gio's

Tuscan villa to visit. He had put them clear across the house to give them privacy. It was too bad that Calen hadn't availed himself of it.

He'd gone to call his guests into lunch only to find them making love in the garden. Calen had pinned his new wife against an ivy-covered wall, her lithe legs wrapped around his waist. He had been whispering something in her ear as he took her, each forceful thrust punctuated by Maia's feminine moan.

Gio had walked away quickly, hurrying back inside the villa. He did his best to forget what he'd seen, but the intimate scene stayed with him, replaying in his mind on a loop.

It was unsettling. He wasn't jealous exactly. Well, yes, he was. But not over Maia—although she was a doll. But it wasn't her he wanted. It was the *feeling* he coveted.

Passion.

That was what he'd seen in the garden, what he saw when visiting his friends. Though he'd had his share of lovers, he realized now he'd never experienced true passion. Lust, yes, but passion was different, wasn't it? With passion came love. Or at least, it was supposed to.

Once upon a time, he thought he'd found both. He'd been dead wrong. Now he knew what the real thing looked like. However, the knowledge came only from observation. He hadn't been fortunate enough to learn the lesson first-hand.

Enough of this. Dwelling on the past would only make things worse. He was done regretting his ill-fated marriage. His tendency for introspection was bad for his soul. It was holding him back and making him bitter.

He downed the rest of his drink and straightened in his chair. A renewed sense of purpose flooded through him. From now on, he would keep an open mind. If his friends had found genuine and loving partners, there was a chance for him to do the same.

One thing was clear—something had to change, and it was probably him.

# CHAPTER 1

## TWO MONTHS LATER

Gio threw the tabloid rag on the seat next to him and swore. *"Puttana d'Eva maiala troia!"*

He wished he was home so he could burn the damn thing in the fireplace. A little dramatic, but fire seemed like a good way to destroy the filth.

Was his marriage going to haunt him forever? Even now, after his divorce had been final for years, it was coming back to bite him in the ass.

It had started a few weeks ago. His ex-wife, Maria Gianna, had gotten involved in yet another car accident. She was cited for reckless driving. A few days after the drug tests came back, she was charged with *guida in stato d'ebrezza*, or driving under the influence. Despite being known as a party girl, the fact she had multiple drugs in her system had been a surprise to him. She'd never been associated with drugs, at least not publicly. And he wasn't the only one who hadn't known.

The press was having a field day with the new revelation. Which was typical. As much as the gossip rags liked to build someone up, they loved tearing them down even more, as Maria Gianna was learning the hard way.

It was a lesson long in the making, one she deserved as far as he was concerned. When he'd first heard the news, he thought it would be a good thing for her in the long run—until she did her first "interview" afterward.

Maria's response to the negative attention was to shift the blame elsewhere. And she'd chosen him as her scapegoat.

It had been subtle at first. The interview had been full of half-truths and barely recognizable innuendo about the role of a "significant ex" in her current predicament. She didn't name him, but Gio had read between the lines, as had many others. She twisted things around, making her drug use his fault. She didn't come right out and say it, but the implication had been clear. He'd been not only the catalyst for her current drug use but the enabler—the one who'd introduced her to that *merda* in the first place.

He'd been so caught off guard by the ridiculous accusation, he'd said nothing. Not that he'd been asked to comment by the press. His name was nowhere in the article. In fact, there were no solid details in the story to identify him, thwarting his ability to bring a libel suit, which he hadn't even considered at first.

He was definitely considering it now.

In the last few weeks, the whispers had continued. And they were becoming more pernicious. The words *"physical and emotional abuse"* had made their way into the rag. Not from Maria Gianna herself, but a supposedly trusted friend, who also went unnamed. Not that he needed the culprit's name spelled out in black and white. Vincenzo's father owned the damn paper.

Gio had done his best to ignore the gossip before, but this new smear campaign was something else entirely. Even his father knew that. His retired parent had dropped in unexpectedly this morning, coming to Rome from their Venetian villa where he spent most of his time. Tobias, Maria Gianna's father, had sent him. They were both worried about what Gio would do.

He was still deciding what that should be. His grounds for a libel suit were getting clearer, although the gossip rags still hadn't printed his name. But Salvatore and Tobias were frantic to avoid an escalation of hostility between their children. His father had even gone so far to suggest that Maria Gianna was simply trying to get his attention, and if they sat down to dinner together, they could work everything out.

Gio's blood was still running hot from his father's rose colored view of his goddaughter.

*I should have told him the truth.*

Maybe if he'd been honest, his father and Tobias would stop their foolish fantasies. But Gio hadn't been able to do it. He couldn't bring himself to destroy his ex in their eyes. It would have broken both their hearts. Of course, now he had to. He couldn't allow Maria Gianna's lies to harm his position as head of the Morgese Bank.

Gio stared at his hands, wondering how he'd gotten to this place. A libel lawsuit was sordid. He had always prided himself on his integrity, in his business and personal life. He had never stolen, lied, or cheated anyone in his life.

Which may have been why he'd taken his divorce so hard. When it was finally over, he no longer loved his wife. In fact, he hadn't ever really known her. But it was as if Maria Gianna's actions had tainted him somehow. Betrayal wasn't a strong enough word to describe how he'd felt. He was *affronted*. His personal sense of honor had been tainted by proxy.

Well, honor would only get him so far. He grabbed the news sheet and tossed it to the floor with enough force to make him glad the privacy partition was up.

His phone buzzed, signaling a text. It was from Charles, his VP of public relations.

*Where are you??? -C*

Three question marks meant Charles was crawling up the walls right now. Gio was supposed to meet him before the event to strategize about the latest tabloid rumors.

*Stuck in traffic,* he typed back.

*The ceremony is about to start. Do you want me to delay? -C*

Gio glanced at his watch. *Damn.* It was already past eight. The annual Morgese Foundation Charity dinner had already begun.

The bank's charity arm was very active. It was a point of pride with Gio. Since he'd taken over, he'd expanded their directive, trying to make it an efficient and lean organization that still managed to fund more programs than in years past. In addition to the usual social improvement endeavors, the foundation now backed ecological and biomedical research. He was eager to meet the two scientists awarded major research grants this year.

Lifting his head, he scanned the traffic. The car hadn't budged in the last five minutes. He was going to have to catch up with Kamal Patel and Sophia Márquez after the ceremony.

He texted back. *No. You're going to have to give out the awards. There must be an accident up ahead.*

Gio put down his phone, simultaneously guilty and relieved that he wouldn't be the focus of all those eyes turned to the stage this evening. Instead, he could slip in afterward, meet with key people, and then duck out after an hour or so.

How convenient for me, he mocked himself. Even though the traffic was out of his control, not showing up in time felt like a cop out. He had been looking forward to this event all week. But now he was letting Maria Gianna's drama get to him.

It was almost nine by the time Gio ran up the steps to the hotel ballroom where the foundation dinner was taking place. He stopped in the lobby restroom to straighten his tie unnecessarily, still reluctant to be the cynosure of so much attention. Taking a deep breath, he left the bathroom and headed for the double doors leading to the ballroom. Briefly, he paused and braced himself before running the gauntlet.

*Okay, enough procrastination.* He opened the doors and walked inside.

Despite the unsavory rumors swirling around him, he was surrounded almost immediately. Hands were shaken, polite small talk was made. People determined to speak to him came and went steadily for the next hour. One or two women even hit on him, which was strange under the circumstances—unless they hadn't heard the rumors. This was an international crowd, and his name had been carefully left out of today's latest gutter story.

Smiling politely, he extricated himself from a conversation with one of the foundation's smaller grant winners from the previous year. They had been lobbying steadily for more funds, but as far as Gio was concerned they hadn't produced sufficient results to justify an increase yet. After making that clear as politely as he could, he escaped to find Charles.

Luck was with him. Charles was with the Kamal Patel. Patel was a water ecologist, specializing in risk resource management. His work assessed drought patterns and made recommendations about the most efficient water conservation methods tailored to local conditions. It was research that areas like California sorely needed, although it was doubtful Patel's recommendations would make much headway in the bureaucracy of local government. Despite that, Gio believed the effort had to be made. Perhaps there was more he could do to get Patel heard.

He'd gotten so caught up in the conversation, that he hadn't looked for the other principal grant winner, Sophia Márquez. Dr. Márquez was a neurologist specializing in Alzheimer's disease and other degenerative disorders. The project the Morgese foundation had funded was for exploratory research on the tie between pathogens and the diseases she studied. One of the pathogens, *Toxoplasma gondii*, was a compelling suspect.

Dr. Márquez's research proposal described how mice infected with the parasite would become reckless. They exposed themselves to cats, effectively courting death so the parasite could pass to a feline host. Pregnant women were already rigorously tested for exposure to the parasite, but it was only in the last few years that a tie had been made between the parasite and altered behavior in humans. Men, in particular, became more careless with exposure, almost as if they too were courting death so the parasite could be passed on. Gio found the idea chilling.

Sophia Márquez's suggestion that parasites like *T. gondii* could be tied to diseases like Alzheimer's or schizophrenia was enough to make Gio sit up and take notice. After confirming the stellar quality of Dr. Márquez's credentials, he put her name at the top of his funding list.

Gio was eager to meet her for another reason, as well. He'd asked all the applicants for a personal anecdote—a reason why they pursued the projects they did. He knew it was uncommon in grant applications to request any personal information, but he wanted a deeper understanding of the people asking him for money.

Dr. Márquez's reason for pursuing her line of research had been the only one that truly moved him. The doctor's mother had died of a fast progressing case of dementia, one that had been tentatively diagnosed as Alzheimer's. Based on her knowledge of her mother's lifestyle, Dr. Márquez suspected a link between a parasite like *T. gondii* and her mother's disease.

Part of the research involved examining brain tissue from hundreds of patients to find such parasites. One of those samples came from her own mother. Since her study had been a double-blind, Sophia had no idea which sample had belonged to her mother, so she treated them as though they all were: with respect and reverence.

The application didn't say whether or not her mother's brain tissue had tested positive for a parasite. It was one of the things Gio wanted to ask her. Hopefully she wouldn't be offended by his curiosity.

"Did you meet Dr. Márquez yet?" he asked Charles once Dr. Patel had wandered off for more refreshments.

Charles scanned the crowded ballroom. "I don't see her. Should I go find her?"

Gio nodded. "I'll be on the balcony," he said, giving the crowd a wary glance.

Charles smiled sympathetically. "What about our other conversation?"

"It can wait till tomorrow," he said, shoulders sagging. All this socializing was draining. "Just try to catch Dr. Márquez before she leaves," he added as he took in the thinning crowd.

Charles nodded and walked away in search of the other grant winner.

*What time was it again?* He checked his watch and stifled a yawn. It was still too early for him to leave. Making his way up the stairs to the less-crowded balcony, he flagged down a waiter and asked for a grappa. The waiter had just finished serving him his drink when he saw *her*.

A buzzing, lightheadedness overcame him as he took in the sight of the woman below him in the center of the ballroom. The stranger was a vision, stunning in a vintage white satin dress reminiscent of a 40's pin-up. Her hair was dark brown with gleaming mahogany highlights, with lips that were red and full. Her skin was a light caramel color that complimented her exotically attractive features. And her body was outrageous...

There was simply no other description for it. Curves that should have been illegal filled out that satin with a flair that dropped his IQ several points.

Gio shifted, uncomfortably aware that he was aroused. He'd never gotten that hot and hard so fast before. Feeling like a stupid teenager, he downed his drink. He was grateful for the protection the balcony wall offered as he stared down at his siren, memorizing her face and every delicious curve.

She was probably married. Or a lesbian. That was the kind of luck he was having these days.

He shook his head and tried to get a grip. Even if she wasn't available, he had to meet her—just as soon as he composed himself. Surely the siren would notice a raging hard-on if he went to shake her hand right now. It was an embarrassing position for a man who prided himself on his self-control.

Clutching his empty glass, he used his free hand to grip the railing. A flare of what could only be jealousy spiked through him when his siren laughed at something the man next to her said—a man he hadn't noticed through his haze of lust. There was actually a cluster of men, all standing way too close to her. Irritated, Gio glared at the men as if he could will them away with the power of his mind.

Footsteps behind him signaled Charles' return. "I'm sorry, I was waylaid on the stairs. I didn't see her. She's probably in the restroom," he said, huffing a bit as he joined Gio on the balcony.

Gio waved the excuse away and pointed at the siren. "Who is that?"

Charles leaned over the railing. "Oh, good. You found her."

Startled, Gio glanced at him. He couldn't mean the siren. "No, the woman in the white dress. Who is she?"

Charles gave him a knowing smile. "That is Dr. Márquez, hiding in plain sight. I spoke to her earlier. Shall I call her over?"

Gio stilled. That couldn't be Sophia Márquez. No doctor looked like that. That woman down there was his fantasy pin-up, not an M.D. who cut up brains for a living.

*Crap.*

Was she married? The grant application didn't include any personal questions about family beyond what the applicant shared in their personal anecdote. Had he at least included marital status on the questionnaire? If he had, he couldn't remember what hers had been. All he could recall was the details of her work.

"Gio?" Charles was waving a hand in front of his face with a smirk.

Feeling himself redden, Gio shook his head. "No, I'll introduce myself. I should apologize for missing the ceremony," he said, straightening his suit jacket.

"Okay." Charle's voice was smug, but Gio didn't care.

Dr. Márquez had broken from the thinning crowd. Worried she was leaving, he hurried after her, taking the steps down from the balcony two at a time.

Getting down to the center of the ballroom was easier said than done. Twice he was stopped by acquaintances eager to network. With poorly concealed impatience, he dismissed them as quickly as he could. When he had finally broken away, there was no sign of Dr. Márquez. He glanced up at the balcony where his friend was obviously trying to stop laughing. Glowering, Gio waved, and Charles pointed at the main ballroom doors.

He swore under his breath and hurried out in pursuit. After checking the richly appointed hotel lobby for white satin and not finding it, he shot to the door and scanned the sidewalk outside. There was no sign of the siren.

"*Merda!*" he vented, startling a well-dressed older couple he hadn't noticed next to him.

Embarrassed, he apologized profusely before going back inside. Missing Sophia Márquez tonight was a disappointment, but he knew her name and where she worked. There would be another chance to meet her. As an important donor, it wasn't out of the question for him to set up an inspection of the lab where she worked.

The grant he'd awarded her was large enough to guarantee she had to meet him personally, maybe even take him out to dinner if he hinted at it. And her laboratory was a short flight away, not far from where his best friend Alex's wife Elynn worked. Placated by the thought of visiting Alex again and meeting the doctor, he headed back inside.

A few hours later, he was home in his city penthouse. Sophia Márquez's bio was open on his laptop, along with several tabs featuring some flattering profiles on her various research projects. There was no mention of a spouse in any of it, but that was no guarantee there wasn't one. On impulse, he shot off an email to Enzo, his head of security.

A little more information on the good doctor couldn't hurt. At least he'd know whether or not there was any point in indulging his sudden and unexpected crush.

# CHAPTER 2

## THREE DAYS LATER

*G*io resisted the urge to throw the phone across the room.

"You can't be serious," he ground out in Italian, pacing his office in the gym shorts he'd been forced to change into.

Across the line, his father sighed, his voice tired but inflexible. "It's not Lucca's fault. He's young and easily led."

"I don't care about that. If he doesn't understand the concept of family loyalty, he's out," Gio finished in a tone of barely restrained anger.

He had never been this close to losing his temper in a long while. He wanted to break something.

"Lucca didn't know what he was saying. He's still a child."

Gio took a deep breath and closed his eyes, but the words still came out clipped and hard. "He's nineteen, not twelve. That's old enough to know better. As of this moment, he's done with the family trust. There won't be a dime for him. If Aunt Perla wants to keep bailing him out from her share, that's up to her, but I'm done with him. He was already on probation as far as I was concerned after that fight he started at the club in Palermo."

Salvatore cleared his throat. "Lucca assured me he didn't start that fight. He was just in the wrong place at the wrong time. Can't you forgive and forget? You were young once, too."

Yes, he had been, but he'd never been stupid. Always the dutiful son, Gio would have swallowed his own tongue before picking a fight with anyone.

"The fact you still believe that shows me how hard you are working at avoiding reality," he said bluntly. "Lucca started the fight. I spoke to the club's manager and bouncer personally. He was drunk and belligerent. As for the latest mess, Lucca has been seen with Maria Gianna around town several times in the past week at all the local hotspots. She has him wrapped around her little finger."

"I'm sure Maria Gianna didn't ask him to lie," his father replied. "He became confused and told the tabloid what he thought she would've wanted him to say. Everyone is aware that there's some tension between the two of you. He was probably just trying to impress her and her circle."

Gio passed a weary hand over his face. His father's gift for understatement was a special kind of blindness. With a sigh he realized part of this was his own fault. He should have told his father everything, but he was, even after all this time, still trying to protect Maria Gianna. And himself.

There was no getting out of it now. But telling his father he'd been cuckolded wasn't something he wanted to do over the phone. It would have to wait till he saw him in person.

His cousin's involvement, however, would end here. The tabloids were spreading Gio's name everywhere now, thanks to Lucca going on record about Gio's "cold and forbidding behavior" toward his wife during their short-lived marriage. Now the abuse rumors were gaining ground, and other so-called friends and strangers were chiming in with their two cents. *Gossip mongers.*

"I don't care who Lucca was trying to impress. He barely even knew Maria Gianna back then. He came to see us once the entire time we were married. And because he's talking out of his ass, I'm getting dragged through the mud. Lucca is cut off. That's my final word."

Out of the corner of his eye, he saw Enzo come in while his father tried to reason with him. He waved his head of security to sit down.

"Can't you sit down with Lucca and explain to him why you're upset?"

Gio ground his teeth before answering. "If he doesn't know already then he's an idiot. Tell him he just pissed away his inheritance and that there will be a lawsuit. If he doesn't want to be added to my libel suit, tell him to keep his mouth shut from now on. And to go back to school. His mother is probably beside herself since he quit."

At Enzo's raised eyebrow, he wrapped up his call. "I'm going to come see you this weekend. We need to have a long talk, all right?"

"*Si*," his father agreed, clearly exhausted. "I love you, *mi figlio*."

"I love you, too Papà," he said, a little flatly, before hanging up.

Enzo was watching him with an expression of benign sympathy. He was a Brooklyn-born Italian who'd spent years in the NYPD. "I bet this isn't what your Aunt Perla intended when she asked you to take over her and Lucca's finances."

Gio leaned back in his chair. "There were no finances to speak of when I took over her accounts. My uncle Cosimo was a great guy, but a lousy businessman. I wish he was still around. Lucca wouldn't be acting out if he was."

His grizzled security chief smiled. "You know, I never believed knowing how to make money would be a burden until I came to work for you. I don't envy you." Enzo paused. "Do I want to know why you're in your gym clothes?"

Gio moved to the wet bar to pour himself a grappa. He rarely used the bar in his office unless he was entertaining clients, but it had been a hell of a week.

"Someone spilled coffee on me," he lied.

The reality was the coffee, a frozen latte of some kind, had been thrown at him on his way back from lunch. He'd wanted to believe it was an accident, but the words the culprit shouted at him had quickly disabused him of that idea.

"So it has nothing to do with the #GetGio hashtag trending on twitter?"

He frowned. "If you already know what happened why are you asking me about it?"

Enzo squinted at him. "Just wanted to see if you wanted me to do anything about it."

Gio shook his head. "It was a teenage fangirl of Maria Gianna's."

"So that's a no?"

"It's a no."

"Well, I have some news that may cheer you up," Enzo said, waving a manila folder at him.

"I don't think there's anything that could," he grumbled.

"This might," Enzo said with a mysterious smile. "I tracked down Sophia Márquez."

Gio stilled. "We already know where she works," he pointed out.

He was a little embarrassed about his reaction to the doctor. He kept telling himself it was an aberration. With all the crap going on in his personal life, he'd been unbalanced and ended up overre-acting to a beautiful woman.

"She's not been at work the last few days," Enzo said with a raised brow, looking down at the sheets in his folder. "She's taking a holiday, so a surprise inspection of the lab should wait."

He nodded, still flushed. Asking Enzo to do a background check on the doctor had been too much. He would visit the lab somewhere down the line, but rushing to Oxford now smacked of desperation.

"I'll get around to that. Maybe next month or the month after. It was premature of me to ask you to look into her personal life.

I'm actually rethinking meeting her right now," he said, not meeting Enzo's eyes.

Enzo coughed. "So the fact that she's still here in Rome wouldn't interest you?"

Gio set down the crystal glass with a loud thump. "What?"

"The holiday she's taking is here in Rome. Or Italy, in general. She went to Milan right after the Morgese Foundation dinner and is back here today for some reason. Tonight she heads out to Florence. There's a train ticket reservation under her name."

Indecision froze him in place. "Oh," he said.

He should have guessed that a visitor to the city would take advantage of the award dinner to take a vacation, especially in a place like this. Not everyone rushed back to work.

"Yes," Enzo said, clearing his throat. "Dr. Márquez checked out of her hotel already, although she left a large suitcase in their luggage storage. Right now she's at a cafe on the Via Veneto. She asked their concierge for specific directions."

Damn, Enzo was good.

The Via Veneto was an elegant street lined with coffee shops that had catered to artists in the '50s and '60s. For the well-heeled and knowledgeable tourist, it was a necessary stop. And it was only a few minutes away. Should he go and see if he could find her?

Enzo apparently thought so. "You don't have time to change, but it's fine to go out in that. You're presentable," he said, examining the simple track shirt and shorts Gio had thrown on after the latte incident.

Still Gio hesitated. Would Sophia Márquez be alarmed or flattered, being hunted down in the streets of Rome? Alarmed, most likely, unless he could pass it off as a casual encounter.

Then again, he was the biggest donor to her research. In her place, he would want to meet his benefactor, especially since the opportunity to do so had been missed at the dinner. In fact, he would have tried to get a meeting after the fact, if possible.

19

Or...perhaps she'd heard the damning rumors about him and wanted to avoid him. In any case, the good doctor was on vacation and probably wanted to be left alone. Drumming his fingers on the bar, he tried to picture surprising her and failed. The idea of chasing after a woman was too much for him. He started to say as much when his security chief forestalled him.

"Oh, and she's single at the moment." Enzo said with a hint of a smile, waving the documents at him.

Gio straightened, his attention caught.

Sophia Márquez wasn't married. An image of her in that white dress came to mind. She wouldn't stay single long...

"What cafe did you say she was at?"

PICKING his way through the crowd on the Via Veneto, Gio marveled at his anonymity. For a man used to being recognized in his home country—and currently whispered about behind his back —it was a welcome change. Apparently all he'd needed to do was shed his standard suit and put on his gym clothes. The mirrored aviators he was wearing might be helping, too.

He stopped in front of the Doney Cafe and scanned the patio seating area first. Seeing no sign of his quarry, he stepped inside the crowded and noisy interior.

She was sitting alone in the corner, drinking a glass of Italian soda. As he watched her bring the glass to her lips, his heart did a funny little stutter, and the blood rushed out of his head in a hurry.

Her lips looked pink and full, even from across the room. Her dark hair was pinned up, and she was dressed in a loose white t-shirt and brown shorts that concealed her delicious curves from the other patrons. It occurred to him that he was disappointed she wasn't wearing the sexy white dress from the dinner, which was ridiculous.

*And if she wore that dress or something equally form-fitting, she definitely wouldn't be sitting alone.*

Walking over to her before he could lose his nerve, he skirted a group of German tourists talking at a near deafening decibel level. He wanted to ask them to quiet down, but unfortunately their volume was necessary to be heard above the din of other conversations and the sound of clattering dishes.

Wincing, he stopped in front of Sophia's table, slipping off his glasses and opening his mouth to introduce himself.

She looked up at him, a relieved expression on her face, and he froze. Up close, she was even more appealing than her online photos or from a distance. Her eyes were remarkable, the color of gingerbread, a few shades more intense than the soft café au lait of her skin.

She smiled at him, and he became aware that he was standing there like an idiot with his mouth open.

"*Bongiorno,*" he said.

"*Bongiorno,* she replied in a mellow American accent. "Are you Gio?"

Shocked, Gio nodded, closing his mouth and blinking. Had she looked him up, too? Was she expecting him?

"Yes. Sophia Márquez?"

Leaning forward, she raised her voice to be heard over background noise. "That's me. I'm so glad you were able to meet me. Kelly would be disappointed if we missed each other again." She gestured to the empty chair in front of her. "Please, sit."

Wondering if Kelly was one of the administrators in her lab, he sat, confused but relieved that she seemed pleased to see him. It had been a while since a woman had looked at him like that, without suspicion. Even his secretary had been giving him the eye lately.

"Am I speaking too fast?" she asked, enunciating each syllable when he didn't say anything.

He laughed. "No, of course not," he said.

Sophia flashed him another brilliant smile. Warmth streaked down his chest, ending at his groin. Shifting to relieve his sudden arousal, he smiled back.

*Stop grinning like a fool and say something.*

It was harder than he'd imagined. Every coherent thought had flown out of his head when their eyes met.

"Kelly said your English was good, which is a relief because my Italian is decidedly subpar. I'm terrible at languages. Anyway, I'm so glad I was able to catch you," Sophia continued with a graceful wave of her hand before he could find his tongue. "I wasn't planning on coming back to Rome yesterday, but when I heard you wouldn't be able to get together later this month, I changed my plans."

"You did?" he asked. Had she been in touch with his office, after all? He leaned in. "I'm glad I'm able to catch you, too. I was sorry to have missed you earlier this week. I was stuck at work and then in traffic."

Her brow creased as if she was puzzled, but she smiled again, and he could feel his tongue thicken and a flush crept up his throat.

"It's no problem," Sophia assured him. "I'm relieved you made it now. Your interview is important to Kelly. Her project met with some setbacks, and she had fewer participants than first estimated," she continued brightly, handing him a thick manila envelope.

"Interview? I'm sorry, what's this?" he asked, opening the envelope and fingering the thick sheaf of papers inside. Had Charles forgotten to mention a PR commitment?

She leaned in again. "It's more intimidating than it looks, but if you like I can go through it question by question. Can you read English as well as you speak it?"

He met her eyes, his brow creasing. "I'm proficient," he said, trying not to sound amused.

Sophia blushed and adjusted the neckline of her shirt. "Sorry, I assumed you spoke it regularly as part of your work, but didn't know if you had occasion to write it often. The questions are fairly self-explanatory. Most are quick ones that can be answered in a sentence or two. The only involved ones are about your personal history—how you got started as a street performer."

Gio's mouth dropped open and he pulled out the papers from the envelope more fully. A small notecard was paper-clipped to the papers with the name *Giovanni Berardi* neatly printed on it.

"Oh," he said dismayed. "There's been a mistake. I'm—"

A sudden burst of loud German laughter drowned out the rest of his words. Sophia reached out and took his hand. A shock of electricity shot through him, startling him with its intensity. Across the table, he saw her eyes widen, and her cheeks flush. She must have felt it too. Quickly, she tried to take her hand back, but he took hold of it, refusing to let go.

It was an instinctive move, a compulsion born from somewhere deep inside him. And suddenly he didn't want to tell her his name. He didn't want to see that light in her eyes turn to wariness and suspicion when he told her the truth of who he was.

*Didn't you wish for a chance like this?* An opportunity to get to know her without the cloud of Maria Gianna's crap accusations hanging over him?

It could be a completely clean start. What if he waited to enlighten her? There was a chance he could make some headway and secure a favorable first impression before he told her his name. *Remember the latte…*

"Can I take you to dinner?"

The words were out before he could rethink them. Across from him, Sophia's lips parted, but if she made a sound, he didn't hear it. The noise of the people around them was too high.

"It's too loud here," he added in a near shout. "You can go over the questions with me," he said, gesturing to the folder for emphasis.

She hesitated. Her eyes darted around the busy cafe, and her color was high, but she didn't say no. And she didn't take her hand back.

"I was only supposed to give you those papers," she said, running her teeth over her full lower lip before continuing. "I'm taking the train to Florence tonight."

He gave her his most winsome smile. "I know of an excellent Florentine restaurant."

# CHAPTER 3

$S$ophia couldn't believe she was doing this. She was sitting across from one of the handsomest men she'd ever met, and he was trying to talk her into having dinner with him—in Florence, of all places.

Despite the noise, they had been talking in the cafe for nearly an hour, a surreal conversation where she'd been gently quizzed about everything she'd visited so far. And, for some reason, she answered every question, totally forgetting to discuss the extensive interview questionnaire in the process.

"It's too far," she protested with a disbelieving laugh when he suggested accompanying her to Florence.

But he persisted, prodding and teasing her gently about taking advantage of a native's offer to act as tour guide.

Kelly had been right about Giovanni. Her best friend had warned her that the wily street performer was a born flirt. He relied on his charm to draw in an audience and make money.

According to Kelly, he made a lot of it compared to other street artists. Gio was practically an institution here in Rome. She was keen to include his interview in her study, a sociological comparison of the life of present day street performers to troubadours of old.

Mailing the documents had proved fruitless. Kelly had sent the papers twice, but Gio was not the kind of man to spend time on a mail-in questionnaire. When her friend had found out Sophia was going to Rome to accept her grant from the Morgese Foundation, she had recruited her to hunt down the elusive man in person.

And after seeing him in the flesh, finally, it wasn't hard to see why he was so successful. The man was indecently handsome, with a square jaw and fine patrician nose. Behind simple wire-rimmed glasses were the most remarkable eyes—long midnight lashes framing irises the color of honey in sunlight. But his attractiveness wasn't the most compelling thing about him. It was the way he looked at her, so earnestly, like she was the most interesting person in the world. That expression, coupled with his bright boyish smile, was completely disarming.

Gio was nothing like she pictured. He was clean-cut and fresh looking, as if the heat didn't affect him at all. In contrast, she was covered in a sheen her mother would have generously described as a "glow," when in reality she was a sweaty mess.

He was also a lot younger than she'd assumed. From Kelly's description, she'd imagined a swarthy man in his forties or early fifties. But this man couldn't have been more than mid-thirties, and he was almost fair for an Italian. With his wire-framed glasses, he looked more like a really attractive accountant, or someone she'd work with in the lab.

*Someone you would have a mad crush on.*

It was disconcerting, this instantaneous and visceral reaction to a stranger. Sternly chastising herself for her wayward thoughts, she tried to nip his flirting in the bud. He obviously tried to charm everyone—it was his bread and butter, after all. She couldn't take this offer of dinner seriously. Although it was tempting…

His gaze was direct, looking at her with obvious appreciation when in reality there was little for him to find attractive. She was wearing a loose t-shirt with boxy khaki shorts that disguised her big body as much as possible.

She had learned long ago that wearing form-fitting clothes tended to attract the wrong kind of attention. Skinny women and a good number of men gave her a *look* when they caught an unencumbered view of her full bust and the exaggerated curves of her hips and ass.

Sophia would never be a size six, and she was okay with that. Most of the time. But there were moments when she'd catch a sly whisper or sideways glance full of judgement, and she'd cringe with something close to shame. Which was stupid. She couldn't help her body type. God knows she exercised and ate right. But no Pilates class or diet could diminish her curves, no matter how hard she tried.

Kelly kept telling her that the Kardashians had made rear ends like her's popular, but she couldn't bring herself to believe it. The unending criticism from her father, Jorge, about her weight coupled with her recent break up had ensured that. But Gio appeared to see through her camouflage, his appreciation obvious. It was a definite boost to her confidence after the way things ended with Richard. And she *was* supposed to get that survey form filled out.

She reluctantly agreed to have a quick meal with him before her train, but he wouldn't hear of it.

"Florence is a quick ride away, and the meals at *Tratto Stivale* are unforgettable," he said, insisting that he had nothing better to do than go to another city to have dinner with her.

"I'm not sure how I feel about you going all the way to Florence for a meal. And it would be *just* dinner," she stressed, one brow raised for emphasis.

Gio gave her another boyish grin. "Of course. And I have family in Florence. It would be a good excuse to see my aunt. I have to speak to her, anyway," he said, a shadow crossing his face for a moment before his expression cleared.

Biting her lip, she stared at him indecisively for a minute. She couldn't argue when he was going to visit family, could she?

Gio put his forearms on the table and leaned forward. "After dinner, I'll take you to the best gelato place in Florence, possibly all of Italy."

Huffing out a laugh, Sophia finally agreed.

They left the cafe and headed for the train station, detouring briefly to pick up her suitcase. He didn't do the same. He hadn't seemed bothered by the idea of spending the night in another town without a change of clothes, which was a good thing. If he'd asked her to go to his apartment to pick some up, she probably would have changed her mind about dinner. Maybe he sensed that, so he opted to head straight to the train after retrieving her bag.

Once Gio had bought a ticket to Florence—which she tried to pay for without success—Sophia started to have serious misgivings about letting him talk her into dinner. And the reason why made her hate herself...but the idea of a date with a street performer was a little difficult for her, as uncharitable as that was.

She was a highly educated professional, a medical doctor with a Ph.D. She could say, without conceit, that in her field she was near the very top. The thought of going on a date with someone who scrabbled in the streets for a living made her uncomfortable. Though Richard had been her one real relationship, she had gone on a few dates with other men here and there. Without exception, those guys had all been white-collar professionals or fellow students headed in that direction.

Her own snobbery shamed her, so she shoved down her misgivings and ignored them. After a while, it became easy. Gio was an incredibly efficient distraction.

The train ride passed in a blink. They sat close together while he asked about her work. Strangely comfortable around him, she described her research project. He asked insightful questions, and she was a little surprised at how well he understood the technical aspects of her job.

28

She'd never experienced this before—an instant sense of ease. The conversation between them flowed so naturally, she forgot her misgivings about Gio's profession. It was only one dinner.

Once she had dropped off her bag at her hotel, they headed back out onto the sun-baked streets, strolling leisurely. Gio didn't try to fill every silence, but the occasional lulls in the conversation didn't feel awkward.

The restaurant he took her to was small and intimate, a family run place where the owner greeted him by name so effusively she was momentarily taken aback. After Gio exchanged a few words with the owner in rapid Italian, they were ushered to a charming table in a private nook—despite the crowd of people waiting to be seated near the entrance.

"I take it they know you well here," Sophia said, blushing as he pulled her chair out for her. She sat down, feeling as if there were in much fancier restaurant. "I thought you were mainly based in Rome."

Gio's brow rose before smoothing. "Er, I am. But as I mentioned, I have family here. The owners are family friends of a sort. My father and I eat here whenever we're both in town. They have the best white truffle pasta. It's a specialty of the house."

Sophia smiled. "Then that's what I'm getting."

After waving over a waiter and ordering two of the dish and a bottle of Chianti, Gio settled back in his chair. When the bottle arrived, he poured her a large glass, and she sipped the deep red wine with pleasure.

"Have you enjoyed your visit so far?" he asked.

She nodded. "I've always wanted to come here, ever since I was little. My mom loved all things Italian. She named me after Sophia Loren."

His eyes lit in understanding. "That explains the spelling, with a "ph" instead of an "f" like the more common Hispanic version."

She cocked her head at him. "Did I spell it for you?"

With a last name like Márquez, most people assumed it was

spelled with an "f". She used to have to spend a while fixing forms whenever she changed schools or jobs.

He pursed his lips and shook his head. "It must have been your friend, um—"

"Kelly," she supplied.

"Yes, it must have been her," he said after a slight hesitation. "So tell me about your mother, the Italophile."

She glanced down at the table, a wave of sadness washing over her. "She was great. She passed away a little over two years ago. Actually, I am retracing her steps from her one trip here when she was a college student. I have a few weeks off work before I start a new phase of my research. I decided, since I had to come to Italy anyway, that this was the perfect way to honor her memory—by seeing all the sights she loved when she was younger. She always meant to come back here for another visit. We even talked about coming here together, but I was always too busy with work. And then it was too late. She was too unwell to travel."

Her voice was low and thin by the end of the explanation.

Gio surprised her by taking her hand. "I'm sorry for your loss. I, too, lost my mother. It was a plane crash, when I was a teenager. It's only me and my father now. Well, and the rest of my extended family, which is rather large."

She met his eyes, grasping his hand before withdrawing it shyly. "Actually, my father also passed away a few months ago, but our relationship was...strained. We weren't close. I didn't see much of him after the divorce. I grew up with my mother in Portland and, though she has family in Mexico, I don't see them a lot."

Gio smiled wryly. "I'm sorry about losing your father, as well. Even if you weren't close, it must feel like something of a missed opportunity."

Surprised that he understood so well, she nodded. "That pretty much sums up our entire relationship, but we were in a fairly good place when he passed. As good as we were going to get." She shrugged.

"Any other family?" he asked.

"None that I see regularly. They're kind of scattered."

"I sometimes wish I didn't have to see my family as often as I do. They can be quite an obligation sometimes."

She narrowed her eyes at him. "You can't fool me. You love them. It's obvious."

He laughed. "I didn't say I didn't love them. It's simply that they can be a handful. And they require a lot of time and energy. I sometimes feel like I'm constantly on call to mediate disputes and help them out of their difficulties." He finished with a resigned shrug.

Tempted to ask what a street performer could do to mediate disputes, she blinked and bit her tongue. His family dynamics were none of her business. But his description made her wistful. It was nice to have people, even if they were troublesome at times.

"Still, it must be good to have them in your life. The closest family to where I live now would be some distant cousins in Spain. My father was Spanish, although he lived most of his life in England. My mother met him there, but we moved to the states after they broke up. I went back to England to be near him after she passed, but work kept us both so busy we didn't see much of each other."

That was mostly true. Her twice-monthly visits to see her father had been regular, but they'd done little to bring them closer. All he had wanted to do was talk about his latest research study, but he hadn't reciprocated in kind and discussed hers. The best she could do was tolerate the one-sided conversations.

Under Gio's gentle prodding, she told him about her father's position at the University as chair of the sociology department and how she first met Kelly when the younger woman had been a teaching assistant for him.

It was also how she'd met Richard, but she didn't tell him that. The last thing she wanted was to do was talk about her ex. But Gio didn't have that problem. Though he didn't go into detail, he mentioned that he was divorced.

"Just the one divorce?" she teased since he seemed pretty casual about it.

"Yes," he laughed.

"Are you sure?"

"Pretty sure. Why do assume there would be more?"

She gestured with an open hand up and down to encompass his whole body. "Cause this, the supercharged-testosteroney-charm-overload thing you've got going on must work on a lot of women. I can see you with a string of ex-wives. Like at least five. And those are just the ones you put a ring on it. Then there are the baby mama's..."

"The what?" he asked, laughing.

"The baby-mamas. You know, the mothers of all your illegitimate children."

It was an unfortunate timing that Gio chose that moment to sip his wine, because he choked on it, spraying it over his place setting.

Pretending the wine-spray was denial, she kept going. "Come on, there has to be at least three or four of those."

Wiping his face carefully with his napkin, he tried to stifle his laughter. "No, there aren't any children, illegitimate or otherwise. Not yet, anyway."

"Ooh, *not yet*. Making plans, are we?"

Looking her up and down, he smiled. A white-hot panty-melting smile. "Maybe."

It was her turn to choke on her wine. She managed not to spit it out and put her glass down carefully on the table. Heat crept up her face. "Hmm. That stuff is very strong. Delicious, but strong."

He kept watching her with those intense gold eyes, the corners of his lips turned up.

She tugged on her collar to move a little air under her shirt, careful not to expose any additional skin. "Hot in here, isn't it?"

His eyes warmed, flashing gold for an unnerving second. He opened his mouth to say something else, but the waiter arrived with their meals. After they dismissed him, she spooned a forkful of pasta into her mouth and promptly rolled her eyes heavenward.

"Oh, good God," she whispered, almost reverently.

"*Yes,*" Gio said, hissing aloud after taking a bite.

Giggling, she took another sip of wine before digging in with relish. Across from her, gold eyes watched her approvingly, which was nice. Richard would have been hiding a disapproving frown if she ordered such a rich meal in his presence. Her ex was tall and naturally whip-thin. The fact he ate like an anorexic rabbit only added insult to injury. It was refreshing to eat dinner with a man who enjoyed food for a change.

Gio launched into a history of Florence, detailing the local attractions she couldn't miss.

"I feel like I should be writing this down," she said, her head whirling with the list of sights she had to make time for.

He leaned forward. "How much time do you have?"

"A little over two weeks."

"And that's for the whole country?"

"Minus Milan. I've done Milan," she informed him.

"Lucky Milan," he murmured softly, and her cheeks flamed.

She threw her napkin at him. "I didn't mean it like that."

Grinning, he waved the waiter over for the check. He ushered her out of the restaurant with a hand on the small of her back. The heat of his touch became the only thing she could feel, and she was glad the streets were darker now so the blush on her cheeks wouldn't be as apparent.

The *Carabe Gelateria* had a line out the door. After waiting their turn, they walked along the bustling streets eating their gelato.

"All the flavors you could have chosen, and you went with chocolate and vanilla," he teased as she spooned more of her dessert into her mouth.

She shrugged. "I'm a dessert purist. But I do plan on going back there and trying those different flavors of granite tomorrow," she said, referring to the slushy-style drink that was popular in hot weather.

Gio glanced at her from under long black lashes. "Speaking of tomorrow, why don't you let me take you around town? I can show you Firenze from a local's perspective."

Sophia frowned. "Don't you need to work? Or can you do your act here?"

"No. I would have to ask for permission. Every town has its own rules. But I could use the time off. Even performers need a vacation," he said, looking down at his feet. "I need to meet my aunt, which I can do over breakfast, and then I'm all yours. If you want company, that is."

It sounded like a huge mistake. She was too attracted to him. Spending more time with him could be dangerous. And she always played it safe. It was one of Kelly's biggest criticisms about her.

*Aren't you tired of safe?*

Accepting his offer as tour guide didn't mean she had to sleep with him. She was a grown woman with a considerable amount of discipline. It would have been impossible to reach the level of her career was at without it.

"I can show you where to find the best *zepoli*," Gio said enticingly.

She laughed. "All right. Meet me outside of my hotel after your breakfast with your aunt."

Those gold eyes gleamed in the night. "I'll be there at ten."

# CHAPTER 4

*G*io's body was alternating between flashing hot and cold as he made his way to the penthouse suite he kept in Firenze. Why didn't he tell her the truth? What the hell was wrong with him?

He'd kept going over it in his head—the perfect words to explain. But he chickened out each time. He let her keep thinking he was this other Gio, the street performer. It had felt so good to be out from under the cloud of suspicion following him that he hadn't been able to go through with his confession.

That, and she thought he was poor. That had been obvious when she tried to treat him at dinner and offered to buy his train ticket. It was the first time in his life that he had the opportunity to get to know a woman without her being aware of his wealth and status. Even as a student abroad, he'd never considered hiding the fact he came from money.

Things were different now. Since his divorce, he was suspicious of women and their motives. But this was a novel situation. Sophia thought he was poor and she liked him, anyway. Or, at least she seemed to. She had even downplayed her efforts to pay his way in an effort to spare his masculinity.

The fact he insisted on paying had been suspicious. He had no idea what a street performer earned, but it couldn't be much. However, he couldn't let her spend her money on him. Thanks to his intimate knowledge of her lab's finances, he knew what her salary was. In fact, in the near future, her salary was going to be paid by the Morgese Foundation grant. For someone in research it was above average, but nothing near what he earned. Her annual salary couldn't touch what he made in a week. Maybe even a day, if he was being honest about the numbers.

He glanced down at the manila envelope she'd given him as he stepped in the elevator of his building. It had to be at least thirty pages of questions. No wonder the real Giovanni hadn't touched it when it had been mailed to him. Whatever else this Kelly person was, she was too damn thorough. Enough to be shooting herself in the foot by making the survey so long.

He was going to have to track down this Giovanni and make sure the questionnaire was completed. It was the least he could do for his small deception.

*Not small. Huge.*

Releasing a pent up breath, he entered the luxury apartment his family kept in the city. He would tell Sophia the truth as soon as he saw her tomorrow morning. In the meantime, he had a few calls to make.

---

BREAKFAST with his aunt Perla had been a serious test of his endurance. His mother's younger sister was sweet, but essentially a weak-willed person. She had been fortunate to marry a man of an equally amiable character, one who didn't run roughshod over her. Unfortunately her good karma ended there. Her son, his cousin Lucca, had grown up to be a self-indulgent and selfish young man.

In her efforts to make up for the loss of his father, his aunt had spoiled Lucca, giving him anything he wanted and covering for him whenever he was into trouble. She was always there to bail him out and would continue to do so, even now as the youthful transgressions were escalating into actual crimes. The fight at the club would have landed a less connected man in jail.

Gio had tried to explain what really happened at the bar brawl to Perla, but she would hear none of it. She bought Lucca's story of being an innocent bystander who was dragged into a fight by circumstance. And she was unaware of Lucca's damning contribution to his tabloid woes.

Determined to put a stop to his cousin's downward slide, Gio was using the only weapon in his arsenal: money.

When his uncle Cosimo had died, he'd left his family deeply in debt. There had been nothing left, and his aunt was in danger of losing her townhouse and everything in it. Even her car had been repossessed.

Though he'd been a young man at the time, Gio had just been appointed CEO of the Morgese bank, replacing his father Salvatore. His father had been a decent, if somewhat middling manager, but the recession had hit all the financial institutions hard. The situation had been pretty grim until Salvatore had made the controversial decision to step aside and let his son take the helm.

Unlike his father, Gio was gifted at making money. His shrewd investment savvy, combined with a thorough restructuring of the bank's assets, had put it back on sound financial footing. Since then it had thrived, and Gio had become renowned in financial circles. Not long after, he established a family trust for all his relatives, his aunt Perla and Lucca included. They had all profited from his hard work, but the life of leisure he enabled for them had some drawbacks.

That was why he'd decided to act. From now on, Gio was taking over the management of Perla's expenses, from rent to food shopping. She would have a small line of credit that would let her shop for herself or eat out whenever she wanted. The older woman normally lived frugally anyway, more than any of his other relatives. Lucca was the one serious drain on her finances.

Knowing his aunt, she would still give her wastrel son what cash she had. But it wouldn't be enough for Lucca to run wild in the fast lane anymore. Gio could only hope losing his trust fund would be enough to shock some sense into his young cousin once and for all.

His head was full of these troubling thoughts, but they fell away when he reached Sophia's hotel and saw her waiting for him outside. She was wearing yet another boxy t-shirt and shorts that fell above the knee. There was no hint of the outrageously curvy body underneath.

*So the outfit from yesterday was not a fluke.* His hot doctor was surprisingly modest. Or perhaps it was something more…

It seemed strange that someone as accomplished as Sophia Márquez might be self-conscious about her body, but that was what he was seeing signs of. All throughout dinner and on their walk yesterday, she had kept fiddling with her clothes, tugging her shorts down and adjusting the neckline of her t-shirt.

However, he didn't mind the conservative clothing. If she wore something like the white dress out in the streets, she might cause a riot. His countrymen weren't subtle when it came to beautiful women. And he didn't want to spend the rest of the day fending off other men. As it was, Sophia was like a carefully concealed present, a gift just waiting to be unwrapped.

While he watched, she pulled out her phone. A flicker of annoyance crossed her lovely face before she pushed a button and shoved it back in her purse.

"Hi," he called out, catching her attention.

She turned toward him, a bright smile lighting her face. It rivaled the sunshine. Suddenly acid pooled in his stomach, and he clenched his teeth behind his smiling lips.

He had promised himself so many times last night that the

second he saw her this morning he would tell her the truth, but he couldn't do it right now. He didn't want that sunny smile to fade away yet. After lunch was a better time. Or even after dinner. There were so many things he wanted to show her first.

Definitely after dinner, he thought as they chatted aimlessly in front of the hotel.

"How did it go with your aunt?" she asked as he led her down the street, toward the center of the historic district.

He shrugged. "As well as can be expected."

"What did you need to talk to her about? Or is that too intrusive?" she asked.

His shoulders dropped.

"Nevermind, you don't have to tell me," she said quickly, pulling the long strap of a travel purse over her head and across her shoulder.

"I don't mind," he assured her. "It had to do with her son. He's been getting into trouble the last few years and it's getting worse. Lucca is quite spoiled, but he's starting to slide into criminal territory." He kicked a stray piece of trash aside. "I'd rather not be involved, but in my family that's not possible. Everybody is in everybody else's business, and if you're not they hunt you down and ask your opinion, anyway. Demand it, in some cases."

Her head tilted to one side and gave him a sympathetic side glance. "I'm sorry. I understand if you'd rather not waste your time acting as tour guide today so you can attend to your family."

"Are you kidding?" he laughed. "You're saving me from them. Don't ever doubt that."

Her mouth pursed. "Only if you're sure."

"Oh, I'm certain," he said, widening his eyes for emphasis before directing her up the *Via dell' Anguillara*.

They walked a little further and he watched her carefully, gratified when her face lit up at the sight of the *Basilica di Santa Croce*.

"This was one of the places at the top of my list," she said, beaming at him. Pleased, he started detailing the history of the church as the burial site of some of the most notable figures in Italian history.

The next few hours were some of the best of Gio's life. He loved sharing this special place with Sophia. They saw the tombs Niccolò Machiavelli, Michelangelo, and Galileo as well as an altar monument to Dante Alighieri, which she assumed was his grave until he told her otherwise. He also showed her the tomb of Rossini, who had composed the famous opera, the Barber of Seville and the rows of inset chapels that lined the walls—including the Bardi chapel featuring the fresco of the death of Saint Francis by Giotto.

Eventually they wandered to the cloister and Pazzi chapel before rounding out their visit by exploring the adjoining museum.

After that, they were both starving, so he took her to a little out of the way restaurant. He ordered a light veal dish and she ordered lasagna, self-consciously citing all of the walking they were doing as an excuse to splurge.

He was tempted to offer another form of calorie-burning exercise as a more pleasurable alternative to walking, but he bit his tongue. Instead, he suggested they spend the rest of the afternoon getting lost in the Uffizi, and was pleased when she agreed. He was able to show her his favorite paintings by Raphael, Titian, and Boticelli before she nudged him along to the neighboring science museum.

"I should have realized this would be a bigger draw for you than some old boring paintings," he teased as she surreptitiously snapped a picture with her camera phone of Galileo's finger on exhibit.

"I loved the art," she assured him with her hand on his arm. "I just didn't want to miss this. Galileo is one of my personal heroes."

He wanted to ask for more details, but she wasn't paying attention anymore. Her rapt attention was fixed on the dried and desiccated fingers, displayed behind glass like priceless treasures.

To each his own, he thought, taking advantage of her distraction to study the lines of her exquisite face.

Her fascination with the macabre display tickled him, particularly when he asked her what she was thinking about. She leaned toward him and whispered, "Cloning him," before releasing a maniacal mad scientist cackle that drew a few stares.

The visit to the rest of the museum went by quickly, but he still had to hurry her out of there to a waiting car. It took them to the Piazzale Michelangelo so they could watch the sunset from the peak. The plaza featured a bronze version of Michelangelo's David overlooking the city and magnificent panoramic views. He took a dozen pictures of Sophia posing with the Duomo, the massive domed main cathedral of Florence, in the background. After they were driven back to town to enjoy dinner from another restaurant he loved, this one with a view of the Arno River and the Ponte Vecchio.

Exhausted, he and Sophia went their separate ways early, but not before he convinced her to spend the following day with him, as well. It wasn't until he reached his penthouse apartment that he remembered he hadn't told her who he was.

*Merda.* He had sworn to himself that he would come clean, but it had gotten lost in their easy conversation and light flirtation. Tomorrow, he would tell her the truth.

# CHAPTER 5

*I*t had been far too easy for Gio to talk Sophia into spending more time with him. Wondering idly where her suspicious nature had gone, she recognized she might be losing an uphill battle.

Her self-appointed tour guide was magnetic and articulate, with a breadth of knowledge that kept surprising her. From his choice of topics of conversation, it was clear that he was well read and spent a lot of time keeping up on current events. He knew more about the world than she did.

As a scientist, Sophia tended to isolate herself in the little bubble of like-minded academics that she spent time with. It wasn't intentional, but happened as a matter of course. Scientists spent time with other scientists. Her friendship with Kelly and her former relationship with Richard were the exceptions to the rule, but both of them had entered her life because of their ties to her father. And both were academics, too, albeit in a different field.

Gio was her first experience of friendship outside the ivory tower, and it was remarkable how comfortable they were with each other. One conversation naturally evolved into another and another with an ease she wouldn't have believed before meeting him. It felt effortless.

He was content to indulge her chosen activities, too. Their second day in Florence began by climbing to the top of the Duomo, the massive domed cathedral of *Santa Maria del Fiore*.

"Are you sure you want to do this?" Gio asked.

The signs at the bottom warned the visitors that is was four hundred and sixty-three steps to the top. There was no elevator. Many tourists had to turn back, unable to handle the narrow winding stairs that led to the fenced-in balcony at the summit.

"I play soccer," she replied. "Don't worry. My legs won't give out."

He looked down. She was wearing shorter shorts today, and her muscular thighs were more visible than the day before.

Her father had hated her legs, along with the rest of her figure. Sophia favored her mother in appearance, a detail he would never let her forget.

"Must you run around chasing a ball all the time?" he would criticize, adding that it made her thighs too thick.

Which was true. She built muscle easily on her legs, and soccer made them grow wide, much to her father's disgust. Richard wasn't much better in his opinion of her body, and she couldn't help but wonder why he had pursued her when she was so clearly not his type. But Gio looked at her legs with ill-concealed appreciation, and she couldn't help basking in the warm glow of his interest.

All too soon, however, that warmth quickly turned to hot sweatiness as the two of them huffed and puffed their way up to the top of the dome. Once at the top, a hot dry wind whipped her hair as she squinted against the sunlight.

"Are you all right?" Gio asked, noticing that she was hugging the wall of the dome, rather than taking a photo from the rickety railing surrounding the circular balcony.

Tense, she smiled thinly. "Um, yes. I just learned the hard way not to stand close to the edge."

"Are you afraid of heights?"

"Not exactly," she said, still plastered against the wall.

Gio smiled and held out his hand. Sighing, Sophia took hold of it and stepped to the edge. She was fine until she looked down, then her head spun and she had to close her eyes as a wave of vertigo swept over her. She swayed slightly.

"Okay, bad idea, bad idea." Gio put his arm around her and herded her to the stairs.

She laughed weakly and they started down the long winding descent, her hand gripping the rails or stone walls whenever she could.

"This is a recent problem," she explained as they reached the street.

"Did you have a bad experience?" Gio asked, his brow creased in concern.

"In a way. It's the damnedest thing. I was in Barcelona earlier this year for a weekend holiday, and I visited all of the Gaudi monuments. I was on the top of *La Pedrera, Casa Milà*. It has those guard-shaped turrets and uneven floors. It's kind of like a cartoon about knights on acid."

He laughed. "Yes, I've been there and it is a little disorienting."

"You won't find an argument here. I couldn't walk up there. I felt ridiculous hanging on to the walls and railings. And now it keeps happening. I step near an edge more than two stories high and bam—vertigo."

He ran his hand up and down her back in a comforting caress. "No more high places."

"But I don't want to miss anything!" she protested. "Let's just stay away from the edge next time."

"Okay," he promised.

After grabbing a quick bite, they wandered some more, soaking up the venerated atmosphere of the city. She snapped a thousand pictures of her favorite statue, Perseus with the head of Medusa, outside of the Palazzo Vecchio. She had loved the piece since she saw it in her favorite movie, "A Room with a View". When she mentioned that to Gio, she was pleased to learn that he knew it well enough to show her where some of the scenes had been shot. It wasn't exactly a guy movie, but he seemed to have eclectic taste in films.

Despite the crowds and heat in the street, Sophia had never felt so energized. It was like swimming in electrified water, the fictional kind that didn't electrocute you. She loved the way the air smelled and the way the sun beat down on her skin. It was a welcome change from English weather.

Later, they shopped on the Ponte Vecchio, a medieval stone closed-spandrel arch bridge over the Arno River. It was lined with stores, most selling jewelry. She bought herself a silver necklace, but had to argue with her earnest tour guide to be allowed to pay for it.

Gio seemed genuinely upset that she wouldn't let him buy her the expensive piece of jewelry, but she was adamant. He worked too hard for his money to let him spend it on her.

"You can buy me a gelato," she bargained with him, teasing until he grudgingly agreed and they headed back to the *Gelateria Carabe*.

Gelato led to dinner and dinner led to tomorrow and another city. She mentioned wanting to see the ancient site of Pompeii and suddenly they were there, walking through the baking hot and dusty streets. They pored over the ancient mosaic frescoes that had been buried in ash throughout the preserved cities of Pompeii and Herculaneum, and refilled a water bottle from quaint spigoted fountains doting the complex. After viewing the famous *Birth of Venus* fresco, Gio bribed a guard for access to villas closed to the public to view even more works of art.

Throughout the visit, Gio was the perfect gentleman, even when she was blushing her way through the lupanar, the well-preserved brothel in Pompeii. Apparently, the ancient Romans weren't shy about sex. The graphic depictions were found outside the brothel too, catching her unawares and sending a periodic flood of heat through her body whenever they came across one. The images wouldn't normally have embarrassed her, but somehow seeing them with Gio made her nervous.

That night, they ate at a casual buffet place called *Todisco*. They filled up on a delicious assortment of food. Once they were finished she was given a tour of the kitchens while Gio chatted with the owner, whom he seemed to know well. Later, when she tried to pay, Gio didn't argue with her because the owners waved her cash away and insisted it was on the house. Then he walked her to the hotel and went off to spend the night with yet another relative.

The next day, they headed to Naples to view more treasures excavated from Pompeii and Herculaneum at the archeological museum. While there, a friend of Gio's led them through a display of mummies and showed them a few treasures hidden in the storage rooms. They also explored some of the Roman water deposits and a few churches off the beaten path.

Completely spent from the non-stop sightseeing, she let Gio convince her to spend a few days lounging on the beaches of Ischia —a gem of an island an hour's boat ride from Napoli. He didn't even blink when she wore a concealing swim tank and boy shorts covered by a gauzy shirt. He simply smiled as if he could see through it and ordered her a cocktail from a beachside bar. They drank them on shaded lounge chairs, enjoying the sun and view of the crystalline water.

Eventually Gio suggested going back to Rome to hit a few ruins and museums she missed the first time, and she went along, content to follow his lead.

By the time they arrived back at the capital, Sophia admitted to herself that she was falling under Gio's spell. He was charming and intelligent while being warm and spontaneous. Every day with him was an adventure, one she was sorry to end each night.

The fact he was a performance artist was his only detraction—one she actively had to chastise herself for looking down on. Gio didn't fit any of her pre-conceived ideas about what he should be or how he should behave. He was at home everywhere they went. The man was connected, and no one else seemed to think less of him for his occupation. Quite the opposite in fact.

Gio was a new experience for her. The fact he didn't try to hide his attraction to her was intoxicating, so much so that she was actually starting to think about having an affair with him.

It was what Kelly had urged her to do after her breakup with Richard. Her best friend had been on her case about finding a man for some therapeutic rebound sex, but Sophia hadn't been able to stomach the idea. She'd never had sex without a commitment before. There had only been one man prior to Richard, in college. Both times she had been in love and believed she was loved in return. In fact, she'd been convinced that Richard was going to propose when everything fell apart.

A vacation fling was totally out of character for someone as conservative as she was, but Gio was proving to be a potent temptation. Though he was an accomplished flirt, he was also romantically old-fashioned. He opened doors for her, pulled out chairs, and always walked on the outer edge of sidewalks, shielding her from traffic. The combination of hot modern man with old-world charm was devastating.

It was driving her a little crazy that he hadn't made a pass. She kept expecting the obvious come-on or physical overture, but it never happened. Which meant Gio might be waiting for her to make the first move. Someone as handsome as he was surely had women throwing themselves at him all the time—street performer or not.

For the first time in her life, she was considering seducing a man. Her experience with the opposite sex was limited. Her college boyfriend had been a virgin, too, and her later courtship with Richard had been polite and formal, mainly because they were being setup by her father.

She had less than a week left of her vacation. There was the sense of an opportunity passing her by. However, making the first move seemed to be beyond her. The idea of letting him see her naked was too much of a stumbling block. So one day slipped into the next without anything happening.

Now that they were back in Rome, she expected Gio to go back to performing, but he made it clear that he had no intention of abandoning her to her own devices. Other than a few hours each morning, he devoted every day to her enjoyment. Together they toured the ancient ruins of the Palatine Hill and the Roman Forum. He even arranged for an exclusive night tour of the Colosseum, a special privilege granted to them because—of course—he knew someone who worked there.

On one of those solo mornings, she rolled out of bed late and had a leisurely breakfast before heading to the lobby to wait for Gio. She sat in a wingback chair, taking advantage of the hotel's wifi to catch up on her emails. Her phone's reception had been terribly spotty so she hadn't filled Kelly in on recent events, including what was going on with her travel companion.

Kelly was going to have a fit when she read her message. Especially if Sophia didn't chicken out and actually slept with Gio. She could practically hear her best friend egging her on to have the affair—although honestly that had been going on *before* she'd broken up with Richard. Kelly wasn't a fan of her ex.

Sophia had just pressed send when her phone buzzed. Glancing at it she frowned at the ID "Dickhead" and declined the call, texting a terse reply instead.

A deep smooth voice startled her. "Who keeps calling you?"

"Oh, hi," she said, dropping her phone inadvertently as Gio sat on the adjoining chair.

She picked it up with a quick grin and gave him a discreet

once-over. He was wearing tan chinos and a long-sleeved button shirt with his trademark mirrored aviator sunglasses. Every time she saw him, he was dressed more and more conservatively. It was a good look for him. Of course, he could make a potato sack sexy.

"It's nothing," she said, tossing the phone in her purse. "What do you have planned for today?" she asked brightly.

Though he asked for her input, Sophia had stopped planning itineraries for what she wanted to see. Gio's ideas were better. He always seemed to know someone who had special access at all the attractions. They got exclusive tours at all hours of the day and night—sometimes even after the site had officially closed. And he always knew the best places to eat.

Sometimes they ate at homey restaurants that served the best regional dishes. Other times they walked blocks out of their way to find some hole in the wall that served awesome street food, like the fried cod they'd had the other day in the Trastevere neighborhood.

Gio leaned in with a gleam in his eye. "I found the *pensione* your mother stayed at when she was here—the Veleria. I thought we could start there and then wander to the Piazza Navona for lunch. Afterward, we can hit the Pantheon and the Trevi fountain before we stop for some *sfogliatella* at my favorite bakery."

Tears stung at her eyes, and she turned away to compose herself. The other day she had randomly mentioned the name of the *pensione* her mother wrote about in her journal. That he remembered and found it was incredibly touching.

"That sounds perfect," she said, her voice husky.

The expression on his face warmed before clouding over. "Before we get going, there is something I wanted to speak to you about. Something I've been meaning to tell you for a while."

The phone started to ring again, and she closed her eyes. Fishing it out, she glanced at the caller ID. Sure enough, it was Richard again. She let out a harsh breath and rolled her eyes.

"I'm sorry, I have to take this," she said.

Her ex wasn't going to stop calling. It would ruin what was left of her vacation if she didn't bite the bullet and talk to the jerk.

Nodding, Gio stood and walked away to let her speak in privacy.

She swiped her screen and put the phone to her ear. "We agreed to deal exclusively through the realtor."

Across the line Richard sighed. "Sophia, darling. It's about time you answered."

Counting to five, she waited to answer. "I told you I was on vacation. In *Italy*."

"There's a few details on the contract we need to discuss."

"Then talk to the realtor," she said from behind clenched teeth.

"I already did, darling. The man can't address these questions."

"I'm not your darling anymore," she said in a flat voice. "If the realtor can't deal with your issues, then talk to my father's lawyer. It's his house you're buying. I never even lived there. Dad's attorney will be more familiar with his estate. And there's no reason you couldn't text me about this instead of always insisting on calling."

Richard grunted. His cultured British accent took on a nasal, and annoyingly superior, tone. "Texting is for teenagers. And you still need to approve sale of the Chevette."

*What?* "You want to buy that too? Since when?"

Her father's vintage 1970 Chevrolet Chevette had been his pride and joy. He had restored the car himself, spending most Sunday afternoons tinkering with it in the garage, regardless of whether or not she was visiting. It still needed a little work, but would be worth a fair amount to the right buyer.

Why Richard, with his aristocratic tastes, wanted it on top of everything else was a mystery. He already had a car—a Bentley.

"Jorge meant a lot to me," he said. "I'm already going to be filling his shoes as head of the Sociology department. It seems right that I be the one to buy his house and the car he loved. It's not like you want them."

That last detail was true. Not being close to her father, she had no real desire to keep his things. Richard's attachment to them, however, was a little creepy. Selling everything to him had seemed like a good idea at the time, but it was turning into a huge hassle.

"I'll think about the car," she said, trying to keep her tone even. "But I'll let you know when I return home. I won't be picking this phone up again until I'm back on English soil. And start texting. You're not a thousand years old. Join the twenty-first century."

She hung up, cutting off whatever else he was going to say next. The phone started ringing again immediately. Resolutely turning it to airplane mode, she threw it back into her purse. Across the way, Gio cocked his head at her before coming back to sit down.

"Everything okay?" he asked.

Collapsing into the armchair, she wagged her finger at him. "Gio, take my advice. Never date a rich guy. Or rich girls, in your case."

He hesitated and frowned. "What do you mean?"

Emotionally drained, she waved her languid hand from her near prone-position on the armchair. "I mean, don't get involved with anyone with money—especially old money. They're too damn entitled and think everything they say is right and everything you do is wrong. *Noblesse oblige* has become *noblesse I'm better than you so why bother having an opinion of your own.*"

For a minute, he stared at her open-mouthed before he recovered. "So that was your ex?"

Nodding perfunctorily, she peeked up at him through her thick lashes.

"And he's from a monied background? Aristocratic?"

*Monied.* What a weird way to phrase it. "Yes," she sighed. "He's a first cousin to an English lord or something. As blue-blooded as it gets, with a matching blue stick up his butt."

Slumping further into the armchair—and she was nearly lying horizontal across it at this point—she put a hand over her eyes. She couldn't believe how much had changed between her and

51

Richard. When they first met, the sun and moon rose and set with him. His good opinion had been everything to her.

Richard's sophistication had been impressive, and as an added bonus, her father loved him. Being with him had seemed like a good way to build a bridge between her and her obtuse parent. But now Richard's condescension rankled. Even his posh British accent, which she had loved, set her teeth on edge.

"Well, it sounds like you're well rid of him." The words came slowly, his voice distant.

Peeking at Gio from behind her fingers, she noticed how pale he looked. Almost sick. Did hearing about her ex bother him? *Must be.* Some men loathed knowing any details about a woman's past relationships. Maybe Gio was one of those.

"I'm sorry. I shouldn't be talking about this. I'm being a total bummer."

Hands clasped in front of him, he shook his head. "Don't worry. Discussing your ex doesn't bother me. I'm sorry that he's harassing you. I suppose he wants to get back together."

His assumption was flattering, but so off-point. "No, I assure you he's not. But we have unfinished business, and I mean that literally, and he apparently can't wait for me to finish my vacation in peace."

She twisted her lips in a lopsided movement that wasn't quite a smile, but Gio stared at her without expression.

"He wants you back," he said evenly.

"Trust me, he doesn't." The idea was laughable. "Why don't we forget all about Richard and head over to the *Veleria pensionne*? I still can't believe you found it. There were no details about it at all online."

Gio stood when she did. "That's because it's no longer in business as a hotel, but I spoke with the owner and she has no problem with us stopping by to visit."

They were heading out the door when she remembered that

he'd wanted to tell her something. "What was it that you were going to say earlier?"

His lips parted and he stopped short on the sidewalk. "Um, I, yes..."

Shuffling his feet, he looked at her and then down, gesturing to the opposite side of the street. When he stayed quiet, she spoke up.

"Is there something across the street you wanted to show me?"

"No. I uh—I have another job."

Stunned, she stared at him blankly for a second. "Are you giving up street performing?"

"Er, no. I mean I've always had another job. I work...at a bank."

Incredulous, she laughed. "Wow. That's incredible. You're moonlighting on your job as a street performer by working at a bank. Are you like a teller or something?"

"A teller?"

"The person who gives money at the counter," she clarified, wondering what they called it in Italy.

Gio tugged on the collar of his polo shirt. "Um, no. I do many different things. Whatever needs doing."

He must be some sort of gopher, an errand runner. Still, it was something that he was open to working in a non-creative field.

"I think that's great," she said and held out her hand. "Well, should we head out?"

Gio hesitated. "Yes."

He took her hand and she beamed, her unpleasant phone call forgotten.

# CHAPTER 6

*I*t had been the most amazing day. Gio had definitely stepped up his game. They saw all the landmarks left on her wish list, and spent hours getting lost in the Museum Capitolini. After dinner, her tour guide surprised her with an unexpected gift, a gorgeous dress she could wear to an exclusive club opening that night.

"Are you sure your cousin doesn't mind me borrowing her dress?" she asked, fingering the material of the skirt.

It was a figure-hugging black silk number with a square-cut bodice and diaphanous Juliet sleeves. Except for the sleeves, the silhouette was similar to her favorite dress—the white vintage satin she brought for the Morgese Foundation dinner. Like the white one, it flattered her figure without making her feel exposed and uncomfortable. She loved it.

"Marina doesn't mind at all. It doesn't fit her anymore."

Sophia glanced down at the dress. "Are you sure she even wore it? It looks brand new," she said, running a hand over the front panel.

He shrugged. "My cousin has a lot of gowns. Too many. She's

always getting more and giving away the old ones. Actually, she mentioned that you could keep this one if you wanted..."

*Ooh.* That was tempting.

She wanted to keep it, but the dress was of such fine quality it had to be worth a lot of money. Several hundred euros, at least. The tag had a design on it, but no name brand she recognized. Regretfully, she shook her head.

"I couldn't possibly accept it. It's too much."

"No, you should take it. The dress will probably end up in a pile for donation." He ran his hot golden eyes up and down her figure. "Besides, I doubt it will look that good on anyone else. It's like it was made for you."

Biting her lip, Sophia stroked the material again.

"Well, as long as it doesn't fit your cousin anymore," she said, her voice reluctant, but secretly filled with covetous glee.

They arrived at the club, *Il Gatto Mammone*, shortly after.

She hadn't known what to expect, but it wasn't this sleek and expensive looking space, complete with velvet ropes and a handsome bouncer in a black fitted suit. The interior was even more impressive. Booths in black leather with white accents surrounded a translucent floor with overlapping circles etched in it. Under each circle a different light shone, shifting from one color to another in an updated version of the dance floor in Saturday Night Fever.

The kaleidoscope of lights was captivating, the effect mesmerizing. The music had a slower beat than she associated with nightclubs, matching the pace of the shifting lights, but it was still a little loud.

"Who do you know here again?" she half-yelled, dazzled by the whole effect of the decor.

"Oh, my friend Calen has part interest in this place," he replied, his mouth close to her ear in order to be heard.

"Really?"

Sophia shouldn't have been surprised that Gio had a connection to such a hotspot, but she would have guessed it would be to one of the bartenders, not an owner.

There was also his appearance tonight. He was wearing an elegant pair of black pants and a tailored shirt. Did he borrow his outfit, too? Puzzled, she studied him out of the corner of her eye before remembering his second job. He probably used his salary as a bank teller to buy this ensemble. No doubt he had a few items like it in his wardrobe, clothes he could wear out on the town or to his moonlighting gig.

*If bank tellers looked like him back home, I'd stop banking online.*

Satisfied at solving that little mystery, she relaxed as he led her through the well-dressed shifting crowd. They sat at one of the booths on a raised dais overlooking the dance floor—one of the prime seats in the club.

A waitress in an extremely short skirt hustled up to them to take their order, her eyes locked on Gio like a love-struck schoolgirl.

Sophia was more amused than annoyed. It helped that her companion didn't notice his admirer's attention. Instead, he asked what she wanted to drink. In the mood to splurge, she ordered a Cosmopolitan while he ordered a Lagavulin whiskey. He continued to ignore the waitress' flirtatious glances when she came back with their drinks; his attention remained fixed on Sophia.

Pleased that he only had eyes for her, she finished her drink quickly. She was feeling festive so she let him order her another one before they went to dance. Wanting to be unencumbered, she slipped her cell phone in his pocket during the first song.

Gio was a little stiff on the fast-moving numbers but moved with fluid grace on the slower ones. Euphoria heightened every sensation, and she forgot all her earlier aggravation with her ex as they danced in each other's arms.

It had been a long time since she'd had so much fun. Richard hated going dancing, and he frowned on her going out with her girlfriends. Eventually, his passive-aggressive disapproval had led her to drop out of her regular girls' night out. But tonight she was making up for lost time.

Gio couldn't keep up on the dance floor, but he didn't seem to mind her partnering with others so long as they didn't get too handsy with her. Which was just fine with her. She didn't want another man's touch right now. Only Gio's. And she soon learned, he liked to watch her move...

Buzzed from the alcohol, her inhibitions fell away. She forgot that she was too heavy to be sexy, and that Gio was nothing but a street performer. Here on this dance floor, she was whatever she wanted to be. Eventually, after finishing her last drink, she got rid of her erstwhile partners and danced for Gio alone. He watched from his perch, the crowd thinning around her as if he'd ordered them to part so he could have an unobstructed view.

Gio's gaze was like a physical caress. There was enough light for her to see that he was smiling down at her, his lips parted. His lust-filled expression spurred her on, making her feel sensual and bold. The beat was keeping time with her pulse, and she danced like she hadn't in years.

It was pretty late by the time she started to tire. Hot and damp with sweat, she went back to the booth where Gio was waiting, watching her with those intense gold eyes. But when she sat down and turned to him, she realized the expression in his eyes wasn't amorous anymore. It was angry.

"What's wrong?" she asked.

Her voice could barely be heard over the music, but Gio shook his head and handed back her phone. She glanced at the screen. Four missed calls from Richard. *Perfect.*

She rolled her eyes and accepted another Cosmo from the waitress. She had apparently been ordered to keep a steady stream of them coming. When Sophia turned back to Gio, he was glaring at her, his burning expression almost enough to singe the tips of her hair.

*"What?"* she mouthed.

"I thought you said you were broken up," he shouted in her ear, making her wince.

There was no hint of a slur in his voice, but she could tell he'd drunk a few more whiskeys while she danced—she could smell it on his breath. Flushed from the dancing and alcohol herself, her temper flared.

*"I am."*

"Then why is your ex calling you so much? And not just today, but this whole past week. He is the one you keep hanging up on right?"

"I told you he was," she said, raising her voice when the next song's bass started to drown out her words. "I also told you we have unfinished business."

He gestured to his ear in annoyance, indicating he couldn't hear her. She tried again, but it seemed like the music grew even louder. After a fruitless minute trying to gesture her aggravation, Gio snapped. He took her hand and tugged her to her feet, propelling them through the crowded dance floor.

Sophia teetered on her high heels, nearly tripping as Gio's grip and quick pace threatened her balance. By the time he pulled her out of the side door into a cobblestone alleyway, she was spitting mad.

"What the hell, Gio!" she yelled, yanking her hand out of his.

He spun around and grabbed her head, pulling her close till she was only an inch away from his lips.

"He can't have you back," he hissed. *"You're mine."*

The declaration sent a heated pulse of pleasure throbbing down to her body as his mouth came down on hers. The kiss reverberated everywhere. It sang in her blood, more potent than the alcohol in her system. Forgetting about their argument, she pressed against him, aching for contact.

Gio was more than happy to oblige. Hot hard male flesh covered her, his heat seeping through their clothing. The warmth was a striking contrast to the cool night air. Instinctively cuddling closer, she was shocked into awareness when he pulled away.

Blinking dazedly, she watched him snap to attention at the sound of voices. A few men and one woman were turning the corner a little ahead of them. Looking back down into her eyes, he took her hand again and pulled them deeper into the shadows until they were in the dark of a dead end alleyway.

She spun to face him and was immediately engulfed by a pair of rock hard arms. Gio crushed her to his chest, the heat crackling between them. His hands were everywhere, rubbing and caressing her curves with possessive impatience.

It was as if a switch had been flipped inside her. One minute she was angry, and the next she was literally weak-kneed with desire. Clutching at Gio's shoulders for support, she fought to stay upright as his mouth flamed up and down her neck with such skill she almost cried out.

She loved necking. It had always been her favorite bit of fore-play, one her ex had sadly overlooked despite her determined hints and suggestions. But Gio wasn't some repressed Englishman. He was all fire and blood-red passion, instinctively knowing how she wanted to be touched.

Her complaints at being man-handled forgotten, she pulled at his clothes, tugging at his shirt until it came loose from his waist-band. He groaned aloud when her hands touched the smooth hard flesh of his back—the muscles tensing and relaxing in a helpless response that told her he was as excited as she was.

He was like warm bronze, a carved masterpiece come to life to give her pleasure.

His breath hitched as she stroked up his back and down the sides of his chest. She felt powerful, heady, but she was unprepared for the sharp hunger that clawed up through her body when Gio grabbed her leg above the knee. He wrapped it around him, opening her more fully so he could grind against her.

Her silky briefs were little protection against the intimidating bulge that seemed to be trying to escape his trousers. Whimpering, she moved against him, matching his rhythm in an effort to stop the maddening ache between her legs.

The friction gave her some relief, but it wasn't enough. Her need had never been this great, the craving so sharp it physically hurt. Heat pooled, her flesh swelling and growing wet. Blind to their surroundings, she arched against him, involuntarily scoring his back with her nails as the pulsing excitement climbed higher.

His hand at her thigh shifted up until he was grabbing a handful of her ass, clutching and kneading while pressing her closer. His other hand was busy under her skirt, tugging at her delicate panties until they tore, the crotch undone at one side.

Her whole body shuddered when his fingers parted the lips of her pussy. He teased and probed, pushing inside her at the same moment his palm ground against her clit, a trick that made her cry out.

"Shh, *bella mia*," Gio panted, sounding almost as out of breath as she was.

He said something else in Italian, but she wasn't listening anymore because his hand was gone and *he* was there, pushing inside her.

His mouth stifled her gasp as his thick cock parted her folds and worked its way inside her. For a second, there was pain. He was long and thick, so much that she wondered stupidly how he found pants that could contain him. She laughed aloud before he shut her up by plunging his tongue deeper into her mouth, that movement mimicking the one below.

*Holy hell.* It had been a long time for her, and neither of her former lovers even came close in rivaling him. But one thrust turned into three and soon she was pinned to the wall, his strength the only thing holding her up.

Lost in sensation, she couldn't hold back her moans as the driving pitch of his hips increased in tempo. His cock plundered, filling her tight channel before withdrawing and filling her again. Her body accepted all of him—but just barely and only because he made her so hot and wet. Otherwise, it might not have been possible.

Suddenly, she was coming, her body seizing and shuddering as she clamped down on the thickness inside her. The spasms rocked her body as she came, harder than she'd ever climaxed before. Her vision blackened and the hot tight tension drained away, leaving her sated and weak. She would have fallen if Gio's body hadn't been pressing her to the wall.

Docile in his arms, she barely registered his movement. He pulled out of her and turned her around, placing her hands against the wall for support before grabbing her hips. In one smooth thrust, he entered from behind, one hand moving to her breast to caress the full mound.

He took her hard, each of his lunges rocking her body into the wall. Struggling to brace herself, she moaned when his other hand left her hip and moved forward to stroke her clit.

"Again," he whispered.

She choked, trying to breathe. "I can't."

There was no way she could orgasm a second time.

*"Again."*

His voice was firm, inflexible. His fingers teased her clit, rubbing in a circular motion that made her bite her lip involuntarily. Tasting blood in her mouth, she arched backwards, trying to bring herself even closer.

Gio moved forward until his chest was flush with her back, his head against hers so he could kiss her hair. The hand that had been at her breast moved up over her mouth and she realized she'd been crying out, begging him to stop or not stop. She didn't know which.

Having her mouth covered, her soft and curvy body held tight against Gio's muscular chest, was more exciting than she could have ever imagined. A few more strokes of his deft finger and she was flying over the edge, the second orgasm stronger than the first because it was so unexpected.

Her eyes nearly rolled back into her head, and she shook violently in his arms. The ferocity of her climax triggered his. His thick staff swelled and spasmed, flooding her with hot seed.

Against her back, Gio trembled and swore in Italian, something unintelligible and harsh. One arm wrapped around her forehead— a shield from the wall as he collapsed, pushing her against the rough concrete.

His lungs worked like a bellows in the silence that followed.

They stood there for an eternity, trying to find the strength to stand and part their bodies. She was still resting her forehead against his arms when bits of awareness started to trickle back. A distant part of her brain was processing and cataloging each sensation; the warmth of the male body behind her and how sensitive her palms were from being abraded by the concrete.

He slipped out of her and, still slightly numb, she staggered upright. A cooling trickle ran down her leg. The realization they hadn't used protection hit her when another seemed to occur to him. He turned her around, his face shocked and pale.

*"We had sex in an alley."*

His voice sounded strangely hollow, almost stunned.

Dumbly, she opened her mouth to reply, but nothing came out. He stood there staring at her so she nodded. It seemed to snap him out of his stupor. He took off the jacket of his suit and draped it over her shoulders.

Looking up at him, she caught sight of some movement in a window over his head and flinched. Someone in the second story of the building was watching them from behind a thin curtain.

She put both hands over her mouth, mortified. Gio glanced behind him. He must have seen the same shadow because put his arm around her to hustle her away. At the mouth of the alley, he stopped and whipped out a smartphone, a newer and more advanced model of the same phone she had. He hit the speed dial and spoke to someone in rapid Italian.

Absently fingering the soft lightweight wool of the suit jacket, Sophia was still in a daze when a shiny black town car pulled in front of them. Gio opened the door and helped her inside, speaking to the driver.

"Do they have Uber in Italy?" she asked drowsily, noting the fineness of the car's leather interior.

The driver was probably using his personal car to make money like they did in the States.

"Um, there are services like it," he answered evasively.

"Are you taking me back to the hotel?" she murmured, leaning on his shoulder.

"You're taking *me* back to *your* hotel," he corrected, putting a finger under her chin so she would meet his eyes.

He smiled at her. "The story of our first time as lovers does not end in an *alley*. It starts there."

# CHAPTER 7

*A*n unfamiliar warmth at his side woke Gio up. Bemused, he lifted his lids slowly. The sight that met his eyes sent a charge of adrenaline through him, waking him more effectively than ten shots of espresso.

Sophia was lying next to him, her glorious caramel curves barely covered by a rumpled white cotton sheet. One arm was thrown on the bed over her head, her fingers curled against the mattress. The heavy lashes of her eyes rested on her flushed cheeks.

With her hair mussed and that color in her cheeks, she looked like they'd just finished making love. He glanced at his watch. It had only been a few hours since the fourth, and final, round.

Gio laid his head back on the pillow and grinned. Last night had been the most passionate and carnal experience of his life.

Images filtered through his head. He'd wasted no time trying to fulfill every fantasy he'd had of Sophia since the foundation dinner. However, she became shy once they were back in her room. He'd had to start over. Not that he minded. Seducing her slowly was exactly what he'd wanted from the start—he needed to savor her after the quick, but mind-blowing, encounter outside the club.

Sophia had blushed pink as he stripped that black silk dress from her glorious body. That color had deepened into a fiery red as he did what he'd been dying to do since he had first seen her. He kissed every inch of her, suckling her breasts and clutching handfuls of her luscious ass as he rode her. Moments passed before she tensed all over and climaxed with a sob.

It was crazy. None of his old insecurities had surfaced, no malicious words had echoed in his head. His sole focus had been on Sophia, and her pleasure. Everything had fallen into place. It had been both natural and so fucking intense, like being on some sort of mind-altering drug.

Instinctively, he knew his life had changed forever. Now, he needed to convince Sophia that hers had too.

*Merda.*

His breath caught, and he sank deeper into the bed. She still thought he was someone else. He had lied to her, and then bedded her under false pretenses.

He'd sworn to tell her the truth before it got that far, but kept putting it off. Getting to know her, talking to her, making her laugh, had become his priority. Most of the time he'd been able to pretend and push the guilt out of his mind, telling himself he was waiting for the right time.

Unfortunately, he wasn't sure when that was going to be. The situation in the press had grown steadily worse in the past week. Enzo had kept him updated about the latest slurs. One tabloid rag had quoted an anonymous source, a former trusted friend of his, that claimed Gio had not only emotionally abused his ex-wife, but he'd pimped her out to his friends and acquaintances.

He didn't have to guess who the "friend" was. After all, he had caught Maria Gianna with Vincenzo Gavazzi himself. Enzo was verifying the source's identity before Gio committed to a course of action. And that needed to be soon. It was only a matter of time before Sophia found out on her own. His picture was plastered on newsstands right now, for crying out loud.

He'd been lucky so far. Sophia wasn't the kind of person who looked at tabloids, even if they were right under her nose. But his luck would only hold out for so long. It was only that it had been so easy to pretend. Far easier than he would have ever imagined. As long as he didn't wear a suit and avoided the financial district, he was relatively anonymous. A pair of mirrored sunglasses and his own countrymen—including the paparazzi—didn't recognize him.

It was disconcerting in a way, being able to step away from his life like he had. Gio didn't enjoy being famous, but as the son of one of Italy's oldest and wealthiest families, notoriety had always been a part of his existence. These past days with Sophia had been a learning experience, in more ways than one.

At least he'd started laying the groundwork. He had admitted that he worked at a bank. She just didn't know that he was the head of it. Or that it wasn't a sideline. What was she going to say when he finally told her the whole truth?

She was going to be angry. There was no doubt about it. Any reasonable person would be furious. A flash of Sophia's face, losing her sunny smile, growing colder and staring at him in distaste ran through his head. And that was the best-case scenario.

*Could the fiery Latin temper be a stereotype?* He could only hope so.

*Never date a rich guy.* Yeah, there was that too. Damn her ex. That son of a bitch had clearly done a number on her. Gio needed to show her that merely because a man had money, it didn't mean he had to bend everyone to his will. A rich successful man could be reasonable and thoughtful, capable of being an equal partner.

Although he hadn't exactly been calm or reasonable last night. He'd been watching Sophia all evening, doing his best not to embarrass himself during her seductive little show on the dance floor. She'd left her phone with him, however, and the cursed thing kept going off.

At first he'd ignored it—until the third call. What kind of pathetic excuse for a man called a woman over and over again when she obviously didn't want to talk to him?

Annoyed, he'd resolved to discuss it with Sophia, but the fucking calls kept coming until he'd been driven stupid with jealousy. And he'd let that jealousy drive him straight into that alley.

Truthfully, he wasn't sure he regretted what he'd done. Letting go of his inhibitions that way had led to the best sex of his life. But Sophia had deserved candles and satin sheets on a king-sized bed for their first time. He glanced around him. This room was nice, but it didn't compare to the bedroom in his penthouse a few blocks away.

He had to tell her the truth today. And he meant it this time. But first, he needed to find out more about this ex and what this unfinished business was. Clearly Sophia's former boyfriend was using it as an excuse to stay in her life...and win her back. The sheer volume of calls was proof of that. He had to put a stop to it.

Gio had finally found his future, and he wasn't about to let anyone take it away from him.

He was thinking it over, making plans, when Sophia shifted, causing the sheet to drift down. The move revealed her creamy café-au-lait thigh and part of one rich globe before she turned over on her back.

Inhaling deeply, he moved lower on the bed and pulled the cover off her body. A man had to have his priorities.

# CHAPTER 8

*S*ophia had always hated getting up in the morning. However, this time she was struggling for consciousness, reaching for pleasure that grew progressively more intense the more she woke.

Stretching languorously, she arched her hips and legs restlessly. Soft hair brushed against the sensitive skin of her inner thighs. Lifting heavy lids, she peeked down. *Oh, God…*It was Gio. And he was…*oh, God.*

His mouth was magic. And holy shit it was aggressive. He was holding her hips down, because even now she was writhing uncontrollably, bucking and straining against his hands. Licking up and down her folds, he ate her with abandon, sucking in her clit to his mouth. He rolled his tongue over it before moving one hand to caress and probe her entrance.

Her pussy tightened and spasmed on his fingers, trying to keep him inside her to rub that magical little spot he'd claimed and made his own. But he was teasing her now. A single finger snaked inside her before retreating and entering again until he was fucking her in a steady rhythm.

But it wasn't enough. What she craved was his thick and heavily veined cock.

It was too big and thick actually. She was a large woman, but not down there. That didn't matter, though. The pain she felt at taking him was minor, not even worth mentioning. Not compared to the ecstasy he gave her.

"Gio, please," she gasped, trying to pull him upward.

But he had other ideas. "No," he said. "One in my mouth, Sophia. Give me one my mouth, please."

It sounded more like a command than a plea. His tongue was in her now, working in and out, withdrawing occasionally to nibble on her clit. Over and over again he penetrated her until she was half crazy, moaning and panting in abandon. She gloried in the sensation, reveling greedily in each wave as the pleasure built.

When it crashed down, it was like being flung on the shore, broken and dashed to pieces. Tensing, she arced like her body had been shot through with electricity. Her vision blurred, and she cried out in a heart-stopping climax.

Gio let her fall, but only briefly. Melting into the bed, she was still experiencing twinges of dissipating bliss when his shaft pushed at her entrance. He thrust inside, filling her completely. The rhythm was rough and deliciously hard before he surprised her by twisting, flipping them around until she landed on top of him. He urged her to straddle him, grabbing her waist and guiding until she was riding him, slowly at first and then faster and faster.

He tugged her forward, cupping her full breasts. Lifting his head, he took one tight nipple in his mouth. Her rhythm broke as he licked and bit the swollen bud. Grabbing his head, she held on tight while the spasms started again.

His hands kept moving, running over every inch of her skin. He palmed her ass cheek, kneading and stroking as he flipped over so he was on top. Then he withdrew, nearly breaking her heart. But her disappointment was temporary. He sat back on his haunches and pulled her on top of him. Happy to oblige, she straddled his lap again, although now they were sitting in the middle of the bed.

Sighing contentedly, her breasts rubbed against the sprinkling of hair on his upper chest with delicious friction. Pressed tightly together, she rocked with him, their movements perfectly in sync.

This was more than sex. She knew it in her heart. Tears stung at her eyes and she clung to his shoulders harder, trying to hold on with a desperation that came out of nowhere.

Gio must have felt the change in her. He caught her urgency, plunging his hands in her hair and clenching them into fists. Beneath her, his hips worked overtime, lunging up forcefully in harsh strokes. Her channel gripped him firmly as she rode him, undulating on his lap in a striking counterpoint. The move deepened and intensified the hot pulses at her core until the ecstasy surged and crested.

She threw back her head, too out of breath to cry out as Gio buried his face in her neck and groaned. Mouth gaping, she bore down, grinding against him in an effort to prolong the high.

The feeling held for a few more precious seconds until it finally spun away, leaving her hazy and weak.

Distantly, she registered his climax. He groaned gutturally as his cock swelled and pulsed inside her, teasing her G-spot repeatedly as she came down from her orgasm with a final convulsive wrench.

He collapsed on the bed with her in his arms. They lay there quietly, breathing hard as he softened inside of her. Eventually, he turned to her and frowned. He reached out and wiped away the tears on her cheeks, which she hadn't known were there.

"*Bella mia*, are you okay?" His voice was hoarse and concerned.

Nodding, she swallowed and took a deep breath. "I often cry during sex," she lied.

"Oh." He relaxed, toying with her hair before moving down to cup her ass—his hand's favorite resting place. "Why don't we jump in the shower and order room service," he suggested, nibbling at her ear and neck.

She wrinkled her nose. "Bad idea. If we shower together we'll take forever. I'm starving and this place doesn't have room service."

Gio's mouth turned down. "No room service?"

She shrugged. "That's what you get when you go with a charming and historic bed and breakfast instead of a luxury hotel." Rolling over onto her stomach, she tugged the sheet over her butt.

His hand snuck up to twitch the sheet back down again.

She smacked his hand. "Why don't *you* jump in the shower, then, and I'll look for a place nearby on my phone. I'm pretty sure we already missed the breakfast here," she said, squinting at the digital clock on the bedside table.

He stood with a grin, unashamed of his nudity. "I'll be quick," he promised before entering the bathroom and closing the door behind him.

Once he was safely out of sight, Sophia collapsed face-first on the bed, burying her nose in the mattress.

Her vacation fling had become so much more.

*What am I going to do?*

What was wrong with her? Why did all of her entanglements with men always get so off track? She couldn't even handle a vacation fling. Other women did rebound sex just fine without getting emotionally involved. Why did she have to be different?

In a few days, she was going to have to go home and it was going to crush her to leave him behind.

The weight in her chest seemed to grow heavier with each breath. She was already mourning Gio's loss, and he wasn't even gone yet.

Rolling over, she stared at the ceiling, blinking back more tears. *What if he doesn't want things to end, either?* He had certainly been acting very possessive since last night. Before then, actually.

*He can't have you back, you're mine.* It had certainly sounded like he meant that. What if he was serious and somehow she could keep him?

*Stop acting crazy.*

It would never work. Gio was a street performer, for heaven's sake. Even if by some miracle he was willing to relocate, could she be with someone so different?

How did you date a man without ambition?

She was honest enough to admit that dating someone beneath her professionally would be a problem. It would be embarrassing to take him to work functions and have him mingle with her academic friends—and she had no others. Gio would never fit into her life...unless he gave up street performing.

Maybe he was already considering it? Why else would he have gotten a second job moonlighting as a bank teller? What if he applied for a job at a bank near her in Oxford? Could he give up his devil-may-care artist lifestyle for a boring nine-to-five job?

*Not if he did it for you.*

She couldn't ask him to give up his life. He'd never be happy as a square peg in a round hole. Artists needed freedom and the right to express themselves. She'd be taking his wings and clipping them. She had to let him go. She couldn't be that person who became involved with someone and tried to fundamentally change them.

*Like Richard tried to do to you.*

Heart heavy, she reached for her phone to check her emails. With a frown she noticed that her phone was on vibrate.

*Shit.* She usually tried to be easy to reach in case something went wrong at the lab, but Gio distracted her. Hopefully work hadn't needed to speak to her because she never noticed when the buzzer went off unless the ringer was on too. Unlocking it, she checked how many times her ex had called last night.

Sophia sat up abruptly. *Ten missed calls?*

Thinking Richard had truly gone off the deep end, she checked the log. But only four were from Richard—the rest were from

Kelly. Worried something terrible had happened, she hurriedly called her back.

"Oh, God, finally," Kelley gasped when the call went through. "Where have you been? I've been trying like crazy to reach you since I got back yesterday from the in-laws."

"I'm sorry, I didn't realize my ringer was off. Is everything okay? Is it Omar? Did something happen?"

On the other end of the line, her friend exhaled a harsh breath and her heart sank. Something must have happened to Kelly's husband, Omar, or her parents.

"It's not me. It's you. Listen about Gio—"

Sophia laughed, relieved. "I know, I know. I'm crazy. I've never done anything like this, but you were the one telling me I should have a rebound relationship. The thing is—"

"No, no! You don't understand," Kelly interrupted. "You're not with Giovanni."

Sophia smiled sheepishly and stood up, wrapping the sheet around her.

"Actually, I am. Right now. Well, almost. He's in the shower. Listen, I know I shouldn't have gotten involved with one of your study subjects, but I couldn't help myself. It's insane, but he's not what I expected, and we…well, I can't go into it or he'll hear me gushing like an idiot. But for once I'm not going to overanalyze. I'm trying hard to live in the moment and just…enjoy him. God, I sound like a schoolgirl with a crush. Don't make fun of me later for the way I'm talking, okay?"

Kelly stayed quiet.

Sophia frowned. "Kel?"

Harsh breathing filled her ear. "Listen and stay calm. You need to get out of there *right now.*"

Apprehension filled her, making her dizzy. She sat heavily on the bed. "Why?"

"He's not who you think he is. The man you are with isn't Giovanni Berardi."

Her stomach tightened. "What?"

"I spoke to the real one," Kelly said. "He emailed me to apologize for not being able to meet you."

Sophia relaxed, almost giddy with relief. "Oh, no, it's all right. I did miss him the first time in Rome. I'd gone on to Milan, and he texted me so I doubled back to meet him."

"No, Sophia. It's not him," Kelly insisted. "The real Giovanni had to miss you in Rome the second time, too. His son was in an accident. He went to the hospital and was too out of it to cancel your appointment. But I got the questionnaire back in the post, so I called him to thank him and he told me everything. A man came to him with the survey and stayed with him till he filled it out. Gave him a thousand euros for his trouble and then took the thing to mail for him. You never met the real Giovanni. Whoever that man is that you are with, *it isn't him.*"

Frozen, Sophia sat there with her mouth open.

"Sophie!"

"But...but it has to be. There must be some mistake. We talked about it. His name is Gio...Giovanni."

There were sounds of movement in the background as if Kelly was pacing and bumping into things. "What does he look like?"

Sophia shrugged, even though Kelly couldn't see her. "He's six-two with black hair and light golden-brown eyes."

"So, he's not a leathery man in his fifties?"

"No," she whispered, her heart sinking. "He's young. Mid-thirties at the latest."

"Where are you?"

"We're at my hotel. I told you. He's in the shower."

Kelly sucked in a breath. "Get your things and leave before he gets out."

She nodded dumbly.

"Are you listening?"

"Yes," she choked out over the lump in her throat.

"Okay, do it now. And Sophia, *hurry.*"

She hung up without another word, looking around wildly. For a moment, she just sat there, the implications of what she'd heard sinking in. What had she done, and who the hell had she done it with?

*Move. You need to move.*

Jumping up, she started grabbing clothes and electronics. She threw her computer in her carryon and her phone in her purse. Her toiletries were in the bathroom, but they didn't matter.

Ransacking her neatly organized drawers, she stuffed everything else into her suitcase and nearly bit her lip open after realizing she hadn't held back anything to wear.

*Not everything is in the bag.*

The black dress from last night was lying on the floor—the one Gio had given her.

*Shit. Not Gio.*

The man in the shower was a stranger and a fraud. She didn't even know his name.

Nearly tripping in her haste, she glanced down at her naked body. *Faster. Move faster.* With shaky hands she pulled on the black dress, fumbling with the zipper. Shoes, she needed shoes. A pair she could run in.

With a wrench, she shoved her feet into her black sneakers, grateful that she brought the kind that slipped on with no shoelaces to slow her down.

Her eyes fell on Gio's discarded clothes, the sleek suit and shirt he'd worn last night. Impulsive, she picked them up and ran to the window, levering it up with one arm. The window faced a quaint little alley behind the hotel, one lined with coffee shops. Heedless of the startled and amused glances of the people below, she threw the clothes down and slammed the window shut, spinning around when the door to the bathroom opened.

"*Bella mia*, did you find a place for breakfast? If not, there's this great little place a few blocks from here I want to take you to."

Sophia backed away, her heart threatening to burst out of her chest. He was standing there naked from the waist up, his chest glistening and a towel wrapped around his waist.

Oh, hell, what did she do now?

He looked at her and frowned. *"Mi amore*, what's wrong?"

She raised her hand and was surprised to see it trembling. In fact, she was shaking from head to toe.

Gio's face filled with concern. He stepped toward her. "What is it? What's wrong?"

*No.*

"Stop!" She tried to yell, but it came of strangled and broken. She couldn't breathe. "Stay away from me! Don't come any closer."

His mouth fell open. "I don't understand."

Sophia laughed, half-hysterical. "Of course you don't. I don't either." Tears stung her eyes. "Why did you do this?" she whispered. *"Who are you?"*

Realization lit his eyes. She could see it washing over him. He closed his mouth, and the blood drained from his face. But unlike her, he wasn't about to lose his shit. His face was solemn…and he looked unbearably sad.

He blinked rapidly.

"I need to explain," he said, holding up his hands, palms out.

It was supposed to be a calming gesture, the kind made when trying to calm a hysterical person. Well, it wasn't working.

He took another step, and she reached for the nearest thing she could find, a heavy ashtray from the nearby table.

"I said, don't come any closer!" she yelled, crouching so she could run in case he tried to jump her.

"Sophia, let me explain," he pleaded, taking another step.

She didn't hesitate. Pulling back her arm, she threw the ashtray at him with all her strength.

He tried to duck, but he was too slow. The ashtray still made contact, glancing off his head. It was enough to knock him off his feet.

He stared up at her, eyes dazed, with a little blood trickling down from his hairline. Her muscles locked in an effort not to run to him. The impulse to kneel and see if he was all right was overwhelming. But there was no time. She had to go now, before he got back up.

Gasping and sobbing, she grabbed her suitcase and sprinted for the door. She didn't look back.

She was half-way to the airport before she burst into tears. Brushing them away brusquely with the heels of her palm, she took several deep breaths. She had to calm down, but the scene in the hotel replayed itself in her mind again and again. And what stood out was him—that stranger—sitting on the floor bleeding.

She turned to her taxi driver. "How do you call an ambulance in Italy?"

# CHAPTER 9

*A* week later, Sophia dragged herself out of bed and into the bathroom of her one bedroom apartment. With forced mechanical movements, she brushed her teeth, staring at her drawn gray face.

It was quite an achievement for someone with her complexion to look pale, but she managed it pretty easily these days.

Sighing, she finished up and moved listlessly to her closet. For several minutes, she stared at her color-coded rows of dresses and shirts without seeing them. She had been back at work for a few days now. She didn't explain why she came back early. The only person in her confidence was Kelly.

Her best friend had picked her up at the airport, prepared with a huge box of chocolates and a bottle of tequila.

It was a tradition Sophia herself had started in graduate school. She had kept chocolate, painkillers, and a bottle of tequila in her desk at work throughout her Ph.D. program. It was her emergency preparedness kit. Science was frequently a difficult and frustrating occupation and more than one of her coworkers had taken advantage of her stash. Kelly had been so taken with the idea that she adopted it as her own for her students.

Sophia had gone over the events in Italy with her best friend, trying like crazy to find an explanation for what had happened.

Who was that man in Italy, and why had he targeted her? Had he been trying to rob her somehow? Scam artists befriended you to get your personal details so they could steal your identity, didn't they? Or did he target lonely female tourists as part of some sick game? Was that how he got off, seducing gullible women and then dining off the stories?

She could picture him now in some shady Italian bar, mocking her body with a group of other gorgeous Italian assholes.

After placing a fraud alert on her bank accounts and changing all of her passwords, she decided to put the whole mess out of her mind. But as hard as she tried, she couldn't forget a thing.

She would close her eyes and see his smile. When she tried to sleep, his hands moved over her body, a phantom touch that kept her awake all night. It was the cruelest form of insomnia she could imagine.

The longing wouldn't go away until she touched herself, masturbating in tears and pretending she was with him—the imaginary Gio who was a real street performer and would never dream of lying to her.

Sophia was only that weak at night. During the day she kept busy, fighting to maintain control with rigid self-discipline. However, in the space between tasks, her composure would crack. It seemed like her every emotion had heightened and run riot. Betrayal, anger, and fear were only the tip of the iceberg. She felt unbalanced and unsure of herself. How could she ever trust her own judgment again?

*Stop it.*

She had to get to work. That's all that was keeping her together right now. When her mother had died, she'd buried herself in it. It was a strategy that had gotten her through some tough spots.

So why did she suspect it wasn't going to be enough this time?

To top everything off, she was going to have to wine and dine her benefactor tonight. Alan Weisz, her research partner, had been glad she'd come back early because he'd received word that a Morgese Foundation representative was coming to tour the lab. Last night, Alan had called her in a panic. No mere lackey was visiting. Instead, it was the man himself, Mr. Morgese, the head of the foundation and CEO of the Morgese bank.

Going out tonight to make polite small talk with some old money blowhard was the last thing she wanted to do. But she didn't have a choice. It was part of her job to charm and impress the big money guys when they came round.

More science was being funded by private donors as government budgets for science research dried up. By and large, it was a good thing, or at least a necessary one. However, the timing couldn't be worse. It was hard to feign enthusiasm for much of anything at the moment. Having to paste a smile on her face for the whole day was going to be a headache.

Once at work, she did her best to finish some work before Mr. Morgese showed up. Some of her ongoing experiments required sampling at timed intervals, and she preferred to do it first thing in the morning. After that, she set about checking the stock of the solutions she needed for the next round.

When she found that one was low, she threw on her lab coat and safety goggles to mix up a fresh batch behind the glass walls of the hazardous chemical room. She had just finished when there was a flurry of activity near the door.

Suppressing a sigh, she prepared for her meet and greet. Cleaning up, she decided to leave the lab coat on. It was always a good idea to play up to the stereotypes around the money people.

Tucking a lock of hair back into place, she pulled off her safety glasses and turned around...only to lock eyes with him.

*Gio.*

Her heart dropped to her knees and she blinked several times, but the apparition didn't change. Her phantom lover was standing there in a fine bespoke suit, a small Steri-Strip bandage at his hairline.

Alan was all smiles, grinning from ear to ear and talking a mile a minute.

"Here she is," Alan said, turning to her and gesturing. "Sophia, this is Giancarlo Morgese. Mr. Morgese, this is our neurobiologist Sophia Márquez."

Her muscles locked, and she could feel the blood draining from her face. "No," she whispered.

That wasn't right. Clearly this man was an imposter. He'd already impersonated one man and here he was doing it again.

Why was he here? What the hell did he want? *Why was it so cold?*

She wanted to run, but she was locked in place—until he moved. He stepped forward and held out his hand. For a moment, she stared fixedly at it. A hint of her horror must have shown on her face because he stepped forward again, in front of Alan, to hide her from view. Then he took another.

*Oh, God.*

Spinning away instinctively, her hand flew out, knocking over an Erlenmeyer flask and a glass jug off the lab bench. She swore as the jug fell and smashed open on the floor.

"Out!" she yelled, alarmed when she realized the flask was the concentrated hydrochloric acid stock—the biggest bottle commercially available. "Everybody out!"

Hands came down on her shoulders, but she pushed them off, turning around and shoving Gio back as the fumes hit them, stinging her eyes and nose. Coughing, she pushed him again until he was past the threshold. Alan pulled Gio back enough for her to close the door. But she wasn't on the other side of it with them.

Quickly donning the safety googles and a mask again, she went to the windows on the other side of the room and threw them open. She grabbed the hazardous spill kit and spread garden lime on the corrosive liquid on the floor, then checked her clothes for places where it might have splashed, ignoring the commotion on the other side of the glass.

Gio, or whoever he was, banged on the glass, carrying on like the world was ending.

"Sophia, get out of there!" he yelled, continuing to call out her name until the whole lab gathered around him and Alan.

Everyone was watching him, watching her. She could see them doing the math, figuring out that they knew each other. For a moment, they stared at one another, her eyes accusing, his frightened.

Whoever he was, he was scared for her.

---

AFTER SHE HAD NEUTRALIZED the spill, the custodial staff came to clean up the wet lime from the floor. A small hole had burned in her lab coat, but her clothes had been spared.

It was also fortunate that she had worn her leather boots today. They had protected her feet from the acid, but she had a persistent cough caused by the fumes. The mask hadn't been adequate protection—or she hadn't put in on in time to avoid a little lung irritation.

The EMTs were currently checking her out. Giancarlo Morgese had insisted.

It was his real name. She had looked him up while waiting in the ambulance. They had checked her vitals and put her on oxygen. One quick Google search later and there was his picture on the Morgese bank website. Her Gio was the CEO of one of Europe's biggest banks—also her donor and the lab's main source of funding.

Sophia could still hear her supervisor doing his best to calm Giancarlo down, explaining that she had done everything right. She followed protocol for a hazardous chemical spill. Closed shoes and clothing that didn't expose too much skin were lab policy for exactly this reason.

It was a rule often broken, especially in the heat of summer, but Sophia didn't. Not when she was doing experiments. So a real disaster had been averted. At worst, her lungs would be a little irritated and she might cough for a couple of days.

When the EMTs told her to rest, she texted her boss. She informed him she was going home for the day and to make her apologies to their illustrious guest.

And then she cried all the way home.

# CHAPTER 10

$S$ ophia had called her, and Kelly had rushed right over with two bottles of wine, proving why she was best friend material.

"This dress is worth thousands of dollars," Kelly pronounced, fingering the fine cloth of the black dress lying across Sophia's bed.

She hadn't showed it to her before. It didn't occur to her that the thing might be worth anything until Kelly had asked to see it.

"So how many billions do you think he's worth?" Kelly asked, still stroking the dress as if she couldn't help herself.

Sophia shrugged. The shock was wearing off, but the anger hadn't come. Not yet. It would, but what she felt at the moment was confusion. Disbelief.

"You know he probably bought this just for you. It's exactly your size."

Suppressing a shudder, she took the dress and looked at the label. Kelly had found the designer online. It was an exclusive brand, someone astronomically expensive and way out of her budget.

"I don't understand," she muttered, passing a hand over her face.

"Well, I think I'm beginning to," Kelly said, turning to Sophia's laptop.

Kelly had been reading everything she could find on Giancarlo Morgese, but Sophia didn't have the heart to look at any of it. Her head was still spinning. She reached for the glass of wine Kelly had poured for her, and winced as it burned on the way down.

Kelly frowned and took the glass. "Maybe you shouldn't have that, after all."

Rolling her eyes, Sophia took the glass back. "Don't even think about it. Right now I need this more than I need you."

Kelly grinned, and then hit her with a pillow. The doorbell rang, and she jumped up to answer before Sophia could stop her.

She put her eye to the peephole, and then turned to raise her eyebrow at her. Kelly didn't even have to say the words.

He was here.

"Do I let him in?"

Sophia wanted to say no, but she couldn't avoid him forever. He'd given her millions in grant money. Money she needed…

"Let him in," she rasped.

It was time to get some answers.

---

GIO HELD his breath and waited for Sophia to answer. An excruciatingly long minute passed. Just when he decided that she wasn't going to open up, the door swung open to reveal a short woman with sandy blonde hair. Her hands were on her hips, and she was giving him the evil eye.

"You better have a damn good reason for doing what you did," the woman said with a scorching glare.

"Um…" He stared down blankly at the woman. Did he have the wrong apartment?

Enzo, who had accompanied him and the lung doctor he had just hunted down, whispered in his ear.

"Oh, hello, Kelly," he said with a heavy sigh.

This was going to be harder than he thought. Behind Kelly, off to the right, there was movement and he looked up to see Sophia watching him from the doorway with her arms crossed protectively over her chest.

"Did you receive the questionnaire from the real Giovanni?" he asked in a low voice.

Kelly twisted her lips, but it wasn't a smile. "I got it," she said.

"I see you brought the whole entourage this time," Sophia said in a low voice, nodding at the men at his side.

Well, at least she wasn't shouting at him. Of course, she couldn't. Not with the lung damage she had suffered, according to the EMTs.

The yelling would doubtless come later, but they needed to take care of something first. He gestured, and the man on his right came forward with an awkward smile. Enzo nodded at the ladies and headed for the stairs before he and the doctor stepped forward.

"This is Dr. Saddler," Gio explained, pointing to the short balding man. "He's a top pulmonary specialist. I'd like him to examine you."

Sophia stared at him for a second and then started to laugh. But it turned into a hacking cough, undercutting all the arguments he knew she was about to make.

The cough was deep. It rattled in her chest, multiplying his guilt ten-fold. His face tightened, and he gave the doctor a little shove.

Kelly was smart enough to get out his way. She stayed for the examination, but once the doctor prescribed an inhalant to soothe Sophia's irritated lungs, she tactfully went to the bedroom. The doctor took his leave, and he and Sophia were finally alone, staring at each other.

She held up the inhaler in her hand. "The EMTs already gave me some of this. A house call was unnecessary, Mr. Morgese."

He closed his eyes for a long hard moment. This was excruciating.

"It really is Gio."

One fine brown brow raised. "Seriously?"

Sitting in an armchair across from her, he nodded emphatically. "It's what my friends call me. And most of my family. That's why I thought you recognized me."

Her eyes bored into him, her hostility palpable. "It should have been obvious after a few minutes that I didn't."

"It was…I'm sorry," he whispered. "I didn't mean to lie."

Inhaling sharply, she turned away, but not before he saw the glitter of tears in her eyes. He felt like an asshole.

"This is the worst thing I've ever done," he said. "Even now, I can't believe that I did it. You are the last person I wanted to lie to. But things were bad for me and they were getting worse. And then you thought I was someone else. It was an insane impulse, but I couldn't stop myself from going along with it. I regretted it immediately. I swear I did. Every day I meant to tell you the truth. However, my situation kept deteriorating. I believed that if you knew who I really was I'd never see you again."

Her fine brows pulled together. "I don't understand."

Exhaling, he leaned back. "I guess you didn't Google me…"

She shrugged. "Kelly did."

"So you know about my ex-wife?"

It was a relief, or it should have been, but Sophia was frowning in confusion.

"What about her?"

Sighing audibly, he rubbed his face. "She's slandering me in the press. We've been divorced for years, but she got in trouble recently. For some reason she decided the best way to get out of it was to throw me to the wolves." He rolled his shoulders in frustration, gesturing with his hands as he went on. "It's a pack of

87

disgusting lies, what she's insinuating. But one of my old friends is enabling her—they're sleeping together. To twist the knife, Maria-Gianna also has one of my young and stupid cousins wrapped around her finger. He's joined in the defamation, so I cut him off."

Her eyes widened, but she stayed quiet. "Well, you can't choose your family, but it sounds like you need better friends," she said eventually.

He smiled sadly. "I do have some good ones. One of them, Alex, is the one who finally told me the truth about my wife. He decided I needed to know after she tried to get him into bed. And he wasn't the first. She pulled the same thing with my friend, Calen, too. He was still trying to figure out how to tell me when Alex beat him to it."

Breaking eye contact, he looked down. He hated talking about that whole sordid mess. But she needed to hear it all or she wouldn't understand why he had made such poor decisions.

"It was the holidays, and they were visiting. Maria Gianna was having one of her fits, and I was already sick of the drama. She didn't like that I didn't react the way she wanted. She needed to be indulged, but I wasn't in the mood. I had just realized how immature and spoiled she was. I'd known her since childhood—she's my father's goddaughter. But it turns out I didn't know her at all. I only saw the glittery exterior. What was underneath was very ugly."

Sophia took a pillow and hugged it to her stomach, sitting back on the couch. "I'm waiting for the part where all that led to you lying to me."

Seeing an open bottle of wine on the coffee table, he nodded and poured what was left into one of the empty glasses next to it.

"I know, it's simply that I wanted to tell you everything for the longest time," he said before letting his eyes unfocus, remembering the ignominious end to his marriage. "As I was saying, not all of my friends were that loyal. There was that one who was sleeping with her, Vincenzo. Every time she was angry with me, she went to him—and she was angry with me a lot toward the end. Vinny and I grew up together...I never realized how much he hated me until the divorce. There were probably others too, but unlike Vinny, they're too ashamed to admit it."

He checked for her reaction.

"Go on," she said.

"Did I mention that Vincenzo's father owns several tabloids?"

Understanding lit her eyes. "I see. So what was she saying and why does anyone care?"

Her pragmatic bluntness made him smile.

"Maria Gianna is a socialite who had small roles in a few Italian movies. The press still follows her around. She was driving while on drugs and was arrested for causing an accident. A man on his way to work was hurt. According to the gossip rags, I was the one who hooked her on drugs—when I've never even touched the stuff. I've never even smoked pot. I'm kind of boring that way."

She didn't smile, but her face softened. "I did. Once." She picked at the fringe on the pillow. "So, what were you doing at the cafe?"

"I was looking for you."

Her lips parted in surprise, and he smiled sheepishly. "I wanted to meet you ever since I saw you in that white satin dress."

Sophia sat up straighter. "You were there? At the foundation dinner?"

"I was late—stuck in traffic—but I did eventually make it. Just not in time to meet you."

"And then you did...and decided it was easier to lie."

Gio shoved a hand through his hair. "No. I mean, yes. I wanted a chance to get to know you without all this *merda* hanging over my head. This is going to be hard for you to believe, but my honor means a lot to me."

She scoffed aloud, making him flinch a little.

"I know how that sounds, but it's true. The last few months, I've suddenly become a bad guy in other people's eyes. Acquaintances have been looking at me like I was some sort of monster who'd been unmasked. Women that I've worked with for years were whispering behind my back at the bank. One woman, an associate who'd been angling for a date for months, was now canceling business dinners because she didn't want to be alone with me. And some kid threw their coffee on me. There's this stupid hashtag going around, pushing my ex's fans to "get" me."

Her brows went up. "All because you supposedly pushed drugs at her?"

"Well, there was the other insinuation—that I verbally abused Maria Gianna…and pimped her out to my friends."

She raised her brows, and he laughed humorlessly. "I know, the irony. If she'd been faithful, I might have stayed married to her, tried counseling or something. My father was crushed by the divorce. So was her father. They're best friends."

Sophia put the pillow aside and crossed her arms. "And you thought I would believe all of these accusations?"

"Don't you?"

She pursed her lips. "I don't know," she said softly, and his heart sank.

"You lied. We slept together, and I didn't even know your real name. How can I believe anything you say now?"

"Because you know me now."

She made a protesting sound.

"*You do*. The real me without all the money and the crazy ex-wife baggage. You know I'd never do drugs, let alone push them at someone. And I sure as hell wouldn't encourage anyone I was with to cheat as punishment, no matter what they did. Think about it… do I seem like that kind of man?"

She was quiet so long he wanted to take that pillow she was holding and rip it to shreds in frustration.

"No, I guess you're not," she admitted grudgingly.

He relaxed incrementally. "I wanted to tell you the truth. I tried a million times, but I didn't know how. And when I had finally worked up the courage, you told me about your ex-boyfriend and how you shouldn't date anyone with money."

She narrowed her eyes. "I stand by that."

"Not every rich man is like your ex," he pointed out. "I'd never try to control you or tell you what to think. But it became a lot harder to confess after you said that."

Her head titled back as she remembered something. "That was the day you told me you worked in a bank..."

"Yes. I thought I would break the news in stages."

"And I thought you had a day job as a *bank teller*, not that you owned the whole damn bank!" She huffed.

"I don't own it. I simply run it," he hedged.

Mentioning that he and his family had controlling interest wouldn't help matters right now. He stared at her downbent head, his stomach somewhere around his knees.

"Sophia, all I wanted was a chance to get to know you. I never wanted to hurt you. Please believe that."

There was another long pause but eventually she nodded. "I believe you...but I think you should go now."

His face fell. He couldn't blame her for how she felt. But it was too soon for him to give up. "All right. Um, I'm going to be in town for a few days. Can we talk later? Have coffee or something? I could come by the lab."

A look of what he hoped was mock horror spread over her face. "Absolutely not."

Gio wrinkled his nose. "I am sorry about that, too. The accident was my fault. I should have done it some other way. Surprising you at work was a bad idea."

"Yeah, no shit," she muttered, looking down at her hands.

He frowned. "I had no idea lab work was so dangerous. You should use some of that grant money to hire an assistant to work with the hazardous chemicals."

Sophia sat up straighter. "I like to mix up my own solutions.

Consistency is better when you do it yourself."

"But if it's dangerous—"

"*Gio.*"

He stood, uncomfortable. He wanted to press her. Her safety was everything to him, but it would have to wait until he was in better standing with her. And he would be. All he needed was one more chance. There would be no need for another.

"All right. I'll go. Is Kelly staying here tonight?"

She shrugged.

"You shouldn't be alone. Ask her to stay. You need to be monitored. Chemical pneumonitis is a possible complication, or so I've learned in the last few hours."

"Look, Gio—"

"I'm *staying*," Kelly called out from the bedroom in a sing-song voice.

Embarrassed to realize everything he'd said had been overheard, he flushed. "I'll be in touch, okay?"

Deciding that giving her a chance to say no would be a bad idea, he took his leave.

---

KELLY POPPED out of the bedroom, wineglass in hand, bouncing up and down in excitement.

"Oh, my freaking God!" she said, sloshing her glass.

Sophia frowned. "I'm glad you brought chardonnay instead of a red...and that I don't have carpet," she said dryly as some of the wine landed onto the hardwood floor.

"Oh, sorry," Kelly said, putting down the glass and curling up on the couch next to her. "*Day-um.* I knew he was handsome from the tabloids, but in person, he's gorgeous! Like knicker-dropping gorgeous. Don't get me wrong, I love my husband, but that hair and those *eyes*. Not to mention that square jaw—doesn't it just make you want to lick it up and down? Did you do that with the billionaire?"

*Yes.*

She shot her dear friend a dirty look and some of that enthusiastic energy subsided.

"Okay, okay. He's a liar, and we hate him. I'm totally on board with that, for however long you want to play it that way."

Sophia collapsed on the couch cushions. She drew her knees up, hugging them to her chest. "You think I should forgive him, don't you?"

Kelly laughed. "Actually, I think you should punch him in the balls...and then possibly maybe think about having coffee with him so he can continue groveling for forgiveness."

She snorted and Kelly held up a hand. "I'm not saying you *should* forgive him, especially if anything his ex is saying has the tiniest kernel of truth to it. But you didn't sound like you believed any of it when you were talking to him. Do you?"

Sophia took the empty bottle Gio had finished and started peeling the label. "I don't know. I want to say no. None of that sounds like him. But there's this huge lie staring me in the face, and I feel like an idiot for wanting to believe anything he says now."

Kelly gave her a sympathetic look. "Oh, sweetie. I'm sorry. I don't know what to tell you. Other than I don't blame you for hitting that—street artist or not."

Sophia snatched up a pillow and smacked her with it until she begged for mercy.

"Truce! Truce!" Kelly yelled before grabbing the pillow and disarming her. She straightened up. "So what are you going to do?"

"Hide until he leaves town."

"You can't. He's your lab's biggest donor."

Sophia groaned. "I had forgotten all about that. I'm not going to be able to avoid him. I can't even show him how mad I am. The lab is depending on his funding this year. If he pulled it at this stage, we'd be crippled. Alan would never forgive me."

"I doubt Gio would be that vindictive."

"One can only hope."

Kelly stood and opened the second bottle of wine she brought. She poured Sophia a very full glass.

"Here's to hope," Kelly toasted.

# CHAPTER 11

*S*ophia straightened the skirt of her dress and made a face at herself in the mirror. She was standing in the bathroom in one of Oxford's most exclusive restaurants. Alan had called her at home, asking—no begging—her to join him for dinner with their biggest donor.

He apologized profusely for making her give up her Saturday night, but they both knew there was no way Sophia could avoid it. Gio had given them a lot of money. A veritable buttload—and she had received the lion's share. Dinner was obligatory. The only way she could get miss it was if her eyes were bleeding.

*Just let me get through this in one piece. Speaking of which...*

She looked down at her dress critically. The simple sheath was loose and too boxy. Most of her clothes were. It had never bothered her before. However, having to walk into a four-star restaurant, knowing that a billionaire banker was waiting for her, made her wish she had gone shopping.

For a second she had considered wearing her white dress, but she nipped that idea in the bud. And there was no way in hell she was wearing the black one he'd given her. So instead she was wearing this dark green sack—a choice she was regretting now.

*Doesn't matter.* At least this way he couldn't assume she dressed up for him. Gritting her teeth, she gave herself a little pep talk before walking into the dining room.

They were seated at a prime table. Gio stood as soon as he saw her. He seemed relieved, and she felt a twinge deep inside that he cared that much, in spite of herself.

He wasn't the only one that looked relieved. Alan jumped up as well, his friendly face splitting into a grin. But the sweat on his brow betrayed his concern. It was unnecessary, though. There was no way she'd hurt the lab by skipping dinner. She would be professional until it killed her.

"Here's our girl," Alan said in a loud voice when she reached the table.

*Too loud.* Several people turned to stare at them as Gio hurried to pull out her chair. Her inner feminist chafed at being called a girl by her research partner, but she bit her tongue. Alan was nervous, and with good reason.

He proceeded to show it by making nonstop conversation for a few minutes before his cell phone rang.

"Oh, really, are you stuck?" Alan said. "All right. It's not a good time but if you're stranded, you're stranded. I'll be right there." He hung up the phone with a good imitation of true regret. "I'm so sorry, but I have to leave. My daughter is having car trouble."

"That's fine. We completely understand," Gio said, not bothering to look at him.

His eyes hadn't left her face since she'd sat down and it was starting to make her squirm. Looking away, she blushed while Alan sputtered a quick goodbye before making his escape.

The silence that followed was broken by a waiter requesting their order. Gio asked for a wine she didn't recognize, but it seemed to terribly impress their server.

"Are you okay? Is your cough better?" he asked.

The concern in his voice was unsettling. "It's gone, thank you."

"I didn't ask Alan to do that, by the way." He leaned forward to pour her some wine.

"Of course not," she replied dryly, taking the glass.

"I promise you, I didn't say a thing. Not about us."

She laughed. "I think the way you were carrying on, screaming like a fishwife over a little spilled acid was kind of a big tip-off that there was an *us*."

He ignored the insult. "Is there still?" he asked softly.

Taking a large sip, she leaned back in her chair and stared at him. "Why do you even want there to be?"

She was at least four sizes too large to be billionaire girlfriend material. She and Kelly had Googled his ex-wife right after he left the day before. The woman was a stick insect...of the gorgeous blonde variety. Seeing the photos had made Sophia sick to her stomach despite Kelly's assurances that Maria Gianna was too skinny.

Gio was giving her a look of mingled frustration and something else she couldn't quite define. "I want a second chance. I promise I won't need a third."

Some deep dark part of her soul thrilled at his words, but it was buried under layers of apprehension and distrust.

"*Why?*"

His hand fisted on the table. "I—because you're amazing. Your research application was head and shoulders above everyone else's. I couldn't forget what you said about why you were pursuing that line of research...By the way, did you ever find out if your mother's sample tested positive for the parasite?"

Sophia swallowed over the sudden lump in her throat. "Her results were inconclusive," she said, her throat tightening.

"Oh. I'm sorry."

She gave him a small nod. "So you were so impressed by my big brain you simply had to meet me?" she drawled sarcastically.

He cocked his head and flashed her a devastating smile. "Well,

97

after I saw you in that white dress and almost swallowed my tongue, meeting you became a top priority."

Her blush crept down all the way down to her chest. Even her décolletage was red. She snuck a glance at Gio's face, but he was politely looking into her eyes.

"I find it hard to believe I'm your type," she said.

He frowned and toyed with his fork. "Why is that?"

"I'm not some skinny fashion plate. I don't dress to show off my body. That white dress is the exception, not the rule. I wouldn't look right on a billionaire's arm. I saw pictures of your ex-wife. She's like a size zero."

"Sophia, that hardly means I only like skinny women. In fact, I always thought Maria Gianna dieted too much. I'm more egalitarian in my tastes than that."

"So you've dated fatties before?" she asked, her eyebrow raised.

His brow creased. "You're *not* fat. I love your curves. I think you know that...and in case you've forgotten, I'd be more than happy to demonstrate my enthusiasm for them," he said, his face sharpening with a predatory hunger that sent a shiver down her spine.

The waiter arrived with their meal, saving her from having to respond to that. She picked at her meal, blushing awkwardly whenever she caught his heated gaze.

He gave her a break for a little while, discussing the lab and its research. Apparently, Alan had given him a tour after she'd gone home yesterday and he was eager to discuss their recent findings and the current state of science in general.

"I do think it's a double-edged sword that we get so much money from private sources these days," she said, warming to a topic that she often discussed with her colleagues.

"So I should take my money back?" Gio asked with a glint in his eye.

Sophia's laugh was a higher pitch than normal. "Bite your tongue. Alan would have me drawn and quartered if he heard you teasing like that. No, I meant that it's a shame government funding of research has stagnated in the last decade. It's not a priority in tough economic times. Politicians forget that science funds innovation and industry. And scientists themselves have become extremely conservative when it comes to what research topics they pick since so much depends on getting the next grant. Innovation is dwindling across the board. Cash-strapped labs can't risk being on the bleeding edge anymore. Most of the time they have to have the research half-done to obtain the money in the first place —to prove a project's viability. At the same time, having to answer to private donors such as yourself comes with its own set of pitfalls."

"Like having to have dinner with your benefactors?" he asked with a wry twist of his lips.

"If only it stopped there," she said, choosing to take his question at face value as they finished up their meal. "Not only do we get accused of conflicts of interest—sometimes with good reason if you do pharma research—but private donor money can come with a lot of strings. The Morgese Foundation doesn't have this reputation, by the way. I'm thinking of experiences other colleagues have had."

He nodded and ordered coffee from the waiter before answering. "I'm glad the foundation has good word of mouth. That work is important to me."

She drummed her fingers on the table. "So, since it has come up, I have to speak to you about the money. I need to know that whatever happens between us, it won't affect the lab's funding."

Gio perked up. "Does that mean you're considering going out with me again?"

"No—I mean I don't know." She bit her lip. "God, just answer the question, please."

He sat up straighter. "Do you honestly believe I would jeopardize your livelihood or that of the people you work with for any reason?"

He sounded angry. Slightly ashamed, she shook her head.

Gio's shoulders drooped. "You earned that grant. You deserve it, and I'm not going to take it away because you don't want to be with me anymore."

He sounded heartbroken.

"I didn't say that."

He leaned forward. "So…dinner tomorrow night?"

"We're having dinner now," she reminded him.

"And tomorrow night, too?" he asked in a hopeful voice.

His boyish grin was completely disarming. Steeling herself, she took a deep breath. Despite what he'd done and her petty desire to continue punishing him, she did miss him. What if she gave him another chance?

He would be on probation, of course, and this time she would be vigilant. She wouldn't take anything at face value. If he lied to her again, she'd take Kelly's advice and kick him in the balls. And she could kick *really* hard.

"If we do this, we start over. You get one, and I mean *one*, more chance," she said, holding up her index finger.

Gio put both hands on the table, his shoulders dropping in relief. "Thank you."

"Don't thank me yet. When I said start over I meant from the beginning." She took a surreptitious look at their fellow diners and leaned in. "That means no sex. As of now, we are strangers who are on their first date."

He was unfazed, an irrepressible grin lighting up his whole face.

"I'm serious," she whispered. "*No sex.*"

THAT LASTED ABOUT A WEEK.

# CHAPTER 12

*D*amn Italian must've drugged me.

Sophia gripped the counter she was sitting on with one hand. The other was busy pulling the hair on Gio's head, which was currently buried between her legs.

"Oh, God!" she cried, as his tongue circled her clit before biting down on it gently.

One of his hands was stroking her pussy lips, two fingers buried deep in her sheath. She shuddered and moaned as they stroked a sensitive spot.

She didn't know how this had happened. They had been arguing just a minute ago in the car. Richard had been calling about her father's Chevette again, instigating yet another argument between her and Gio when all of a sudden they had been kissing—a heated clinch with tongues and teeth that had them climbing all over each other in the backseat of his town car.

Thank God it had tinted windows.

Getting to Gio's place was a blur. She barely recalled being ushered out of the car. His hands had been busy under her skirt, and she had come close to being fucked in an elevator.

It had been a long ride to the penthouse.

She remembered him opening the door to the place, but for the life of her couldn't remember how she'd ended up sitting on the marble countertop in the kitchen getting oral from a billionaire.

Gio had been lent the glorious apartment by a friend of his from university so he could stay in town to "court" her. The place was ridiculously large with a dozen rooms, including a private gym and a home theater. Last night she had watched a blockbuster new release in there snuggled in Gio's arms.

It had taken Herculean strength to go home to her cold bed alone yesterday. She was proud of the amount of willpower she'd displayed around him. But her resolve to take things slow flew out the window mid-fight.

"We have to stop settling arguments this way," she managed to say between breathy little moans.

His laughter sent delicious little vibrations up and down her pussy. She buried both hands in his hair and held him closer, her hips pumping up helplessly. Worried that he was in danger of suffocating, she tried to back up, but his hands moved to hold her against his mouth. He sucked and licked in an aggressive rhythm that made the blood pound in her ears in a matching beat.

When his tongue stabbed into her, she tightened and throbbed around him. A broken sob escaped and her hands trembled on his head as he snaked in and out of her channel, extending the ripples of her orgasm until she was limp.

Gio pulled her off the counter. He was wrapping her legs around his hips, his cock probing at her entrance when there was a sudden loud crash somewhere behind them.

She gasped and pulled her skirt down while Gio hastily zipped up his fly. He was looking over her head, his face beet red.

"Alex!" he said.

"Oh, God," she moaned, her hands covering her face.

Slowly she turned around and peeked out from beneath her fingers. There was a very tall, very embarrassed, dark haired man standing there with his mouth open. He closed it and opened it a few times, desperately trying not to laugh.

"I am so sorry," he said, holding up his hands. "The doorman let me up." He looked down sheepishly at the broken lamp beside him.

"I didn't mean to intrude...It's just that I haven't heard from you, and Elynn and I were worried that it wasn't going well...but I'm glad to see that I was wrong."

Gio made a choking sound.

"Not that I saw anything!" Alex assured them before breaking out into a shit-eating grin. "Well, nothing good anyway..."

Sophia laughed despite her humiliation, and Gio gave her the most adorably abashed look of relief.

"Um, Sophia this is my friend, Alex Hanas. Alex, this is my Sophia," he said, moving to stand behind her and put his hands on her shoulders.

*My Sophia.*

The possessiveness was enough to make her put her hands down to peek at the two men standing there looking so bloody handsome and...handsome.

*Damn,* they were both so attractive. Of course, Alex was nothing compared to Gio, whose square jaw and light gold eyes were far more devastating than the other man's more generic model looks.

"Er...I am going to be right back," Gio said holding up a finger.

She twisted her head around to give him a don't-you-dare-leave-me look.

He ducked his head.

"I'm sorry," he whispered. "I need to clean up," he added pointedly and she blushed because up close her intimate scent was noticeable all over his face.

"I'll be right back," he called, practically running out of the room.

She and Alex stared at each other awkwardly, and she laughed again. He relaxed and laughed with her.

"I am *really* sorry," he said. "We were worried about him and the doorman didn't mention he had company. Gio and I went to school together, and we've been pretty tight ever since. Anyway, he called last week and told us the whole crazy story. For what it's worth, he's never like that. Gio is the most honorable man I know. This whole thing with his ex, the bitch from hell, really messed with his head."

Her brows went up. "Bitch from hell?"

"It's her official title."

"Not a fan, I guess."

He shook his head emphatically. "We hate her."

She smiled. "*We?*"

"My wife Elynn and I."

Moving from the protection of the counter, she joined him in the living room. "Does that mean you're one of the friends that Gio's ex…"

She trailed off with a gesture.

Alex wrinkled his nose. "I was. Me and our other friend, Calen. It was…bad. Horrible woman. Which is why I am so glad to meet you." he gushed. "Gio hasn't been serious about anyone in a long while."

His enthusiasm was genuine, and she was a little flustered. Alex was a forceful personality. Sophia could feel herself being carried along by it—instant relationship, just add water. The sensation was a little overwhelming, but not entirely unpleasant.

"So, I guess he tells you everything…"

Had Gio actually said he was serious about her, or was Alex inferring it?

Alex put his hands in his pockets with a little shrug and smiled. "Like I said, we're close. By the way, my wife is dying to meet you too. We're hoping the two of you can come to dinner soon. Calen and his wife are going to come out for a visit next week and, if you come, I'm pretty sure I can convince Sergei and his wife Eva to fly in as well." He leaned in. "They're dying to check you out, too."

Her smile was awkward. "Oh, that's great," she said weakly.

Who were Sergei and Eva?

Gio hurried out of the hallway at speed. He almost skidded to a stop before Alex, moving to hug him with one of those hearty pats on the back masculine men tended to give each other. They spoke in what sounded like Greek before Gio walked to the bar and poured a glass of something brown and terribly expensive. Then he poured Sophia a glass of her favorite Madeira with a wink.

Sipping it, she watched the two men interact. So this was Gio's version of Kelly. Alex seemed like a nice man. She hadn't been expecting somebody so GQ, but perhaps that was because in the back of her mind she still thought of Gio as a man of limited means.

Which was a bit stupid of her. Looking at him now, she wondered how she could have ever believed he was uneducated or poor. Both of the men in front of her screamed money. Their wealth and breeding were obvious in the clean lines of their suits and strong masculine features.

With a little grimace, she glanced down at her utilitarian sheath dress, one of a dozen in her wardrobe.

She might need to do a little shopping. It wouldn't kill her to buy a few outfits that fit a little better. The idea had made her uncomfortable for years. But it was doubtful anyone in the lab would call her a slut if the outline of her breasts were visible for a change. She was a fully grown woman with a high-level research job. The days of falling victim to a few cruel taunts were behind her. *You hope...*

*Stop that.* Besides, Gio loved her curves.

*You can do the sexy librarian look.* She could probably pull that off...and Gio would go nuts. He'd already asked her to wear her reading glasses for him when they made out last night, so it was a pretty safe bet he was a fan.

As the men caught up, she only replied when spoken to. She was silently planning the marathon shopping trip that would be required to overhaul her wardrobe. Gio seemed thrilled to hear that his other friends were coming to town.

She loved the boyish eagerness he displayed as the pair regaled her with stories from their old University days.

*Don't go there.* It was way too soon to be using the word love in any context.

Alex left soon after, but not before making her promise to attend dinner. Gio closed the door behind him and gave her a commiserating smile.

"I apologize for that," he said. "Alex owns this place, and several others, all over town. He and Elynn used to stay here, but now that the baby is walking they commute from their country estate."

She collapsed back onto the sofa, a little dizzy. "A country estate? How very Jane Austen."

Exactly how rich were these people? A penthouse was a big apartment, but a whole estate? Did Gio have one of those? *Probably several. B is for billionaire.*

Oh Jesus, her head was starting to spin.

Gio sat next to her. "It's just a house," he said softly, reading her mind.

"Yeah...I get that. But it's an adjustment, knowing you have obscene amounts of money."

She'd been worried about the opposite—how he would fit in with her friends. Now she was concerned about how she would fit in with his.

Gio laughed. "It's not obscene amounts. And most of it is not mine. The money belongs to my family. I'm simply this generation's caretaker of it."

Yeah, that did not make her feel better.

She stood up and went for her purse. "Right. Uh, I should go."

His face fell. "Already?"

"I need to pick up a few things at the store."

*Lingerie.* She should buy lingerie. *Hope it comes in plus sizes.* It was always hell for her to find a decent bra with enough support, let alone a pretty one.

The disappointment on his face lightened fractionally. "You know I can send out for anything you need. I can have my UK shopper give you a call. He'll even do grocery runs if you need him to."

Wow. Gio had someone to shop for him? *Probably more than one...*

"You have a personal shopper for every country, don't you?"

Gio stood too, following her to the door. "Only the ones I do business in a lot."

"How many is that?"

"Well, it's in the ballpark of a dozen or so."

There went her equilibrium again. "*Damn.* Um, okay. Have your UK guy give me a call."

As much a she hated the idea of taking advantage of Gio's wealth, she was going to need professional help finding lingerie that wouldn't make her look like a parade float.

"I will," he promised, still looking at her wistfully. "Are you certain you don't want to stay?"

"*I'm sure,*" she said decisively, picking up her coat and clutching it protectively in front of her.

"All right. I'll call down and have the driver take you home."

She paused halfway out the door. "Really, it's not necessary. I'm going to hail a taxi."

He folded his arms in mock disapproval. "Absolutely not. Sam is an excellent chauffeur. You never know about taxi drivers."

"Gio—"

"If you're leaving me to sleep alone tonight, at least give me that."

Slumping visibly, she conceded defeat. "All right."

"Good...and I'm sorry for letting Alex railroad you into dinner. I was going to give it a few more weeks, but with Calen and Maia coming into town—"

She held up a hand. "I'm good. I want to meet your friends," she said, hoping they were as friendly as Alex appeared to be.

He beamed at her. "Excellent. I want them to get to know you, too. Goodnight."

Leaning in, he stole a hot hard kiss before she could summon the willpower to leave.

On the way home, she called Kelly. Shopping for attractive form-fitting clothes was going to require major reinforcements... and several bottles of wine.

# CHAPTER 13

Gio smoothed a covetous hand over Sophia's ass as they rode in the elevator to the penthouse.

He was proud of his restraint all through dinner. Sophia's new dress was simply too tempting. He'd been unable to keep his hands to himself the whole night. But he'd kept it G-rated when they were in company—waist and hips only.

He had to give his UK shopper, Gavin, a bonus. Of course, he wasn't supposed to know that Sophia had used him to buy clothes. She swore the man to secrecy, but Gavin knew which side his bread was buttered on. As a result, Gio had secret approval of Sophia's new wardrobe. Without her knowledge, he had been able to make several suggestions she had ended up loving. One of them was this velvet dress.

Unable to restrain himself, he nuzzled his woman's neck, running his fingers against the nap of the luxurious fabric.

"I love you in velvet," he murmured, intensely disappointed when another couple joined them in the elevator.

Sophia gave him a pointed look and pinched his hand. He

refused to move it, though. It was her fault for wearing the velvet instead of the wool.

Dinner with the gang had been a resounding success. Calen and Sergei had joined Alex in his effusive approval of Sophia. Everyone had loved her, although he'd had to smack Sergei a few times for making an hourglass figure with his hands behind the women's back and mouthing "*wow.*"

Sophia had hit it off with Elynn and Maia, too. That had been a nice bonus. The other guys had thought so too. In fact, Sophia was going to meet them for lunch when Eva, Sergei's partner, joined them after her business trip later in the week. But tonight she belonged to him…

His patience eroded the moment they walked into the penthouse. He pressed Sophia against the front door, leaning down to cover her mouth with his.

"Did I…mention…how happy…I am that you agreed…to spend the night," he said between biting kisses.

Sophia gasped as he rubbed against her rhythmically, his hands cupping her full ass to pull her in closer.

"I don't know how you do it…I have no willpower with you."

He pulled back his head enough to grin down at her. "Good," he said, picking her up to carry her off to the bedroom.

"Gio, put me down! You're going to throw out your back!"

Maneuvering into the hallway, he laughed. "You weigh nothing."

"Liar!"

He smiled down at her. She looked so uncomfortable that he felt a little bad. But not enough to put her down. "Sophia, *mi amore*, does it seem like I'm having trouble?"

She scowled at him as he moved into the master bedroom and put her down on the large four-poster bed.

"No," she admitted. "But that's just because you're a gym rat." He laughed and took off his shirt and she waved at his chest. "It's not funny! Look at you. You're practically photoshopped!"

He glanced down at his six-pack. "I exercise when I'm frustrated. And I'd like to add that no one has complained before now."

Sophia groaned and collapsed backward on the bed. "Why can't you eat cookies when you're upset like a normal person?"

Hiding a smirk, he took advantage of her prone position on the bed, kicking off his shoes and climbing over her.

Wiggling underneath him, she put her hands on his chest. "Wait!"

Kissing along her neck, he murmured. "Hmm?"

"Stop that, or I'll forget what I want to say," she said, trying, and failing, to push his head away from the soft skin next to her ear.

"Go ahead," he said before sucking on her earlobe.

A little purr escaped her, and she went boneless underneath him until she came to her senses and pushed him away.

"This is not a sexy conversation."

He rolled over and sat up. "All right. What kind of a conversation is this?"

"The uncomfortable STD one."

His throat almost closed up. "You have an STD?" he choked out.

"No, you do!"

"I don't have an STD," he said with a laugh.

"I didn't mean you actually had one. That was supposed to be *"do you have one"*? This is the belated sexual history talk. The one we should have had before I lost my mind in that alley in Rome."

*"We* lost our minds. But believe me when I say that I am completely one hundred percent clean."

She studied him solemnly. "Okay...it's only that some things don't show up right away. And with you being you..."

He narrowed his eyes. "What does that mean?"

A hand moved to encompass his naked chest. "You're so much more experienced and if you're sometimes careless then—"

"I am *not* careless."

"But—"

He held up a hand. "Sophia, I've never had unprotected sex

with anyone other than you and my wife. I'm fastidious when it comes to my love life. You are the exception…and well there's only been you since my marriage ended."

Sophia shot up to a seated position. "Wait, you got divorced like a year ago!"

He straightened uncomfortably. "More than two years actually."

Her mouth dropped open. There was silence while she stared at him for a painfully long minute. "*Oh.*"

"Yes, oh. Additionally you should know that given the reason for my divorce, I felt it necessary to get every STD test known to man."

"Oh."

He pushed her back down on the bed. "Can I have another syllable please?"

She giggled and reached up to put her arms around his neck. "Would you settle for an *oh, God?*"

He didn't. He settled for four.

---

GIO'S HANDS rubbed over the naked skin of her back.

Sophia was asleep on her side, her forehead pressed into a pillow, sheets tangled around her waist.

"Mmm," she murmured, fighting her drowsiness.

Even in her half-conscious state, she wanted to be awake and back in her lover's arms. Last night had been devastating in the best sense of the word. Gio had clearly been making up for his almost two years of abstinence. They had gotten precious little sleep, but she didn't give a damn.

A long strong finger slipped between her ass cheeks, making the short journey to no-man's land. Suddenly wide awake, she turned her head to the side, giving Gio access to her neck. His warm breath tickled her ear.

"I want to take you here," he said, making her catch her breath. "Have you ever done that with anyone?"

"*No.*" Her voice was small.

He continued to rub, pushing at her rosette with his thumb. His index and middle fingers moved down until he was rimming her front entrance as well. She was already soaking. His thumb pressed down harder.

"Would you want to, with me?"

"I..."

Tracing her slippery folds, he licked that sweet spot next to her ear, the one that made her shiver. "'Cause if I didn't know any better, I would think you like it, judging by how wet you are."

His voice was smooth and dark, like bittersweet chocolate. Coherence was impossible when one finger and then another entered her sheath, twisting and teasing until she moaned.

"Yes, I want to."

The words were out before she could analyze them. There was no desire to take them back. Gio was her chance to fulfill every forbidden desire and secret fantasy she'd ever had. True, she hadn't ever thought about *that*, but if she didn't like it, she didn't have to do it again, right?

Her heart skipped a beat when he took hold of her hips and pulled until she was on her hands and knees on the bed. Withdrawing his hand, he moved behind her, stopping when he was only a hairsbreadth away. The heat from his body warmed her skin, but he wasn't touching her—nothing but his cock. His thick naked shaft rubbed against her wet lips, slipping and teasing. The friction was just right.

The man always did *everything* just right.

The anticipation had become excruciating. Her sheath was clamping down hungrily on nothing, silently begging to be filled.

"Please, please," she begged shamelessly, pushing back against him.

She didn't care where he put his cock, as long as he filled the aching emptiness inside of her. He made a pleased little growling sound and then he was there, pushing inside her tight pussy.

She gasped, clawing at his Egyptian cotton sheets.

"I thought—" she managed to say before he laughed.

He ran a loving hand over the smooth skin of her left cheek. "That's the sort of thing you have to work up to," he said, slowly working his member in and out of her in forceful strokes.

Of course, he was right. A man of his proportions could not be accommodated easily. She had read enough guilty-pleasure erotica to know it would take some preparation before they made the attempt.

And apparently we're starting now, she thought as one of Gio's fingers pushed past the constricting ring of muscle of her back entrance. Her pussy reacted instantly, tightening like an anaconda around his thick cock. He made a strangled sound, and she giggled in response and did it again.

"Someone is being bad," he muttered. "Which can only mean one thing...punishment."

The spank from his free hand was a complete surprise. It was hard, startling her into jumping forward. It knocked the breath out of her and his cock nearly fell out. Taking hold of her hips he pulled her close again, sliding deep. Then he smacked her butt again until it was hot.

"Gio!"

"Too hard?" He lovingly caressed the smarting skin.

"I don't know!"

He hummed and gave her another little tap, softer this time. "Is that better?"

It was. God, she could feel herself getting wetter—if that was possible. Then the finger in her backside twisted around and she cried out, pushing back blindly.

"Guess that *is* better," he said.

"*Yes*," she breathed hoarsely.

She pushed back again, trying to encourage him to keep

moving but he was too distracted by her ass to do anything. He kept stroking her skin, rubbing and kneading while he thrust like the consummate multitasker that he was.

Bracing herself against the mattress, she moaned shamelessly while he pumped inside her, working that naughty finger with each stroke. The sensation of being so filled overwhelmed her. The dark wave of forbidden pleasure swept over her. Her channel spasmed violently, clamping down on him.

He stroked into her hard, extending her orgasm to a record-breaking length. She damn near passed out, falling forward when her trembling arms wouldn't support her. He followed her down, moving his hand from her ass so he could embrace her from behind. His body enveloped hers, hips driving inexorably until his cock swelled and jerked, flooding her with heat. She ground against him, holding tight, letting his climax trigger a second one of her own.

For a long while afterward they stayed liked that.

"I like that you're so tall," she said after a comfortable silence. "You make me feel small."

"You are small," he said sleepily, nuzzling her neck.

She hummed happily and waited until his breathing deepened, signaling that he'd fallen asleep.

"I love you," she whispered, before burrowing deeper into his arms.

She closed her eyes, pretending to be asleep when Gio went to the bathroom a few minutes later. She didn't know if he'd heard her, but he did squeeze her extra tight when he got back into bed.

# CHAPTER 14

The scent of good strong coffee woke her early the next morning.

"Hrmph," she muttered, pushing Gio's hand away before reluctantly sitting up in bed. "Unless that tiny espresso cup has cream and sugar, take it away."

"Sacrilege!" he said, chucking her under the chin and setting the cup aside.

He sat down next to her with a graceful economy of motion she envied. She squinted at him, resenting his bright-eyed and bushy-tailed attitude. "I hate that you're a morning person."

He smiled, his gleaming teeth almost blinding in the sunlight.

"Stop that. You're like a toothpaste commercial. And why are you so dressed up?"

He was wearing a fine dark gray suit with a pearl colored tie. She'd never been into suits before, but his normal wardrobe made him look like he fell off the cover of a men's magazine. She was quickly becoming a fan of the style.

"Work," he said, picking up her coffee and drinking it himself.

"But it's Sunday. And don't you work in Rome? That's the bank's headquarters, right?"

"I'm working out of the London office until further notice. Also, I have a few things to take care of, tasks that piled up while I was away."

*Away pretending to be a street performer.* She bit her tongue to keep from mentioning it and then her fuzzy brain caught up.

"The office is in London? What's the commute on that?"

He shrugged nonchalantly. "It's not too bad on the chopper."

She opened her eyes so wide they hurt. "You have a *helicopter*?"

"It's not mine. It's part of a service I contract with."

"Oh," she said. "Still crazy, though..."

The man took a helicopter *to work*. She drove a Saab.

He smiled, leaning over to play with her hair. "I should be back by early evening...unless you want dinner in London. In which case, you can get dressed and come with me now. You can squeeze in some shopping or go to this spa Elynn recommended."

*Crap.* She was going to have to tell him about her plans for the day.

"Err. Sorry. I can't. I have to meet Richard."

Gio's expression turned frosty.

"Oh. Why?" he asked very casually.

"That unfinished business I mentioned. He's buying my father's house. We're signing the papers today."

He leaned back, surprise replacing the coldness of his expression. "Why are you selling it to him?"

She shrugged. "He wants it. I don't. Not much more to it than that."

His brows lowered. Sophia took the espresso cup from him and finished what was left, flinching as it went down. God, it needed sugar.

Gio continued to stare at her.

"*What?*" she asked defensively.

"I suppose I find it odd that you would sell your childhood home to an ex-boyfriend."

Sophia stared at him, scowling. "Um, did you not notice the American accent? My dad's place isn't my childhood home. It's not my anything. I only visited there as an adult, and I hardly ever went inside."

"Ah," he said, his expression shifting to sympathy. "I know a lot about your mom, but not your father. We've never talked about him that much."

"And were not going to start now," she said resolutely.

"Why not?"

"Because you don't have ten hours or one of those really long psychiatrist couches."

He exhaled heavily. "Okay. Can you sum up why you're giving this Richard your father's house?"

"Not *giving*, selling," she insisted. "He's way more attached to the place than I am. Richard is the son he never had—his heir, literally. He was my father's protégé at the University. Richard has even been awarded the position my father had, the Sotheby chair of Sociology."

"So he's inherited your father's job *and* he wants your father's house?"

She shrugged. "He says it's more convenient to the University than his place—which it is, but only slightly. Personally, I think he just misses the old man. They were tight."

"It would seem so," he said with a nod, still watching her with a mushy expression of sympathy.

"It's actually a little creepy. Richard also wants his car."

Gio's face soured. "I'm sorry, what?"

"My dad had a 1970 Chevette. He was always tinkering on it during the weekends. I used to have to sit out in the garage with him if I wanted to talk to him at all."

Gio snapped his fingers. "That's why you hardly went inside the house."

She smiled sardonically. "Yes, smart alec, that's right. Even in the freezing cold I sat in the garage huddled next to a space heater so I could have a twenty-minute long conversation with him every Sunday. Then I would go inside for a cup of tea—alone—and then I would go home."

He nodded. "And you sign the house over to Richard today. Are you going to sell him the car, too?"

"Probably. I have a car. One with a backseat that isn't held in place with armature wire."

"So...where are you meeting Richard? At the house?"

"No, at a coffee shop near his office. It's across the street from Kelly's place, which is where I'll be heading for the bitch session I will be sure to need afterward."

His laugh was forced. "Well, that sounds like a plan. I'll call you after my meeting."

"Sounds good," she said, watching him from beneath her lashes.

It wasn't that difficult to guess his mood now, but he was doing a good job of faking acceptance as he leaned over to kiss her cheek. Impulsively, she grabbed his tie and kissed him on the mouth instead, hard.

"Don't hit any birds in that chopper. That's an order."

The light in his eyes warmed, making them a shade closer to honey. "I'll be sure to relay that to my pilot."

"Do that."

With that, he left and she dragged herself to the shower to get ready. It wasn't till after she'd finished that she finally glanced at the bedside clock.

It read six-thirty am.

*Damn morning people.*

---

SOPHIA PAUSED in front of the coffee shop, straightening her skirt in an attempt to procrastinate before facing her ex. She was wearing one of her new outfits, a figure-hugging dress with a black skirt and attached white silk top. It was cut with an empire waist, a style she'd avoided for years because she thought it made her bust look too big. Gavin, Gio's UK shopper and her new favorite person, had convinced her otherwise.

She was now wearing cuts and silhouettes she'd never considered dressing in before. They flattered her figure without making her appear unprofessional, giving her a boost in confidence she hadn't been aware she needed.

Yes, her size had always been an issue, but she was smart and driven. Her confidence came from her ability and success at work, not her appearance.

It was a familiar pep talk, one she'd given herself many times around Richard and her father. But now she knew she looked good. Richard's issues with her body were exactly that—*his* issues.

He was early of course. She hated that about him. He always made her feel as if she'd been late when she'd been right on time.

He was sitting in an intimate corner with two armchairs pushed close together over a small round table. There was a pile of papers on it, presumably the deed to the house.

"Are these them?" she asked without preamble, sitting in the empty chair next to him.

Richard choked on the sip of tea he was drinking, standing formally to greet her, although she'd already sat down.

"Hello, darling," he said standing there awkwardly, waiting for her to get back up before giving up and bending to kiss her cheek.

*Whatever. You don't have to follow his Emily Post rules of etiquette anymore.*

"Hi."

He sat back down after her lackluster greeting, looking her up and down.

"Sophie darling, you look smashing. New dress?"

"Yes," she muttered, ignoring his scrutiny while she went over the paperwork.

*Wait for it.*

"It's a little form-fitting, isn't it?"

*There it is.*

She clenched her teeth before forcing herself to relax and answer.

"That's the idea," she said, managing to keep her tone pleasant.

"Darling, you know that I didn't mean anything by that. You were always so sensitive about your outfits," he said, smoothing an imaginary wrinkle on his lap.

*Because you were always criticizing them.* He'd been like her father that way. If her curves were visible, she would be gently chided about "flaunting" herself.

"Sometimes it's nice to change things up," she said leaning back with a cool glance. "I see you're still sporting the same urbane professor uniform."

He was wearing a button-down shirt paired with a tweed sports coat, the kind with suede patches at the elbows. Since it was Saturday, he'd gone with an informal chino in place of his usual pair of slacks. She used to think his was the perfect style on a man, but these days she much preferred the GQ look. A clean tailored suit and tie was much more sophisticated.

Without waiting for him to answer, she stood and went to the counter to order something to eat. She was disappointed when she was given a little number to display on her table, instead of waiting up front for her food.

"New system?" she asked the barista.

He gave her a big grin and nodded. Refraining from giving him a dirty look, she turned back to the table, stiffing him on the tip. But true to form, she immediately felt guilty and returned to stick a five pound note in the tip jar.

The walk back to the armchair was exhausting. She sat down with a thump, taking out her pen. Wasting no more time, she started signing and initialing as needed.

*Just think of that big bottle of Bordeaux Kelly has waiting for you.*

"Darling…"

"I thought we established that I'm not your darling around six months ago."

Richard gave her a little moue of distress. "You know that was a mistake. In fact, I've been wanting to speak to you about our relationship," he said, leaning over to put his hand on her arm to stay her pen.

Stiffening, she shook his hand off.

"My parents are in town," he said. "They're here to see the house. I thought we could have dinner with them."

Her mouth dropped open, but nothing came out. She was literally speechless. Gaping like a fish, she clenched her hand around the pen until the boiling white hot rage caught up with her.

"Are you *fucking* kidding me?"

Richard gave her one of his patented disapproving glares, the one that made his face thin and pinched. He had an assortment of them, although this was his favorite.

"Darling, don't be vulgar."

Sophia took a deep breath and counted to ten. "We were together for two years and not once did you offer to introduce me to your parents!"

"Sophie be reasonable. They retired to Spain and never visited, or you would have met them."

She pointed the pen at him, resisting the urge to throw it at his face. "I know for a fact they visited twice, once for your birthday and another for your cousin's wedding—a wedding you didn't invite me to."

He huffed and picked at his sleeve. "You were busy at work the weekend of the wedding. And we had just started dating when they visited the first time. It was too soon."

*Do not stab him with the pen. Do not stab him with the pen.*

"We were together for four months by then," she ground out. "And I would have rearranged my work thing if you'd asked. Not to mention the fact you went to see them in Spain twice a year, and you never asked me to go with you."

"Their place in Seville is too small to entertain. You know that."

It was the same excuse she'd heard a million times. The truth was that Richard hadn't wanted her to meet his parents because he'd been ashamed of her. It didn't matter that she was his mentor's daughter. She was her mother's mirror image in looks and demeanor, and someone like her didn't fit in the Selwyn's aristocratic world.

Richard had made that clear often enough with his less than subtle hints about her weight and his gifts of gym memberships and exercise equipment. His was an existence best suited for skinny blondes who could wear jodhpurs without looking ridiculous.

The arrival of her cream tea interrupted her inner rant. Richard's opinion of her no longer mattered. She was in a good place with Gio. That man was crazy about her. He loved her body exactly the way it was. The fact that he was a gorgeous billionaire was the universe's way of making up for her past relationship.

*Plus all the sex is making me toned.*

With that thought, she calmed down and reached for one of her scones. She spread a generous amount of clotted cream on top and took a big bite.

"Mmm." It was delicious, and she berated herself for giving them up when she started dating Richard. With a little smile, she added more clotted cream and took another bite.

She glanced over her pastry to see Richard staring pointedly at her scone. Smiling like a cat who got the cream, she slowly reached for her knife and added another dollop, making a production of polishing off her plate. She ate the whole scone and then the other, in the most eloquent *fuck you* gesture she could manage.

Richard sat there with an air of resigned patience while she finished. "Have you decided to sell me the car?"

"Yes, you can have it."

It was unreliable anyway, and she only had one parking space at her apartment.

"Thank you, darling. Now about dinner—"

"I won't be attending," she said with a sigh.

"If you're worried about them not approving of you, you shouldn't be concerned. I told them all about you, and your recent accolades. They're excited to meet you."

She held up a hand. "Oh my God, stop! I won't be meeting them because my boyfriend would think it was weird, like *I* think it's weird. You and I aren't a couple anymore, and I've moved on."

Richard's head drew back, and he frowned. "I wasn't aware that you were seeing anyone."

"It's recent. I met Gio on vacation. He's Italian."

"Oh." His lips pursed tightly. "So…this man followed you home? Is he unemployed or something?"

There was the condescending note again. "Actually, he's a banker."

A polite nod. "Is he a clerk?"

She suddenly hated herself for assuming the same thing once upon a time.

"No. He runs the bank. He's Gio Morgese, of the Morgese Foundation."

Richard couldn't hide his surprise. "The one that gave you your grant? Well, that's…nice. I suppose you met at the awards dinner."

It wasn't a real question so she didn't bother to correct him. In fact, she didn't want to talk to him about Gio anymore.

As much as she wanted to rub her new relationship in Richard's face, it felt wrong. What she had now was too precious to discuss with her ex. She had no desire to sully her bright and shiny new memories with Richard's judgments.

"You should take Bernice to dinner," she added blandly, flicking a crumb off her lap.

Across from her, Richard's mouth tightened. "I told you that was nothing. She kissed me, not the other way around."

"Sure she did. And you tripped and fell on her lips the second time."

"What?'"

"I saw you kiss her twice. You kissed twice in your office."

"Darling—"

"My fault, really. I should have called ahead to let you know I was coming by for my keys. Although, I should add that having an affair with your teaching assistant is a little cliché. But you were my father's protégé, so of course you learned from the best."

"Really, Sophia. I explained that. And technically you had broken up with me the night before. Bernice was trying to console me—not that I wanted her to. I had to have a very uncomfortable talk with her afterward."

He sounded genuinely aggrieved and hurt by her lack of trust. There had been a time when she would have felt guilty for doubting him. Richard had a way of doing that to a person. Everything he said sounded so reasonable and dignified that you forgot he was a condescending lying jerk.

Truthfully, she didn't have proof that he cheated with Bernice. The only physical contact she'd witnessed between the two of them was post-breakup. *Immediately post break-up.* But she had her suspicions before. She'd let them go at the time, but now in hindsight she *knew* he had cheated.

"I remember your explanation," she said. "I also remember saying I never wanted to see you again, but you wanted the house, so here I am."

"What about the car?"

*Count to ten. One...two...*

"We can handle the car by email," she said, trying not to sound as irritated as she felt.

He pursed his lips. "If you insist. But you should stop by your father's house. I've been going through his study. I think there are some of your mother's belongings in there."

*Perfect, just perfect.* Couldn't the universe cut her some slack? "If that's the case, I want them."

"So when would you like to stop by?"

Gritting her teeth, she silently conceded defeat. She didn't want to go to her father's house but what choice did she have now?

"I'll get back to you. My plate's a little full right at the moment."

"Yes, it would appear so."

Richard's tone was distracted, and she realized he wasn't looking at her anymore. Confused, she glanced over her shoulder through the plate glass window behind them.

A gorgeous Italian billionaire was standing on the sidewalk, staring at her possessively. His suit still appeared as crisp and clean as it had this morning, but then he always managed to stay neat and perfect. It would have been irritating if he wasn't so hot.

"So that's Gio Morgese. He looks very...sophisticated." Richard's tone implied just the opposite. "I didn't realize he was going to be picking you up."

*Neither did I.*

"He's shorter in person, isn't he?"

*No, he's taller.*

Outside, Gio gave her a little nod, his hands in his pockets.

She shot to her feet and grabbed her purse. "I have to run, Richard. I'll get back to you about coming around to the house."

"Fine, darling, fine," he said absently, trying to be subtle about the close inspection of his replacement.

Resisting the urge to roll her eyes, she hurried outside before Gio decided to come inside—she could smell the testosterone from here.

# CHAPTER 15

*R*ichard is trying to get her back.

It was obvious. The man kept leaning in and trying to touch her hand, even when she was signing paperwork, for crying out loud.

*And there he goes again.*

One more, and Gio was going to go in there to beat the crap out of the good professor. He looked like an academic, too—of the overbred chinless variety.

Except he had a chin. Richard wasn't hideously ugly, as much as Gio wanted to believe otherwise. He had those pale good looks of the English upper class, the weak kind that would fall apart in middle age. No doubt Richard did well with women in the University environment, where sheltered co-eds were easily impressed by a clever turn of phrase and a tweed coat.

Gio stood outside stewing until his fixed attention was noticed by the occupants of the cafe. Sophia turned and saw him waiting on the sidewalk. She didn't look happy to see him. Perhaps he should have warned her he was coming back early.

She didn't waste any time saying goodbye to her ex. Fortunately, for his equilibrium, all Richard received was a distracted wave as she headed for the door.

"*Bongiorno, mi amore*," he said, putting his arms around her and giving her a warm and very visible kiss.

He didn't fool her for a second. She gave him an exasperated glare and pulled him down the street, away from the cafe, putting on her coat and scarf as they went.

"What are you doing here?"

*Merda*, she sounded mad.

"You said you were meeting Richard at the cafe near Kelly's place. That is her place, isn't it?" he asked, gesturing across the street.

"I meant, why aren't you in London?"

"My meeting was rescheduled so I headed back early."

"Of course it was."

Red warning lights started flashing in his head, but he ignored them. "What does that mean?"

She stopped and spun around to face him. "It means, did you reschedule it or did the other guy?"

"My associate canceled," he lied.

Sophia's lips pursed and she tapped her foot. Even when she was angry, she was so damn sexy.

"*Gio.*"

Distracted by the delicious fullness of her lips, he'd lost his train of thought, a dangerous thing when a woman was irritated with you.

"Yes, *bella mia?*"

"Don't *bella mia* me. I know you came back early because I was meeting Richard. But there was no reason to. You don't have to be jealous."

"I'm not jealous," he protested, growing warm despite the sharp bite in the air.

"If you're not, then what are you doing here?"

"I was concerned," he said, reaching over to adjust the scarf inadequately covering her. He wrapped it around her neck and closed her coat more firmly against the wind.

Her face softened, and she put a hand over his. "There's no reason to be."

Was she serious? He threw up his hands, finally losing his patience.

"Sophia, that man called you ten times a day when we were in Italy. He's stalking you!"

She laughed.

*"It's not funny."*

Sobering, she wiped the smile off her face and tilted her head at him. "It would be if you knew him. Richard never does anything if it's the slightest bit inconvenient for him. Stalking anyone would be too much of a strain. But he is a pest 'cause he refuses to text on principle. He wrote a paper on how texting and instant messaging is destroying civilization. And if you're ignoring his voicemails, like I have been since the breakup, he calls and calls until you give up and answer."

"So he's a luddite. Doesn't change the fact that he's trying to win you back," he said.

Sophia stopped and for a moment she looked young and confused. "Yeah, maybe, but I'm not sure why."

Her voice was soft and her eyes were distant like she was mulling it over.

"For the obvious reasons," he said, a little sharply.

That got her attention. Her eyes met his and she cocked her head at him. "And what are those?"

Time seemed to stand still while as he gazed into her ginger-bread brown eyes. "You're beautiful, smart, funny...you're everything."

*"Damn."*

"What?"

"I want to stay mad at you, and then you go and say a thing like that."

His shoulders relaxed. "I'm not wrong about any of it. I didn't like the look on his face now. He's not safe to be around."

He could tell she was trying hard not to laugh again, so he threw an arm around her and pulled her into his side. "But you're right. I have no reason to be jealous. This is the end. You signed the papers for the house and you don't have to see him again, right?"

Sophia wrinkled her nose and mumbled something.

"I didn't catch that."

Hesitating, she glanced up at him and then away. "I told him he could have the car, too."

"Sophia, really!"

"Calm down and stop waving like you're being attacked by a bee. People are starting to stare."

He looked around, spotting a pair of track-suited geriatrics watching them curiously.

"I'll buy the car," he said.

"*No.* I don't want it around. It's a piece of junk with terrible mileage. The backseat is broken, too. I'd rather let Richard have it since he cares so much. If my father had bothered to leave a will, he'd probably have given it to him, anyway."

That didn't make him feel any better. "Are you sure that's what you want? You might regret giving that last piece of your father away someday. Then you'll have to deal with your ex to get it back."

"Trust me, I won't want it back."

Her phone buzzed, and she glanced down at the screen. It was a text from Richard, with a message he could see clearly over her shoulder.

*Please call me if you need help with the Italian.*

"*Figlio di troia.* Is he serious?" Gio growled, snatching up her phone. "I thought he didn't text on principle."

Sophia avoided his eyes. "It's the first text he's ever sent me."

And it was about him, offering help as if he was some kind of villain.

Because God hated him, the phone buzzed again and he lost it. He snatched the device from her hands and threw it into the middle of the street where it was immediately run over by a passing car.

"Gio!"

Shocked at his own behavior, he froze.

"Goddammit, Gio, all of my contacts were in there, my calendar—"

He grabbed her hand. "I am so sorry. I don't know what came over me."

He looked at the phone, wondering if it had survived when another car, a bigger one, ran over it a second time. Wincing, he squeezed Sophia's fingers until she met his eyes.

"I'll buy you a new one—a better one. The most expensive one money can buy."

She glared at him. "I don't want a more expensive one. I want *that one*," she said, pointing at the wreckage that used to be her phone.

He cringed. It was in several large pieces now.

"I can run out and grab it. My tech guys from the bank might be able to recover some data from the SIM card," he offered, preparing to dart out into the busy street.

Sophia clutched his arm. "Don't. You'll get hit by a car...I have a backup of the data on my laptop."

Relieved, he hugged her. "That's great!"

But she was still upset. Putting a hand between them, she shoved him away. "Go home, Gio."

Oh, he'd fucked this up.

"Sophia, I am so sorry."

Her eyes closed. "I know that, but it doesn't make this okay. You can't keep flying off the handle like that and expect an apology to make it all better."

"I don't. I swear I'm not usually this insane. But you can't trust this guy," he said, gesturing back to the cafe.

She passed a hand over her face, and he hung his head. He was losing ground rapidly. He shouldn't have come, but it had been hard to stay away knowing she was going to be alone with a former lover.

And now she was selling her father's car to him, too? He should have Enzo make Richard an offer for the damn thing after Sophia rid herself of it. One he couldn't refuse.

*Merda.* His possessiveness was turning him into the godfather. Also, Richard looked like the type to whine to Sophia the minute Gio had his back turned. It was best to leave things alone. He would have the man watched, however. If his friend Alex's situation with his wife's stalker, Stephen Wainwright, had taught him anything, it was to proceed with caution—and to trust no one of the opposite sex around his woman.

Giving up, he kissed her forehead. "I'm still sorry, and I'm going home now to think about what I've done," he said in an appropriately chastised tone.

Sophia's lip quirked. "Good."

"I don't suppose you want to come with me?" he asked, waving to his driver.

The man was standing next to the car down the block.

"No. Kelly's waiting for me with a very large bottle of wine. I'll see you at your place later. Besides, I drove here."

Disappointed he couldn't sweep her off, he nodded.

"Okay. Do me a favor. Wait a while after the wine before getting behind the wheel. I'll wait for you at home."

He bit his tongue, but Sophia didn't notice his sudden distraction. Instead, she gave him a narrow-eyed glance before walking away.

He made sure she was safely inside Kelly's apartment building before he left, thinking over his little slip.

Home was where Sophia was. It was just a matter of time before she became aware of his intentions—and heaven help him if she was this mad at him when she did.

# CHAPTER 16

"*I*'m going to get you for this."

"Sophia, *mi amore*, calm down. Keep your eyes on me—"

"I'm going to smash all of your espresso cups and throw out your grappa!"

"It's only a few more minutes before we reach the airport," Gio assured her, pulling her to him and rubbing her back.

In the headset, he heard his pilot snicker.

He and Sophia were in the back seat of his Eurocopter EC 135. They were on their way to the airport, where his private jet was waiting. It was a long weekend and he'd talked Sophia into spending it in Rome with him, instead of working through it the way she usually did.

The trip was originally intended as a romantic getaway, but he'd heard from his father a few hours ago. Salvatore had organized the whole family to come over for cocktails tonight.

Sophia had taken the news that all of his relatives were assembling to meet her rather well. She didn't even mind traipsing all the way to Rome—giving up her rare and precious free time—to do it. No, what she minded was the helicopter ride.

"I'm going to use my dissection tools to cut microscopic holes in your favorite suits. You won't be able to see them, but you'll know they're there and it will haunt you!"

"*Tesoro,* I'm sorry I forgot about your issue with heights," he apologized, continuing to rub her back while the pilot choked back his laughter. "And it wouldn't haunt me."

It would *destroy* him. She knew him so well already.

"Say goodbye to your perfectly organized sock drawer! The minute we get back I'm going in and mismatching every pair! No more ROYGBIV color order!"

He suppressed a chuckle. "We're almost there. Look, I can see the airport now," he added, pointing.

Sophia looked up instinctively, following the direction of his hand before covering her eyes and groaning loudly. Shutting her eyes, she grabbed blindly until she caught his tie and yanked on it. "I'm going to scratch up your Doctor Who Blu-Rays!"

*Ouch.*

"It's over. We're here."

The flight on the jet went much smoother. It helped that the plane was outfitted with a full bar. He poured Sophia a brandy and then had her lie down in the back bedroom for a while. That went *really* well for him—after he properly apologized for forgetting to mention the helicopter ride. It went really well for her too, but, of course, that was part of the apology.

The flight to Rome was over in a blink. Before he knew it, they were climbing into his town car at the airport. His local driver had picked them up. Sophia narrowed her eyes when she recognized him and then pinched Gio's ass cheek as they climbed into the car.

"I can't believe I bought that he was an Uber driver. He wears a suit. No Uber driver wears a suit. And their cars smell like take-out. This one smells like cognac and expensive leather. Does filthy rich have a smell? 'Cause I think it smells like this."

Amused by her observations, he cuddled her closer and pointed out the sights, places he wanted to take her to eat or to shop and occasionally a building he owned. She was refreshingly unimpressed about the latter. All she did was nod and grumble adorably about moguls and their "damn helicopters."

It was such a relief to be completely honest about his background. He couldn't wait to show her Rome—for real this time. Now that she knew everything, he could take her to his favorite restaurants and the theater. He knew she would love them. They liked the same things, from music to their taste in movies. None of his other friends liked science fiction or fantasy beyond the latest season of Game of Thrones. In fact, Sophia was the only person he knew who'd read the books.

"I should warn you the penthouse is on the top floor," he said, once they were in the elevator on their way up to his apartment in the Parioli district.

Sophia rolled her eyes at him. "Buildings are all right. Buildings don't fall out of the sky."

"They do during earthquakes," he couldn't help teasing.

"And you have a lot of those here in Rome?" she asked sarcastically

"No, not really," he admitted as the elevator doors opened, revealing the penthouse foyer…and his father.

"Papà," he said, taken aback. "You were supposed to come over with everyone later."

His father was standing there in his favorite sweater vest and faded black slacks. He was a small man, around Sophia's height, with dark hair that had gone gray at the temples. Gio resembled him, except for his size and stature.

"I thought I would meet your friend before everyone arrived," Salvatore said, extending his hand.

The words were friendly. His father even had a smile on his face. But Gio knew the tone and it wasn't good. Especially the emphasis *"friend."* Also, Salvatore didn't shake hands. He kissed on the cheek like any good Italian.

Gio had hoped his father would warm to Sophia on sight, but apparently it wasn't going to be that easy. Salvatore had lobbied hard for him to marry Maria Gianna, and he still wasn't ready to let the dream die.

"It's a pleasure to meet you," Sophia said, a fixed and overly large smile on her face.

They shook hands and exchanged pleasantries about the flight. It was very polite and completely awkward. She fidgeted with her hair, which was still a little mussed from their lovemaking session on the plane, and then shot him a meaningful look over his father's head.

Hopefully, his father hadn't noticed. Gio offered him something from the bar and Sophia excused herself, presumably to find the nearest mirror.

Salvatore turned to watch her walk away. "She seems nice, although not in your usual style," he said in Italian

"I don't have a style, Papà," Gio replied flatly, pouring himself a drink.

"All I am saying is most of the girls you've dated were on the thin side." *Like Maria Gianna.* "And this new girl is..."

"Perfect the way she is," he said in a noticeably colder voice.

"Maria is more beautiful," Salvatore muttered.

Gio slammed his drink down on the mahogany surface of the bar. "Only on the outside."

And it wasn't true. Sophia was far more beautiful and exotic. She just wasn't model thin and blonde.

"*Mio figlio*, I don't have anything against this girl. I think it's fine for you to spend some time with her for now. But eventually you and Maria Gianna will reconcile. I know there's been some bad blood recently—"

"It's more than bad blood. Reconciliation is not possible."

"But—"

*"No."*

Salvatore templed his hands. "Tobias and I were speaking about your problem. We think if Maria gets a little counseling, she can turn her life around. All she needs is a man to take charge of things, someone to encourage her to stay out of trouble."

*Unbelievable.* They wanted him to be his ex-wife's keeper. Didn't his happiness matter to them?

"That someone is not going to be me."

His father was not above pouting. "Think of my grandchildren."

Gio put up his hands. "Any children that woman had wouldn't have been *your* grandchildren. Trust me on that."

Behind his father, Sophia stepped out of the hallway, but after hearing that last sentence, promptly turned around and went to hide.

Passing a hand over his face, he decided it was time to tell the truth about Maria Gianna. It was long overdue. He couldn't allow his father's blind allegiance to the idea of him with his best friend's child bias him against Sophia.

Salvatore drew himself up to his full and unimpressive height. "I'm aware there were rumors, but you can't listen—"

"They were more than rumors. I caught her in bed with Vincenzo Gavazzi."

His father's face fell, the air leaking out of his tires until he sagged, seeming to shrink before his eyes.

"Sorry," Gio huffed. "I didn't mean to blurt it out like that."

Silence.

*"Babbo."*

Salvatore took a big sip of the drink in his hand. He cleared his throat. "Why didn't you say anything before? You let me go on and on about her and all this time she was a...a..."

Gio reached over and gently took the glass his father was waving around, spilling his best grappa on the marble tiled floor. "She's still your best friend's daughter and your goddaughter. I should have told you before. I thought to spare you and Tobias some of the ugliness, but I can't let you go on thinking that Maria Gianna and I are still a possibility. We're not, and I don't want you to have anything against Sophia. She's very special to me."

Salvatore blinked. "How special?"

"*Very* special."

His father dropped down on a bar stool and reached over to pour himself a refill. "So where did you meet this girl? Has she ever been married? Does she like children?"

Relaxing, Gio laughed. "She's a woman, not a girl. And I haven't asked her if she likes them. And she hasn't been married, although she was engaged once, to a professor. I met her at the foundation dinner," he said, stretching the truth. "Sophia's one of this year's research grant winners."

Salvatore straightened on his stool. "The ecologist?"

"No. The neurobiologist."

The surprise on his father's face was comical, if slightly insulting to Sophia.

"So…who were her people? Is she Catholic?"

"Since neither of us goes to church anymore, I don't see how that last matters. Her mother was Mexican and her father was Castilian. She was an artist, and he was a professor of Sociology."

"Another professor?"

He shrugged. "The ex-fiancé was the father's protégé. But he's out of the picture. So is her father. Actually both of her parents have passed away."

His father crumbled like the softie he was. "Oh, how sad. She's probably a bit lonely. Find out if she wants children."

"Shh," he whispered as Sophia poked her head back into the living room. "Enough of that for now, or you'll scare her."

He waved Sophia over and poured her a glass of red wine. She took it with a polite smile and sat on the barstool next to his father. Salvatore asked her about her research and Sophia relaxed, clearly glad to be talking about a safe subject.

Things were going well, but he needed to have a little time

alone with her before his relatives descended. After a few more minutes, he ushered his father out, promising to see him later at his house in the outskirts of the city.

"Oh, I forgot to tell you we moved everything over here for tonight," Salvatore said innocently. "It's more central for everybody and you've never entertained here, but now that you have Sophia that's going to change, isn't it?"

Gio smiled in defeat. "Yes, it is."

"Excellent. Plus your cousin Carolina sprained her ankle and we didn't want to make her drive out to the house. This way she can take a cab." He waved and headed to the elevator.

"You could have started with that," Gio called after him.

Once the doors closed, Sophia raised her glass. "He doesn't like me," she said before drinking.

"He will. You're his only hope for grandchildren."

Gio almost bit his tongue off when Sophia choked on a sip of wine. She coughed a few times, waving him away when he tried to pat her back.

"So, who all is coming tonight?" she asked brightly, changing the subject.

*That's not good.*

He let it go and proceeded to tell her all about his relatives, especially who to avoid. It wouldn't do to let her get cornered by Uncle Nunzio, who became pretty handsy after a few drinks. And God knew those curves were an unholy temptation for a normal man. In fact, a large number of male relatives were coming over. He needed to keep a close eye on everyone tonight.

It turned out those words were prophetic...

The gathering had been going fine until his cousin Lucca showed up with Aunt Perla. Gio had been furious, but his aunt insisted that her son was sorry and had come to tell him so.

The grudging apology he received from a sullen Lucca was woefully inadequate. Fortunately, Lucca had taken off almost immediately afterward so there hadn't been a scene. But his cousin's appearance had put a damper on the rest of the evening for him, and Gio was glad when everyone departed.

After his family left the rest of the night took a decided turn for the better—right after he showed Sophia the master bedroom. Neither of them got much sleep. He was looking forward to an equally sleepless Saturday night when the vice president of one his subsidiaries called early in the morning.

Negotiations over some real estate in Germany had taken a turn for the worse. It was partly his fault. He hadn't been able to finalize the purchase himself because he'd been in England courting Sophia.

Feeling responsible, he reluctantly broke the news to her and made plans to spend the rest of the weekend in Berlin. He consoled himself by organizing a special treat to make it up to his siren.

"Stop apologizing," Sophia laughed as he packed. "I'll head back home early, and we can try again in a few weeks. You're always so understanding when I have to work on the weekends, surprising me with dinner in the lab and hanging around working on your computer while you wait. It's only fair that I be as understanding when you need to do it. In fact, there's a few experiments I'd like to try on my newest samples since I have the time."

"No! I promised you a break and I'm going to give you one," he insisted, throwing a few pairs of socks into his bag. "I have it all arranged. You have a full spa day planned at this place my cousins swear by. After that, I have arranged a few tours at some of the museums we didn't hit the last time we were in town. And if there is someplace you want to see a second time, ask Carlo, my driver, and he'll organize it for you."

"You didn't have to do that," she said, trying to convince him to let her go home.

He was determined, however, and in the end he left when she did. He headed to the airport and she went to the spa for her first appointment, a massage in the preferred style of her choice.

She chose deep tissue, as well as a seaweed wrap and the spa's signature fourteen karat gold facial. And he didn't even have to bribe the spa personnel to keep him informed, as he originally intended. Instead, he had asked Sophia to keep him updated and she did with a series of texts.

Marveling at the simplicity of dating a reasonable woman, he attacked his work in Germany with ruthless efficiency, cutting down the negotiation time to a third of his original estimate. By evening, he was already on his way back, eager to surprise Sophia with his early return.

Unfortunately, an airport strike delayed his arrival until well after midnight. When he got inside the penthouse's master bedroom, Sophia was already asleep. He put down his suitcase next to the bed and stopped to kiss her soft lower lip.

She cracked an eyelid and smiled at him with a sleepy little purring sound.

"Go back to sleep," he whispered. "I'm going to take a quick shower before coming to bed."

Humming a little sound of acquiescence, she snuggled deeper in the covers. The sheets shifted enough for him to see that she was wearing one of the new nightgowns Gavin had picked out for her.

*Yes, Gavin definitely needs a raise.*

He picked up his suitcase, deciding to take it into the office, before coming back to take the fastest shower in history.

# CHAPTER 17

*A* banging sound jarred Sophia out of the light sleep she'd been in since Gio had come in. Still drowsy, she struggled to open her eyes, wondering what he'd dropped to make such a racket. But she was too relaxed to do it quickly. It had been a full day of pampering, and all the massage and specialty treatments had left her body pleasantly drained and lethargic.

"Hmm," she hummed when the covers pulled back and Gio climbed into bed with her.

He must have changed his mind about the shower, because he was still dressed in pants and a shirt. She threw a languid hand over his shoulder, embracing him as he crawled over her.

Gio must have missed her a lot because he was pawing at her more aggressively than usual. His hand squeezed her thigh painfully before moving up to pinch her breast—too hard.

Upset at the rough treatment, she made a protesting sound and put a hand up to push him away. But he was rubbing against her so closely, she couldn't budge him.

It wasn't until he kissed her that she realized something was wrong.

His lips were unpleasantly wet, and he reeked of alcohol. And then she felt him down there—the long thin manhood pressing against her.

It wasn't Gio. Someone else had climbed into bed with her.

Sophia craned her head away from the mouth trying to cover hers and screamed. The noise didn't seem to bother her attacker. Instead of running away, he tried to remove her panties with bruising force. Panic flooded her and she screamed again, but it was muffled this time.

Heart pounding uncontrollably, she fought with everything she had.

For a second, it didn't make any difference. The person on top of her was tall and strong, but a lucky elbow in the throat caused her attacker to rear back.

In the dim light from the window she could see who it was— Gio's teenage cousin Lucca, the one he was mad at. The boy was stinking drunk.

Her fear catalyzed to anger. Suddenly furious, she struck out with her fist.

She was strong, but the little shit climbing all over her must have been numb in his drunkenness. He murmured something unintelligible in Italian and pulled back enough to put a little distance between them. With a wrench, she drew back her head and snapped it forward the way her self-defense instructor had taught her long ago.

The flat part of her forehead crashed straight into his nose. He fell back, crying and clutching his face.

Using the strong muscles in her thighs, she pushed him away with her powerful legs. He hit the floor as she scrambled away, standing on the other side of the bed.

No sooner had Lucca hit the floor than a roar filled her ears. Gio came out of nowhere. He took it all in an instant, running toward them to grab the drunken idiot by the collar.

She had no idea how strong Gio was until he picked up Lucca

with one arm, swinging him like a rag doll. He dragged him farther from the bed and started pounding on him. His fist came down over and over, the dull thudding sounds of flesh being beaten filling her ears.

Lucca was crying and weeping openly, gibbering on in Italian. He was trying to cover his head and face, curling into a ball while pleading for Gio to stop. But that wasn't going to happen.

Sophia stood frozen in shock until she caught a glimpse of the cold rage on his face. It was chilling.

*He's going to kill him.*

Sick to her stomach, she realized it was up to her to save the man who'd attempted to rape her.

"Stop it, Gio!" she said, running up to him and putting her arms around him.

But he was too far gone to listen to reason.

He shrugged her off. She landed on her butt on the floor. Picking herself up, she reached out and took his arm, stopping it from connecting with Lucca's head.

"Gio, please!"

The boy was still conscious, covering his head and sobbing with a harsh wheezing sound. Desperate to stop her enraged lover, she jumped on his back, wrapping her legs around him and squeezing with all her might.

"Sophia!" Gio yelled, finally acknowledging her.

"Stop it!" she shouted back. "Stop it now, or you're going to kill him!"

*"That's the idea."*

"No! He's drunk. He doesn't know what he's doing."

"I don't care! He's dead!" he said, trying to shrug her off without hurting her.

She wasn't as gentle. She squeezed harder until she could swear his ribs groaned in protest.

"For fuck's sake," Gio wheezed.

Coughing raggedly, he stopped struggling, so she relaxed the muscles of her legs. They stayed like that for a long moment, their breathing fast and ragged.

"Are you going to get off me now?"

Still holding tight, she craned her neck, trying to look at his face. "That depends. Are you going to stop?"

He didn't answer, so she held on and waited.

"All right," he finally ground out.

She slid down, clinging to his shoulders with shaky hands.

In front of them, the teenage boy curled into himself and cried harder. He was saying something, but her Italian was too poor to understand properly.

"What is he saying?" she asked, grimacing at the pathetic sight.

Gio passed a hand over his face. "That you wanted him. She told him so."

His voice was full of disgust.

So she hadn't misunderstood. "What the hell does that mean? Who is *she*?"

Gio didn't answer. He snatched up the phone on the bedside table and barked something into it. One long terrible minute later, Enzo, Gio's security chief, came into the bedroom at a dead run. He was followed by two other men she didn't recognize.

"Get him out of here," Gio ordered, pointing to his sad heap of a relative.

Face ashen, Enzo nodded abruptly. He and one of the other men stepped forward and took hold of Lucca, one at each arm. They hustled him out, his groans and the sound of his heart-wrenching weeping carrying back to them.

"Stop!" Gio called out.

He ran over to Enzo and hissed something in his ear, pointing and waving his hand back and forth, slicing the air with quick abrupt motions.

Sophia wrapped her arms tight around her middle, mentally transported to her one fraternity party in college. Her roommate had convinced her to wear a tight V-neck sweater, one that had displayed her cleavage. The outfit had attracted the attention of a large drunken frat boy. After less than a minute of incoherent conversation, she'd been grabbed and pinned to the wall.

It had happened in full view of everyone, so it hadn't been long before someone noticed she was being mauled against her will and pulled the guy off her.

Intellectually, she knew it hadn't been her fault. She put the incident behind her and moved on, but the same irrational feeling of shame was back. She felt dirty.

*You are dirty.*

Glancing down at her breasts, she saw red spatters. Sophia reached up to her chin and flinched when her fingers came away with blood. It must have been Lucca's.

Nauseated, she turned on her heel and marched into the bathroom, stripping off her nightgown and throwing it on the floor. She stepped into the shower and turned it on full-blast.

She was still scrubbing herself raw when Gio came into the bathroom. He was fully dressed in his suit and tie, but that didn't stop him from walking into the shower stall with her.

He pulled her hands away, stopping her compulsive washing by wrapping his arms around her. He held her to him, letting the water run over them both, ruining a suit that probably cost more than her car.

"I'm so sorry," he whispered. "I don't know how this happened, but I swear from now on no one will ever touch you. Not even me. Not if you don't want me to."

Tears stung at her eyes and despite all her resolve to be strong, she threw her arms around him and started crying.

"What is wrong with that kid? Does he have mental problems?" she asked, hiccuping, her face buried in his shoulder.

"Yes. It's called terminal stupidity." He pulled her away and held her at arm's length. "Look, this is my fault. My doorman took my open door policy with my family too literally. I never dreamed

Lucca was this messed up, but he's going to pay for this. I promise you. This is it for him."

Only half listening, she nodded listlessly. He took her in his arms again and held her until the hot water finally made her feel warm.

# CHAPTER 18

*G*io had never been so furious in his entire life. His suspicions had been correct. Lucca didn't decide to attack Sophia on his own. In fact, he'd been so drunk he could barely walk last night.

Enzo had pulled the security footage from the front of the building and they'd seen what happened.

A car with tinted windows had dropped off Lucca a little after Gio had arrived home. His cousin had staggered out of the back and started walking to the building before turning around. Lucca had tried to climb back into the car, but whoever was in the rear seat had stopped him. Lucca had bent, listening at the window before nodding and lurching into the building.

None of the camera angles caught the driver, who kept their head down, or the passenger in the back. But his cousin had been seen at a local club with Maria Gianna and her entourage just an hour before. Enzo was still trying to trace who the car belonged to, but Gio already knew whose it was. Vincenzo had a car just like it.

He could imagine what happened. After that begrudging attempt at an apology at the party, Lucca had run straight to his ex-wife to blab about Gio's new woman. Once Maria Gianna knew there was someone else in his life, she lost her drug-addled mind and plied his idiot cousin with booze. Then she sent him back to assault Sophia.

*"Find her,"* Gio hissed at Enzo after watching the footage.

He wasn't a violent man, but right now he wanted to break every bone in his ex-wife's body. But since he could never hit a woman, he was going to have to settle for Vincenzo's head on a platter.

In light of what happened, Enzo had offered to resign, but Gio wouldn't accept it. He couldn't. What had happened was his fault. He'd avoided dealing with his ex-wife, preferring to keep the peace than doing what he should have done in the first place. He'd been too nice. For all his life, he'd been conscientious and proper, a dutiful son and nephew.

He'd even been a good husband. But despite all the effort he'd made, the gifts he'd showered on her, it had never been enough for Maria Gianna. The jewelry had always been wrong, the diamonds too small or the settings too old-fashioned. She wanted to go to parties and travel to the latest hotspots at the drop of a hat—things he couldn't do with his job.

For a long time afterward, he believed the divorce was his fault. He was too boring and dull for someone as bright and exciting as Maria Gianna. She had said as much herself—taunting him about his prowess in bed when he'd caught her fucking Vincenzo.

His was a world of numbers and keeping up with tax codes. Sex was scheduled. It happened at night three times a week—four if it was a special occasion like a birthday or an anniversary. When his ex-wife cheated on him, he blamed his own rigid rules and quiet lifestyle. Now he knew the truth.

Maria Gianna was spoiled and vindictive. She'd targeted his friends for her affairs to try and hurt him as much as possible. But he hadn't been hurt. Embarrassed, yes—even repulsed. His ex had been infuriated that he didn't care more. But now she had found a way to hurt him that was far more effective.

He'd been dragging his feet about the libel suit because he didn't want to make waves. Now she and Vincenzo thought of him as a pushover, someone who'd take their crap without complaint because he didn't want to upset anyone. Well, *fuck that.*

Last night had been a step too far. Sophia had been targeted. He was going to find that bitch and her lapdog, and he was going to make them pay.

Unfortunately, Maria Gianna and Vincenzo had skipped town. Enzo had three of his men trying to track them down, so whatever he was going to do would have to wait. In the meantime, he was going to take Sophia home.

SOPHIA HELD onto her patience with effort. "I'm fine, Gio."

She had been saying those words a lot recently.

"Humor me, please."

She rolled her eyes at Elynn. Alex's wife was waiting in her extra office chair as Sophia talked on the phone with her overprotective Italian lover.

"Enzo doesn't mind driving you," Gio continued, trying and failing to hide the possessive concern in his voice. "He can be there in five minutes."

"Tell him I have my car," Elynn stage-whispered.

Since Sophia had already mentioned that she had *her* car, she didn't think Gio was about to be reasonable. He wasn't about to give up the idea of an armed escort to her girls' night out with Elynn and her friends. He certainly hadn't when she pointed out the pub they were meeting at was only a few blocks away.

Since their labs were fairly close together, she and Elynn had met up on their lunch hour several times since first meeting. Tonight they were also seeing Maia again. The little redhead and her husband Calen had been traveling in Spain, checking on some of his clubs on the Costa del Sol. She would also be meeting Eva Stone for the first time. Sergei's partner had been on an extended business trip for his company—part of which he'd joined her on with their new son. But they were back in town, stopping for a week before heading to their home in Manhattan.

Sophia had been looking forward to this evening all week. Ever since they returned from Rome, Gio had gone into overdrive. He checked on her ten times a day, and she was pretty sure he'd assigned her a security detail without asking. It would have been sweet if it wasn't so insane. She knew he was still beating himself up for what happened, but being monitored twenty-four-seven was going to drive her batshit crazy.

"Gio, I'm hanging up now. I'll see you at home later," she said firmly.

Pulling the phone away from her face, she took a deep breath and pushed the end button on her screen with a little wince.

"Be strong," Elynn said, amused.

Slumping in her chair, Sophia wrinkled her nose at her new friend. "Gio has lost his mind since Italy. Did I tell you Enzo followed me into the ladies room at the restaurant last night? It's too much."

Elynn giggled before growing serious. "He's worried. Trust me, it's better to let them have their way when it comes to security concerns. I speak from experience. I'm pretty sure my husband *still* has me followed around and my stalker is never seeing the light of day again. Not if Alex has any say about it."

Sophia shot her a commiserating look as she put on her coat. Elynn had told her all about her experience with Stephen Wain-wright, as well as the terrifying situations both Maia and Eva had faced in the past. Compared to those experiences, the thing in Italy seemed like small potatoes.

Except it still bothered her...which was why she needed to go out tonight. All she wanted was to have four or five margaritas with some ladies so she could bitch a little. Kelly had done her best to console her over the phone, but she was out of town at her in-laws' again, so Sophia was leaning on Elynn and Co. tonight.

"Bodyguards are unnecessary in this case," she said as they left the building to walk the short distance to the pub. "It's not like I'm in danger now. Gio's drunken cousin is drying out in some sort of high-security rehab center, and even if he wasn't, I doubt he'd come within ten feet of me."

Once Lucca had sobered up, he'd been horrified by what he'd done. At least that's what his mother had told her. Both she and Gio's father had flown out to beg them not to press charges against the boy. Sophia hadn't even known that Gio had been determined to prosecute him until they arrived.

The rehab issue had been a source of contention. Gio didn't think it was a severe enough punishment. Part of her agreed, but she was conflicted about the whole mess.

"It is a good idea to set limits now," Elynn said, distracting Sophia from her troubled thoughts as they reached the restaurant. "Our men are a little too powerful—too used to having their way. But in this case, there's a bit more to it than you may be aware of. I'll tell you after we order. You're going to need alcohol for this."

She waved her inside where they found Maia waiting for them with a pitcher of mojitos. Sophia gratefully accepted a glass and sat down.

"I didn't think this place made these in pitcher form!" she said in appreciation.

"I asked for it specially," Maia said, sipping her own glass. "I figured you were going to need it."

She frowned. "So you heard too? About Lucca and the rehab drama?"

Maia smiled apologetically and shrugged. "The guys are gossipier than a bunch of hens. We all know everybody's business. I hope that doesn't bother you, because I don't think it's going to change anytime soon."

"Amen to that," Elynn muttered, staring longingly at the pitcher. Sighing she waved over a waiter and ordered a virgin piña colada, patting her pregnant stomach absently.

"I don't mind it, really," Sophia said with a laugh. "I've been looking forward to venting for days now. God knows, I can't talk to Gio about it. He just goes nuts—simultaneously apologizing to me and ranting in Italian about *puttanas*. I'm not sure what that means, but it doesn't sound good."

Elynn winced. "Yeah, it's not. That's what I wanted to tell you. Gio thinks his ex-wife may have had something to do with the attack. She's the *puttana* he's talking about. She's some kind of minor celebrity in Italy, and Lucca is a groupie of hers. Gio thinks she loaded him up on booze and sent him your way on purpose to get back at him for the divorce. Alex agrees with him."

It took a second to process, but once Sophia understood what Elynn was telling her, she was incensed. "Are you fucking kidding me? What kind of woman does that? I mean, I knew she was a piece of work—that whole tabloid thing totally messed Gio up—but seriously this? *Christ.*"

Elynn sat up straight. "I know. Maria is a witch with a capital "B". She tried to seduce both our husbands while she and Gio were still married," she said, gesturing to Maia. "They're the ones who had to tell him. It's why they divorced."

"I thought they got divorced because he found her with that Vincenzo guy," Maia broke in.

"He did, in *their* bed," Elynn confirmed. "But he had already decided to divorce her by then. Once Alex told Gio about her attempt at seduction, he was done with her."

"Ugh. I hate this woman," Sophia said with a scowl. "This whole situation makes my skin crawl. Do you know I had to talk Gio out of pressing charges against Lucca? I didn't want to do it, but the moron is only nineteen." Pausing to take a fortifying sip, she continued with what was disturbing her the most.

"Never did I imagine I'd be in a position where I had to defend someone who attacked me," she confessed. "It makes me sick, but given the extenuating circumstances I didn't feel like I had a choice. This thing was tearing Gio's family apart. His cousin is still a teenager. Not that it excuses what he did. He should be punished. But I'm not sure sending him to jail would help, or just make him worse. Not that it's going to happen now. I just have to hope that getting disowned and being sent to rehab is enough to knock the stupid out of that kid."

Elynn put a hand over hers. "I'm sorry. I know how you feel—dirty and violated. Maybe a little helpless too?" she suggested softly.

"But she broke his nose!" Maia protested, refilling her glass from the pitcher. "You're my new hero. I wish I could have done that to that guy in the woods, but he was *huge*."

"I didn't think I did that much damage at the time," Sophia pointed out, finishing her drink and accepting a refill herself. "It should be empowering, but it's not. I'm frustrated. I feel off. Like my skin is the wrong size or something. I mean, I've taken self-defense classes and I play soccer. I'm not a small woman. I always pictured myself going totally Buffy on anyone who tried something like that. But none of my ass-kicking fantasies included getting ambushed in bed. I'm still berating myself for not doing more. The broken nose was a lucky shot. I was still half-asleep."

"You got him off you, too," Maia pointed out. "I wouldn't have been able to and I've been training with a self-defense instructor ever since my daughter was born. I keep getting overpowered because I'm so small. My trainer insists I'll learn to use my size to my advantage, but it's not happening. Which is why I'm never going to be rid of my security detail." She leaned forward. "You should be proud of yourself. Someone had you at a disadvantage and you kicked their ass. If Gio hadn't jumped in, you could have dealt with Lucca all by yourself. You were half-way there."

Sophia wasn't sure. She remembered that feeling of helplessness when she realized it wasn't Gio on top of her. If Lucca hadn't been drunk, it might have been a different story. But she didn't say that.

She raised her chin. "I guess that's the one blessing to being the size of a house."

"You're a normal healthy size," Elynn insisted loyally. "We're just shrimps. Eva included—" She broke off. "Speak of the devil."

They were joined by another adorable petite woman. This one had blonde curls. She was so cute, Sophia would have pegged her for a ditz if she hadn't known the woman was brilliant, the daughter of a famous inventor who'd inherited his talent and then some.

A few minutes of conversation later, and Sophia knew she had found a kindred spirit—especially since the first thing Eva did was offer to help kick Maria Gianna's ass. Like Maia and Elynn, she had been told everything.

Eva Stone was bright and funny, but she had an edge the other two women lacked. Sophia appreciated the hint of cynicism in others, since she possessed it herself. Her admiration went up a notch when they discussed Eva's business trip.

Eva had been inspecting the early construction stages of a new manufacturing plant that Damov industries was building. The company was going into solar panel production using innovations based on her father's work. It sounded interesting to Sophia, but Eva didn't seem too enthusiastic. Her glum demeanor prompted Maia to ask if anything was wrong.

"It's nothing serious," Eva said, waving away her concern. "I had to sleep alone last night, so I'm grumpy."

"How did that happen?" Elynn said with a laugh. "Sergei can't keep his hands off of you. Seriously, it's gross."

"You're one to talk," Eva laughed before wrinkling her nose. "And that's usually true, but I arrived here early—last night, instead of this morning. Sergei wasn't expecting me. He'd been drinking with the guys. And he won't touch me when he's had any alcohol. He even slept in the second bedroom of the hotel suite and left the baby with me. Not the homecoming I'd been hoping for."

"Oh. Is his drinking a problem?" Sophia asked with concern.

"No. Not for a Russian," Eva said, finally breaking out into a grin. "He just likes self-flagellation. Let's get back to you. Are you sure you don't want to kick Maria Gianna's ass? Cause I'm sure Elynn and Maia would be happy to help, and I'll join in too for the principle of the thing. We can take turns holding her down. We'll take a bat to her knees cause that bitch is tall."

"I knew I liked you," Sophia said, toasting the tiny blonde terminator. "And as much as I want to, I can't see myself getting on a plane to get even. It's a little too Kill Bill volume three. But if I ever see that biatch, I will throw down. She better stay out of dark alleys anywhere near my vicinity."

"There's no reason you have to do it in person," Eva said as if it was the most reasonable thing in the world. "One of Sergei's subsidiaries makes drones. We can have one rigged up to follow that skank around and dive bomb her in the face."

Sophia was tipsy enough to giggle. "Tempting. Let me get back to you on that."

The others laughed and the conversation veered away from Gio's ex to the man himself.

"I can't believe he's being so aggressive," Elynn said. "He was over telling Alex all about Rome—or rather yelling about it. I've never heard him raise his voice before. He's usually so sedate and proper. I never expected to see him so angry."

Sophia, several drinks in by now, swallowed a large sip of mojito and held up a hand. "Seriously? The man has a *filthy* temper."

Three pairs of wide eyes stared at her in collective surprise.

"No way," Maia said. "He's always been the calm center of the group. Almost zen, if you can describe a compulsive organizer as zen."

Sophia guffawed. "Zen my big Mexican butt! Did I tell you how he threw my cell phone in the street cause my ex texted me? If I even mention Richard's name it turns into an argument."

Maia's mouth dropped open.

"He *fights* with you?" Elynn asked in disbelief.

"All the time. Well, not all the time. It's usually only the subject of Richard which makes him go ballistic. And now this thing with his cousin. But mostly it's my ex-fiance."

Wide-eyed Maia thumped the table. "Oh, my God! He loves you."

Sophia shook her head. "That's what Gio says, but he doesn't. It's really this weird hero worship Richard had for my father—"

"No, no! I meant Gio," Maia said waving a little over-enthusiastically and spilling a bit of mojito.

"Because they fight?" Eva asked, sounding as confused as Sophia felt.

"Yes! She's right," Elynn said, pointing at Maia and nodding. "Gio never fought with Maria Gianna. He didn't even throw a punch at that guy she was in bed with. He didn't care enough."

Sophia's brows rose. "So he fights with me because he loves me?"

"*Yes,*" Maia and Elynn said at the same time.

Sophia couldn't help it. She started laughing, but Eva cocked her head and seemed to think it over. "They're right. Sergei says he's never seen Gio behave this way about anyone before. The other three guys are loving it too. Probably because he's starting to act more like them."

"I'm not sure that's a good thing," Sophia said wryly, but inwardly she was pleased.

So Gio was different with her than in his previous relationships. That knowledge warmed her, inside and out. Of course, it could have been the rum, but she was still secretly delighted. It almost made the arguments with Gio worth it.

*Not almost.* They were totally worth it if he loved her.

"Is Gio moving here?" Elynn asked. "'Cause Alex would love that."

Okay, there went her warm and fuzzy feeling.

"I don't know," she confessed. "We haven't talked about it. I can't possibly relocate. My research project just started. The whole lab would have to move and my research partner would never go for that."

"Well, don't worry about it," Elynn said quickly. "Gio can fly out to the London office of his bank when necessary. Alex does it all the time."

"Does he? Maybe they should carpool or heli-pool. Whatever you call sharing a helicopter ride," Sophia muttered, remembering her one trip in the Eurocopter with distaste.

Her tongue was getting a little thick. She squinted at the bottom of her glass and poured a smaller refill.

Across from her, Eva smiled. "I think we should order some food."

She waved a waiter over and ordered nachos and mozzarella sticks for the table. They had demolished most of them when another touchy subject came up.

"I should warn you that Gio is over at Alex's place right now covered in babies," Eva said. "The guys are staying in with the kids tonight instead of going out."

"Why should I worry about that?" Sophia asked, reaching for a particularly cheesy tortilla chip.

"Oh," Maia said, "You haven't seen Gio around a baby yet, have you?"

*Uh oh.*

She straightened in her chair. "No, I haven't...I don't suppose you're about to tell me that he hates them and wants me to get my tubes tied."

They froze.

"Oh, no! You hate kids!" Elynn said.

Maia looked crushed, and even Eva appeared a little concerned.

"Don't panic. I don't hate them," she reassured them. "Granted I haven't spent a whole lot of time with them, but I do want children eventually. Maybe in a couple of years. But I'm starting a whole new phase of my research—ironically because of Gio and the grant he gave me. So if you're trying to tell me he's baby crazy, it's going to complicate things."

The other three ladies exchanged loaded glances.

"I hate to be the one to tell you this, but yes. That man's biological clock is *ticking*," Eva said, shooting straight as expected. "When I left, he was giving Alex junior a piggy-back ride while rocking Ethan Patrick to sleep at the same time. Gio wants a son so bad he can taste it."

"Or a daughter," Maia chimed in. "He's wonderful with my little girl. He calls her his *princessa* and never comes to see us without a gift for her. Granted the last one was a pink calculator, but it's the thought that counts."

"A calculator, really?" Sophia asked with a giggle. It was such a Gio gift.

"It's actually her favorite thing right now. She likes mashing the buttons."

Sophia digested the new information with some trepidation. She did want children, but the prospect of them had always been far in the future. She was only twenty-eight. There was still plenty of time. But if Gio was hellbent on having babies now, could she put him off? Did she even want to?

*Calm down.* Gio hadn't discussed the future at all yet. They hadn't even settled on where they might live if they stayed together. He did seem to be crazy about her, but that didn't mean he was going to get down on one knee and propose marriage anytime soon. And there was a chance he didn't even want to remarry. God knows being saddled with a crazy ex-wife like Maria Gianna was enough to turn anyone away from the institution.

Of course, one didn't need to be married to have children. Eva and Sergei still hadn't walked down the aisle yet and they had a son. Would that be enough to give Gio ideas?

It was entirely too much for one drunk neurobiologist to think about.

"You know, I think it's time for a second pitcher," Sophia said.

# CHAPTER 19

ophia should have been surprised to see Gio leaning on his town car door, waiting for her outside the pub, but she wasn't. The unexpected part was that Alex was with him. When he saw their group exiting the pub, he hurried up to Elynn and threw his arm around her.

"Eva, Maia, you're coming home with us," Alex said, bending to kiss his much shorter wife. "Sergei and Calen are waiting for you back at the house."

Sophia sidled up to Gio and cuddled into his warmth. "By house, does he mean huge honking mansion?" she asked as the other ladies waved and walked away to a waiting stretch limo.

Gio smiled down at her, that hot dark grin that he saved only for her. "Yes, he does. We're invited to brunch there next Sunday, by the way."

"Ooh, I love waffles," she said, burying her face in his chest.

Pleasantly warm despite the chill in the air, she leaned on him heavily, content to feel the pressure of his body as the other car pulled away.

"*Cara mia*, are you drunk?"

She looked up at him and smiled. "Maybe a little," she said, closing her eyes and humming a nonsensical tune.

His chuckle was deep and sexy. Embracing her, he opened the door behind them and pulled her into the darkened backseat of the car.

"Home," he said to the driver before raising the privacy screen.

As soon as the partition went up, Sophia climbed on top of him with a giggle.

"Hi," she said stroking his jawline with her fingers.

Kelly was right, his square jaw was incredibly sexy. Bending down, she flicked her tongue out to lick his closed lips before leaning back. Smiling seductively, she undid the top buttons of her blouse and opened it wide, revealing a deep red lacy bra.

Gio's eyes widened. "I think I'm going to like girls' night out," he said burying his face in her décolletage.

"Mmm," Sophia murmured, growing wet as his mouth covered her nipple through the sheer material of the bra. "How far is it to the apartment?"

"Four minutes." His voice was muffled.

"Too soon and at the same time too long," she said, rolling her neck in a circle.

Her body was warm and her limbs felt heavier than usual. Each touch seemed magnified, the sensations heightened by the alcohol. It made her want to rub all over him like a cat.

"Then let's make the most of it," Gio said huskily before taking her mouth and kissing her hard.

She leaned into him, following his lead and taking as much as she gave. Her hungry response seemed to drive him crazy. His hands ran all over her breasts and hips, his tongue tangling with hers.

He broke off for a moment. "Okay, definitely a huge fan of girls' night," he said, his hands fingering a lock of her hair.

Sophia giggled and shifted again on his lap, making him groan.

The quick ride passed in a heated clinch that overshadowed

every other make out session in her life. They fondled and groped at each other impatiently, but it was only four minutes, and before she knew it, they were pulling up in front of Gio's building.

When the car stopped, she climbed off him in a rush. Gio made a sound of complaint and grabbed at the empty space where she had been, making her giggle again.

"Come on," she said, reaching for his hand and tugging.

They managed to control themselves on the elevator ride up to the penthouse, but the second the front door closed behind them, their restraint disappeared. Hands went for zippers and buttons in a disorganized grappling session that made them both laugh and pant at the same time.

Shedding clothes like a debauched breadcrumb trail, they burst into the master bedroom, landing on the bed with a thump. Determined to take the lead, Sophia climbed on top.

"I have an idea," she said playfully.

Running his hands up the bare skin of her waist and back, Gio grinned up at her. "And what would that be?"

"I want to do that thing you wanted, the one I haven't done with anyone else."

Gio's gaze unfocused, trying to remember before his expression cleared. "You want to do *that?*"

"Yes, I do."

"Really? You're sure?"

"I'm sure, but if you don't want—"

"Oh, I want to," he interrupted, running a covetous hand over her ass. "As long as you want to."

"I already said—" Sophia stopped and squealed as he flipped her over, apparently deciding he was giving her too many opportunities to change her mind.

Pulling her to her hands and knees, he bent his head until his cheek was leaning on one of hers.

"Any reason why you want to do this tonight?" he asked curiously, pressing a kiss to her backside.

Sophia giggled again. "Yeah. Because this can't get me pregnant."

"*Okay.*"

She could tell he didn't understand, but as a man, Gio wasn't about to look a gift horse in the mouth. He continued to stroke her back and butt, peeling her bra and panties off as he went.

Still buzzed from the alcohol, she undulated sinuously, eliciting a harsh groan as the satin skin of her derrière slipped back and forth under his hands.

"God, I love your ass," he said, pressing a hot kiss to the center of her left cheek. "Have you been using your toy?"

Toy? Oh, the buttplug.

Gio had presented her with one not long after she agreed to try this one day. It was a black silicone cone with a softly pointed tip and a flared base. She'd worn it a few times but hadn't used it regularly, and not at all in the last few days. But she reasoned the alcohol had made her warm and willing. If she was ever going to try this, tonight was the night.

A hard spank surprised her. "I'm waiting for an answer, *cara.*"

"I used it," she said, deciding not to elaborate on the precise details.

"Good," he said, kissing her right cheek now, before shifting to spank her again.

A little huff escaped her parted lips, and she rested her forehead on the mattress when Gio ran his hands over the seam of her pussy. Parting her inner lips with a finger, he hummed approvingly.

"This makes you wet. I think you like it," he said in a low gravelly voice.

Before she could reply, he spanked her again and she moaned, her hands fisting on the silky sheets. One of his fingers entered her pussy, sliding easily in her wet channel. She moaned and pushed back against his hand, wanting more of him.

But he disappointed her by withdrawing and getting off the bed.

"Where is it?"

"Where's what?" she asked, clearly aggrieved.

"The plug, *cara*," he said laughing a little.

"Oh, in the drawer," she said, collapsing on the bed with her head to the side, watching him.

He moved to the dresser on her side of the bed and then disappeared for a second into the bathroom. When he returned he climbed back into bed, setting the plug, a tube of lubricant, and something else she couldn't see on her other side.

With both hands, he started to rub her shoulders and upper back. "You should be totally relaxed for this."

Sophia's laugh turned into a drawn out sigh as Gio's muscular hands kneaded her back and shoulders. Relaxing, she gave herself over to his skilled fingers.

Damn, the man was talented. *If he cooks, too, you may have to marry him.*

He massaged her back, working his way down until he was over his favorite spot. Every inch of her backside received his detailed attention. His obsession with that area was a bit much, though, and she was about to request that he speed things along when he stopped and reached for the plug. Applying a generous amount of lube, he pressed it to her puckered rosette.

Sophia pulled her arms in, her hands tightening into fists as the narrow tip penetrated the ring of muscle. Moaning, she pushed back until the flared middle reached her entrance. Gio paused, spinning the plug so the thickest part stretched her wide.

Little sparks of pain mingled with pleasure lit up the dark behind her closed eyes. Then Gio stopped working the plug sideways and pushed it all the way in, the flat flared base resting against her sphincter.

Crying out, she raised her hips reflexively. Gio growled in

approval, caressing her upturned cheeks reverently before spanking her hard.

"*Ah.*"

It felt different with the plug, both hotter and weirder.

"Still feeling good, baby?" he murmured in a voice like dark velvet.

"Yes," she whispered.

"Then this will feel even better." He withdrew the plug slowly until only the tip rested inside her, then he pushed it back in. He repeated the motion until he was fucking her with it in smooth strokes. Pushing her down until her weight rested on her forearms, he pulled her hips up until her butt was raised high off the bed.

"Oh, *oh God.*"

Gio's cock teased her pussy, rimming her entrance before pushing inside her.

It was tight, so much tighter than before. His cock barely fit inside her normally, but with the plug she was at her limit. He started to move, instantly transporting her into another place, one where that delicious slippery friction was the center of her world.

She thought there was no way it could get better, and then it did. Gio's thick cock plundered her pussy hard and rough, the way she liked it, but his hand was gentle, moving the plug back and forth—fucking her in both holes.

Involuntary little cries escaped her as she went into sensory overload. This time, she couldn't help by gripping or fluttering her inner muscles. The best she could do was hold on while Gio took complete possession of her body.

Sophia had never felt so vulnerable. She had ceded control over herself to another person and it was devastating. It would have been impossible to do this with anyone else. But this was Gio, and she was as captivated with him as he was with her. And she wanted to give him everything.

It took her a minute to register that he was speaking to her, murmuring hot dirty words in both English and Italian. As he urged her with his hands and speech, she rocked back into him, impaling herself on his cock and the probe until she was at the edge. Vision hazy, she rode the line of pain and pleasure. One of his hands slipped from her hip to her clit, teasing and pinching until she screamed, the violent contractions of her orgasm obliterating her senses.

When she came to, she was resting on her side on top of one of Gio's arms. He was hugging her to him with his left arm, pressing her to his chest. The plug was gone, and in its place was the heated head of his cock.

Despite their preparation, Sophia was having a hard time accommodating him back there. Gasping, she grabbed his left hand with both of hers, leaving his right free to guide his staff, feeding it into her inch by inch.

The pain wasn't unexpected, but she hadn't anticipated its sharpness. It cleared the haze of the alcohol and she was suddenly sober, holding tight to Gio's hand as she whimpered, bucking despite her intention to stay still.

Both of Gio's arms wrapped around her. "I'm almost there, *cara*, just a little more," he said, pushing forward a few millimeters. "Relax and push back."

Digging her nails into his hand, she sobbed and shifted, doing as he asked. It was a little better, but still not good. She was going to ask him to stop when he pressed home, his thighs meeting hers. Somehow he'd managed to fit all of himself in.

"Holy shit," she breathed.

"Do you want me to stop?"

"Of course I do, don't ask stupid questions," she said, half-laughing, with a little wince.

"I'm sorry, *cara*, I'll stop," he said, his voice threaded with disappointment.

She smacked his hand with one of hers. "No, you've gotten this far and I'm still a little buzzed. I want you to keep going, 'cause this is the only time we're going to do this."

Gio laughed and stroked her hip. "I'd rather stop if I'm hurting you, but I do have something that might help."

He reached over and picked something up, holding it in front of her. It looked like an oversized vitamin capsule with a little loop of string at one end.

"What is that?"

"It's called a vibrating egg. Did you know these can be controlled by your phone now?"

"No," she giggled, obliging him by parting her legs as he touched it to her pussy, running its smooth surface in a circle over her slit and entrance.

He pushed it inside and she closed her eyes. A few seconds later and it started vibrating.

"Shit! *Oh, God.*"

The crazy little device sent her already over-stimulated body into instant orgasm. She bucked wildly, so much that Gio had to hold her down, taking advantage of her reaction to add a little lube to the base of his cock and begin thrusting.

The cold gel quickly warmed as he pinned her to the bed. Helpless in his arms, she strained against him as he fucked her ass with quick short strokes.

She was holding on, but only just. She was too full, her nerve endings screaming. Behind her, Gio's breath grew shallow and rapid. His palm pressed against her clit hard, and he growled, swelling and coming with a hoarse grunt. The continued vibration inside her pussy, combined with the action of his grinding palm sparked another orgasm. The stormy surge of pleasure built up, spilling over in a blinding rush that left her weak and boneless.

"*Cavolo,*" Gio swore, collapsing next to her.

She laughed. "Not sure what that means, but I second it."

He didn't answer for a minute, but when he did he sounded

hoarse. "Does that mean you'd be willing to reconsider doing this again?

"It is entirely too soon for this conversation considering you are *still* in my ass," she said, twisting to try and smirk at him over her shoulder.

Gio bit his lip to stop a smile and pulled back, his spent cock slipping out of her.

"We can discuss it later, after a shower, but *bella mia* I want you to know it doesn't compare to taking your tight little pussy."

She laughed and shook her head. "Your friends think you're so straight and proper. They have no idea how dirty you are, do they?"

He bent to nip her nose. "Our secret," he whispered, tugging her up and leading her to the shower.

# CHAPTER 20

$\mathcal{D}$ays passed in a haze of sexual bliss.

There wasn't a repeat of the anal intercourse that blew both of their minds. Although Sophia had enjoyed the prelude and had loved the end, that middle part had been difficult for her. A man Gio's size couldn't be taken casually, and he admitted afterward that, while it had been good for him, it wasn't as good as he'd always imagined.

"Hadn't you done that before?" she asked, surprised, at breakfast one morning when they finally got around to talking about it.

"No, you're the first. Like I was your first," he said with a trace of smugness.

She narrowed her eyes at him. "Yeah, well, I think we're going to save that particular act for special occasions. Like your birthday. When is your birthday by the way?"

"It just passed."

"Perfect!" she cried out, raising her hands over her head in a V for victory.

He laughed so hard he spit eggs all over himself and had to change before leaving for work.

Gio didn't seem to mind letting her dictate hard limits in the bedroom. He was happy to resume their sex life in whatever form she chose—and he performed with an enthusiasm that left her sated and exhausted every night. They made love everywhere in that penthouse, preferring to stay in unless Alex managed to coax them out to dinner or Sunday brunch at his gargantuan estate.

Being around people with money was a surprise. Despite being what could be safely classified as obscenely wealthy, both Gio and Alex were kind and considerate men whose primary focus was their family. It was simply that being a part of their family meant being surrounded by luxury—mansions, penthouses, and town cars. Not to mention the bodyguards.

Sophia was becoming increasingly certain that Gio wanted to build a family with her. He'd begun to drop hints about marriage and children, and even asked if she would be willing to relocate to Rome after her research project with Alan ended.

Crazy as it was, Sophia was actually considering relocating— enough to start looking up details on research labs over there. Whatever she decided, it would have to have to wait a few years until a move was practical. And she probably wouldn't be spending those years alone. All of Gio's hints about the future made it seem like he was planning on sticking close by. At least, she hoped it did.

But she was reluctant to ask him if he was thinking of moving to Oxford, or if he planned on them having a long distance relationship.

Though she was willing to do long-distance if she had to, she wanted Gio to make this city his home base. To a billionaire with his own jet and access to a helicopter, the distance between Rome and Oxford was small, but she would miss coming home to him every night. Not to mention waking up with him every morning.

If it came down to it, she knew she had allies in Alex and Elynn. They could lobby Gio to relocate with her if the need arose. In fact, Alex had already taken her aside to say as much at brunch last Sunday—after acknowledging that he didn't think Gio would need any convincing. All Sophia had to do was ask. And she would...in a few days. Or next week...

It wasn't that she was afraid to talk to him. It was just that things were going so well, she didn't want reality to intrude on her happy new relationship bubble. And the likelihood was Gio would be going back to Rome. He had an empire to run.

Unfortunately, her bubble was burst prematurely the day Gio disappeared leaving behind a note with a single line.

*I found my ex-wife, and I'm going after her.*

"ARE you sure this is the place?" Gio asked his security chief as they arrived in front of the hotel.

Enzo nodded. "They're here. They checked in yesterday and closed down the bar last night. The key card data indicates they haven't left their suite since. Probably too hung over."

Gio snorted. "Not exactly laying low, are they?"

"Well, unfortunately, we can't prove they've broken any laws so they know the authorities aren't after them. And, honestly, they're not expecting you to come busting down their door."

His fist tightened. "I know. That's the problem. Maria Gianna is used to living in a world without consequences and she thinks I'm a fucking pushover."

Enzo's lip curled. "I don't think she's gonna believe that after this," he muttered.

Taking a bracing breath, Gio stepped out of the car. They were outside of an exclusive hotel in the party town of Malaga, Spain. It wasn't a city high on his list of vacation hotspots. Too many young people partying. If this place was Maria Gianna's idea of a good time, he'd severely overestimated her taste. The hotel might cost more than a thousand dollars a night, but the streets around it were clogged with drunken students moving like a sea of inebriated lemmings.

Across from the car, a young man bent over and started throwing up while his friends patted his back. Disgusted, Gio turned to the hotel and went inside. He let Enzo pave the way, securing a key card to Maria Gianna's room from housekeeping with a healthy bribe.

"Sure you don't want to break the door down?" Enzo asked him.

"Don't tempt me."

He was angry enough to do it. This confrontation had been put off too long, and his temper had finally reached the breaking point. Actually, he wouldn't be here at all if they hadn't messed with Sophia.

"Let's go," he growled.

They went up to the top floor where all the luxury suites were located. The room Vincenzo had rented was at the end of the hall. There were no security staff stationed anywhere on this floor, so he went up to the door and slid the card in.

The little light embedded in the card reader flashed green.

"Wait here," he told Enzo.

"You sure you don't need backup?" he asked, gesturing to the gun holstered at his side.

"They're degenerates, not gangsters," Gio said dismissively.

Then there was the fact that Maria Gianna had sent a drunken teenager to do her dirty work. It was the act of a coward, not someone who would be lying in wait with a weapon, ready to do violence.

"I'll stay out here then, but if I hear something I'm coming in."

Gio inclined his head in assent and handed the card over to his security chief before stepping inside. The room in front of him was empty, with clothes and shoes strewn about the sofa and floor next to dirty dishes. One of the lamps was broken, lying on its side on the carpet, next to an empty bottle of Crystal champagne.

It was unbelievable that they'd done this much damage in less than twenty-four hours. Silently thanking God that he was no longer married to the slob who created this mess, he headed for the suite's bedroom.

His ex-wife was sprawled across the bed. She was still wearing last night's cocktail dress. Vincenzo was snoring next to her, naked.

Furious at seeing the two of them lying there, the evidence of their debauchery all around them, he let go of his restraint. The iron control he normally had on his temper burned away like a flash fire.

Raising his leg, he kicked the end of the mattress repeatedly.

"Wake up, assholes," he said in Italian, his jaw tight.

Vincenzo woke up first. Rolling over, he stared, wide-eyed into Gio's wrath-filled face. Without taking his eyes off Gio, he reached over and shook Maria Gianna awake.

"What is it?" she mumbled, annoyed, her voice thick with sleep.

Following Vincenzo's eyes, she looked to the foot of the bed and saw him standing there like an avenging angel.

She flinched. "What are you doing here, Giancarlo?" she asked, making an effort to mask her surprise.

"What the hell do you think I'm doing here, you *bitch?*"

"Gio!" she exclaimed, genuinely astonished at the heated response.

He didn't blame her for being surprised. In all the years they'd known each other, he'd never raised his voice in her presence. He'd never gotten mad about anything. Not even finding her in bed with the idiot next to her.

"Listen to me carefully, *puttana*, because I'm only going to say this once. If you ever come near my Sophia again, I will *destroy you.*"

"But we didn't do anything—" Vincenzo started.

Gio cut him off with an abrupt gesture of his hand. "Don't even start. I know what you did that night, getting Lucca loaded and sending him to rape my fiancée. The only reason you're not sitting in a jail cell right now is because I can't prove it."

The flicker of emotion that crossed Maria Gianna's face gave her away—not that he needed confirmation of her involvement. But Vincenzo looked confused.

"Don't look so fucking relieved, you bitch. I don't need proof to ruin your life."

"I haven't done anything wrong," she said, her mouth twisted in a petulant frown.

"Save it. I know you did it, and it was the last straw. You can smear me all you want but the second you went after Sophia, I was done. You've had all the chances you're going to get with me," he hissed, his blood pumping hot through his veins.

"I don't want another chance with you," she said smugly. "You're far too dull for me. Vinny is so much more exciting."

Gio's eyes narrowed on her thin sallow face. What had he ever seen in her?

"You misunderstand me. I wouldn't touch you with a ten-foot pole. What I mean is that I'll ruin whatever is left of your reputation—the way you tried to ruin mine. Don't forget the Morgese bank has ties to every major industry in Italy and most of Europe. One word from me and all those silly endorsements you receive from fashion designers and clubs will disappear. And forget about any future movie roles. No one will touch you if *I* say they shouldn't."

He drew himself up, looking down on them with the distaste he felt all over his face. "You'd still be able to live like a parasite off your father, of course, but make no mistake. I have men watching you now. They will continue to watch you wherever you go—whatever you do. Anything illegal and I turn their surveillance over to the authorities."

Her face was ashen pale. "You wouldn't do that."

"*Try me.*"

She stood up then while Vincenzo watched, his head swinging back and forth between them like a spectator at a tennis game.

Maria Gianna's face twisted. "All this for *her*, that fat slut!

You're willing to make my life a living hell, but you wouldn't lift a finger to fight for me."

"Why the hell would I fight to keep a faithless *whore?*"

The venom in his voice hit her like a physical slap. She shrank away from him, backing away until her legs hit the edge of the bed.

"And don't call Sophia names unless you want the shitstorm to start now. Sophia's ten times the woman you are."

Maria Giana turned away with a smirk. "Literally," she muttered.

Gio took another step closer, then another, until she had to sit to avoid bumping into him. He stared her down with a glare hot enough to burn.

"Don't test me. I'm done looking the other way to protect your father." He turned his black expression to Vincenzo. "And don't think you're getting off the hook. As of Friday, you no longer have a platform to print your filth."

"What does that mean?" Vincenzo asked, sweat beading on his forehead.

"It means I bought the Gavazzi newspapers."

Maria Gianna stood back up, her face flushed red now. "You can't do that!"

"It's already done."

"Even you don't have that kind of money," she sneered. "The Gavazzi group is a media empire."

"You're kidding," he scoffed. "Old media is dead. Newspapers and magazines are closing all over the world. I bought the lot for a song."

"Papa sold you everything?" Vincenzo looked like he was going to be sick..

Gio didn't bother to answer. He turned away and headed for the door.

"Giancarlo, wait!" Vincenzo caught up with him at the door, hastily wrapping a sheet around himself. "I didn't know about the girl. I saw Maria Gianna talking with Lucca that night and buying him drinks, but I didn't hear her say anything to him about your new woman. I had to fly out to New York the next day for a meeting the next day so I took off early. "

He stopped and looked back at Maria Gianna sitting on the bed. "You don't think she would actually do something like that, do you?" he asked in a low voice.

Pausing, Gio took a good hard look at his former friend. There were new lines on his face that hadn't been there only two years before. His skin was ruddier and the whites of his eyes had yellowed. Being Maria Gianna's yes-man had taken its toll.

"Do yourself a favor and get away from her now, before there's nothing of the old Vinny left," he said, his heart heavy with old memories. They had been good friends once.

Vincenzo looked down, unable to meet his eyes. Gio opened the door. Enzo was waiting outside.

"Let's go home," Gio said, the rush of adrenaline from the confrontation wearing away.

Sophia was waiting for him.

# CHAPTER 21

*I*'m going to kill him, Sophia thought as she paced across the penthouse living room. Gio had been gone all night and he hadn't called or responded to any of her texts.

She had hurried home from the lab, eager to spend another night in with her man. Instead, she'd found an empty apartment and that damn little note.

What the hell had he been thinking? Didn't he know leaving like that was going to drive her crazy? Especially after that little bombshell message. So he was "going after" his ex-wife, was he? Well, what exactly was he planning on doing once he found her?

*It's not to get back together, so stop picturing him naked with the Italian stick insect.*

Sophia knew better than that. After everything Elynn and Alex had told her, she didn't believe that Gio was after some sort of reconciliation with Maria Gianna. But there was still that tiny insecure part of her that was comparing herself with the glamorous and svelte, evil ho-bag.

No, what Gio was after was some sort of revenge. What he had planned was a mystery. He was too much of a sweetheart to do anything violent, even if his note did make him some like the lead in a bad gangster movie.

Knowing him, Gio was going to hit them where it hurt—their wallets. It was what he'd done with Lucca, and if the updates from Salvatore were to be believed, the little shit was remorseful and reformed.

What Gio's exact plans were for his dreadful wife and her co-conspirator didn't matter. As hateful and wretched as those asshats were, what actually bothered her about his little disappearing act was something else.

And he gets to hear all about it right now, she decided, when the penthouse door opened to reveal her aggravating Italian in one of his trademark charcoal suits.

The smile he gave her in greeting threatened to take the wind out of her sails, but she was determined not to get sidetracked by his looks and charm. Crossing her arms and tapping her foot, she waited while he crossed the suddenly endless expanse of the foyer.

"I missed you, *cara*," he said, his steps slowing as he reached her.

He bent his head to give her a kiss, but she was having none of it. Reaching up, she grabbed his puckered lips.

"Don't even think about it."

"What's wrong, *cara*?" he asked.

At least that's what she thought he said—she hadn't let go of his lips so it came out somewhat garbled.

"Are you serious? You take off to go see your ex-wife and don't pick up your phone the whole night?"

He squinted and gently pried her fingers off his lips.

"*Cara*, I'm sorry if you were worried, but I couldn't talk to you. I needed to stay mad."

"*What?*"

His shoulders went up to his ears and stayed there. "I had to confront my ex-wife about her involvement in your attack. She egged Lucca on, got him drunk and put the idea of coming after you in his head. She even drove him to my place."

179

Sophia closed her eyes. "Yes, Elynn told me all that. And might I add that sucks! You should have been the one to tell me. I had a right to know what kind of psycho you married."

He held up his index finger. "And divorced. I may have married her, for the wrong reasons, might I add, but I got out when I saw what she really was."

Throwing up her hands, she bowed sarcastically. "If it's credit you want, fine, you've got it. But as long as we're keeping score, can I point out that my ex has never sent anyone to attack you!"

Gio's face darkened. "So this is about Richard?" he asked incredulously.

"No!" Sophia yelled, before changing her mind. "Yes, all right! It is. You go on and on about Richard, like he's some kind of thug when your ex-wife is this unbelievable bitch who is *actually* dangerous. And I'm supposed to sit here and do nothing while you go and confront her!"

He stared at her for a moment, his mouth open. "Only because it's my fault she even knows about you. The only reason she tried to hurt you is to strike out at me. So I went and made sure it would never happen again. It's my job to protect you."

"I don't need protecting. I can take care of myself. If I were in the same town with your ex, I would have dealt with her myself."

"You don't have to do that. She's my ex—my problem to deal with."

She put her hand on her hips. "You mean like Richard is *my* problem, not yours."

His head drew back. "That's not the same thing at all."

"And how is it different?"

He put his hands out in a supplicating gesture, but they were tensed so hard she could see the veins in them. "I have a bad feeling about him. I think he's obsessed with you. He's still trying to win you back. Or am I wrong? Tell me he hasn't called or texted you more than once since I've been gone."

She pressed her lips together and didn't answer.

"*See*, he still isn't willing to let go. Considering how long you've been broken up, not to mention the fact that you're with me now, it's unhealthy that he hasn't given up yet."

"He's buying my father's stuff—crap he's welcome to. After that, I won't hear from him."

Gio laughed humorlessly, making her boiling mad.

"*Hey*," she snapped, "where do you get off telling me what to do with my ex, when you won't give me the same right with yours? If I have to get constantly lectured about Richard, I should have the same right to tell you what to do with Maria Gianna. It's only fair."

"But that's not the same thing. I don't speak to my ex."

She threw up her hands. "Except you just left town to go and see her!"

"Only to make sure she never came after you again!"

"Then you should have taken me with you. I would have had a hell of a time convincing her that would be a fucking stupid idea!"

Gio stared at her like she was some species he'd never seen before. A little piece of her knew she was being irrational. She certainly wasn't explaining herself well. The subject of douchebag Richard wasn't where she wanted to take a stand in their relationship. But she couldn't let Gio decide how she should deal with her ex while he went off and did the exact opposite. He had to learn to trust her judgment and accept that they should both be held to the same standards.

Inhaling deeply, she went for her coat. "I'm going to go home and sleep there tonight."

Gio's face fell. "Sophia, don't leave."

She paused at the door. "Look, I know I don't get to tell you how to deal with the people in your life. But you don't get to dictate those things to me, either."

He followed her to the door. "I'm just concerned because I love you!"

"Yeah, well, I love you, too!" she yelled back before slamming the door in his face.

# CHAPTER 22

*S*ophia stormed out of Gio's high-rise in her brand new heels. Her fury lasted all through the trip across town and up the three flights of stairs to her apartment. She yanked off her dress and threw her shoes across the room with a satisfying hard kick.

She'd most likely be on her hands and knees checking them for scuffs later because she suspected the red soles meant they were Louboutins. She should have checked before she tossed them.

Kelly had taken a good look at her wardrobe and pointed out the luxury labels. Gavin had clearly been ordered to buy her designer clothes and not tell her what they actually cost. Or he'd found the mother of all trunk sales.

Irritated with herself, and even more annoyed with Gio, she jumped in the shower, washing off her makeup with extra rough scrubbing.

After that, she turned off her cell phone and took a very large glass of wine to bed to re-watch "The Holiday" on her computer for the twentieth time.

She woke up the next day a great deal calmer. After making

herself coffee, she puttered around her apartment in her flannel pajamas, studiously pretending her cell phone didn't exist. She needed a little more time before she talked to Gio.

Forgiving him wasn't a question. It was a matter of when. However, her stubborn streak wanted to make him stew a little. It hadn't been terribly mature of her to walk out, but she couldn't let him dictate to her the terms of her relationships. Elynn was right. She needed to set limits now, or he'd walk all over her.

She sat on the couch and hugged a pillow to her middle before picking up her mug and looking around. Her coffee table was dusty. It had been a while since she stayed here. And damnit—it felt tiny after Gio's palatial penthouse.

Her apartment had always been her haven. Every piece of furniture, every picture and knickknack had been chosen with relaxation in mind. It was a cozy space, comfortable while still being orderly and neat. She was extremely attached to each and every item in the place. But as soon as Gio rolled into town with his deluxe apartment in the sky, she hadn't looked back.

It should have felt good being surrounded by her possessions again. It didn't. And it wasn't because she missed the luxury of Gio's penthouse. This place seemed…empty.

She was too much of a feminist to admit it aloud, but being alone felt strange now. Gio hadn't taken over her life, but he had carved out a big space in it for himself. Even now when she was mad at him, she wanted to see him or hear his voice.

It wasn't like those times she'd missed Richard. Each time her ex left town without her, for work or to see his family, she'd marked his absence and told herself she missed him. But it was nothing like this whole-body longing. She hadn't yearned for him like she was doing now for Gio.

*Ugh.* Sophia took a deep breath. This whole being-in-love thing was turning her into a big pile of mush.

And this situation wasn't anything like her time with Richard. Gio didn't take her for granted. It was quite the opposite, in fact.

Her former relationship had chipped away at her self-worth and made her feel unattractive and unimportant. Richard had taken his cues from her own father, constantly picking at her appearance and downplaying her accomplishments.

Now she was with a man who not only delighted in her success, but he made her feel beautiful and sexy. The way he had introduced her to his friends and family, with such obvious pride, had meant everything to her. It felt good to be important to someone so accomplished and kind in their own right.

She could only hope that things would settle down the longer they were together. Gio had no reason to be jealous of Richard. Or of any other man. Yes, her ex was being oddly tenacious, but she knew that he didn't really want to reconcile.

Could it be that Richard's hero worship of her father was inspiring this effort to win her back? If so, it was a half-hearted attempt at best. A few phone calls, and that one text. He had dropped by the lab once to try and take her to lunch, but she had already left for an early meal with Elynn.

Hopefully, once she sold him the Chevette, it would be the end of her involvement with him. She knew Gio didn't understand why she wanted him to have it, but in her mind her father and Richard would always be tied together. Mentally she compartmentalized them in the same box—and their possessions belonged right there with them. Getting rid of it was her clean start.

Reassuring herself that she was doing the right thing, she finally turned on her phone. Only one missed call from Gio and one text that read *Please call me when you feel like talking.*

Considering how they'd left things, he was showing remarkable restraint. There was a missed call from Richard, too, probably another inquiry about getting the car's ownership papers.

Procrastinating, she decided to check her email before calling him back. At the top of her inbox was one from Kelly with the subject *"Have you seen this?!!!"*

Concerned something was wrong with Kelly or her husband

she opened it. All the message said was, "Isn't this what your father was working on?" and there was a link to the Sociology Department's Homepage.

There splashed at the top of the page was a feature on Richard and his new appointment as the head of the department. It was the next paragraph that had her seeing red. It was praising Richard for his groundbreaking and insightful work on the evolution of online trolling and its impact on gender identity in the internet age.

*No, it can't be.*

With a sinking sensation, she clicked on the link to Richard's most recent paper. Scanning the abstract quickly, she found her suspicions were correct.

Richard had stolen her father's research and published it as his own. Sucking in a breath, she went back to the original article on his appointment. The story praised Richard as a bright young star. It credited his most recent advancements in the field as the reason he was chosen for the prestigious Sotheby chair of Sociology. With the position came a sizable research grant and tenure.

*I don't believe this.*

How could Richard do something so unethical? And how had he gotten away with it? Didn't the other faculty know what her father had been working on during the last days of his life?

Probably not many of them. Her father had been a perfectionist. It was likely that he hadn't detailed his work to his colleagues until he was ready to publish it. She was an exception, but only because he didn't see her as a real scholar. In his eyes, she was a mere experimentalist who enjoyed getting her hands dirty—not a pure abstract thinker like him.

Her father had been about to submit his research project for publication the last time she'd talked to him. It hadn't occurred to her to check and see if he'd actually done it.

But she should have thought of it. They hadn't been close, but she still owed it to him to ensure that his legacy as a scholar was recognized. His work had been the most important thing to him—

far more important than his marriage or his daughter. If anything, the fact that he'd bored her senseless detailing his research all those Sundays while he puttered in his drafty garage, meant the damn thing would be published under his name.

Was that why Richard wanted the house? Had he known her father's unpublished work was sitting there unclaimed? And why the hell had he wanted the car? Was it guilt? Did he think claiming all the old man's possessions somehow made it right to plagiarize his research as well?

At the time she had been grateful when Richard agreed to take her father's personal belongings. Anything she hadn't wanted was going to charity anyway, and she'd decided it should all go.

Well, it seemed that her decision to avoid the painful memories of her relationship with her father was coming back to bite her in the butt.

Furious, she picked up her phone and dialed Richard.

He picked up on the second ring. "Darling! I'm so glad you called!"

"You won't be when I'm through with you!" she said.

*"Darling?"* The tone was simultaneously hurt and condescending.

"How could you? He was your mentor, you bloody thief!"

There was complete silence on the other end of the line.

"Well? What do you have to say for yourself? And how has no one in that damn department realized you stole my father's research?"

More silence.

"Richard, so help me God, I'm going to go over there and I'm going to kick your ass into next week if you don't start talking right now."

There was the sound of someone taking a fast quick breath. "Yes, come over. That's exactly what I need you to do. I can explain everything. You'll understand once I tell you what happened.

Come over here to your father's house. Everything will be clear. Just don't do anything rash before you hear what I have to say."

Even angrier now, Sophia fisted her free hand. "There is nothing you can say to explain this away!"

"Yes, there is! But I need to talk to you in person. Will you come?"

Sophia ground her teeth and exhaled slowly. "All right. I'm on my way now. But I'm warning you, Richard. I'm not letting this go."

"I know that. I'll be expecting you," he said in a hollow voice.

Sophia hung up and stormed to her bedroom, pulling off her shorts and t-shirt and taking out jeans and sweater. She started to put them on and then changed her mind.

Her old clothes weren't going to work for this confrontation. On impulse, she picked out a deep pink bodycon dress. It was part of her new wardrobe—one of the pieces that made her feel empowered. Deciding she could do with a bit of armor, she threw it on over her head. Finally she grabbed a pair of black motorcycle boots and tugged them roughly on her feet.

She was about to run out the door when she remembered Gio. Right now, their conflict was nothing in the face of Richard's deception. She needed to let him know that he'd been right all along to distrust her ex.

*God, he's going to love that.*

Letting Gio tell her, "I told you so" was going to have to wait. First she had to go kick some ass. Grabbing her phone, she typed a brief message to her know-it-all Italian before snatching up her car keys and slamming her apartment door shut behind her.

# CHAPTER 23

Gio should have been exhausted. He'd been up all night, unable to sleep since his argument with Sophia. Instead, he felt strangely buzzed, the lack of rest making him twitchy.

It had taken all his willpower to keep from going over to her apartment last night. One phone call, which had gone unanswered was all he allowed himself. He couldn't push her right now. She needed time to cool off. To that end, he'd sent her a text at two in the morning before trying to rest. But sleeping alone had been impossible.

The bed felt empty without Sophia in his arms. She belonged there. It was the only thing that made sense. Deep down she knew it too, and he was sure they were going to be fine once they were past this point of contention regarding their exes.

They had to be.

His body needed more convincing. There was a rock in his stomach, a tangible reminder that he'd mishandled the whole thing.

Sophia had a point that he was being unfair. If he was being honest, he knew she had a right to deal with Richard any way she chose. But something inside of him couldn't accept that.

His strongest instinct was to protect her, and it was telling him to keep her away from that man. Keeping her from hurt or harm was his priority. Those protective feelings had always been there, but after the incident with Lucca they had gone into overdrive.

Intellectually he knew that overstuffed shirt Richard didn't look like a threat to anyone else. An impartial observer would probably side with Sophia. Gio was being unreasonable about him, but he couldn't seem to stop—which was disturbing in and of itself. After a lifetime of deliberate and rational behavior, he was acting like a madman. His only justification was this gut feeling that something wasn't right with his rival.

He spent the rest of the day trying to bury himself in work. It was a tried and true technique that had served him well in the past. Only this time it failed him completely. He kept checking his phone for messages every ten minutes, hoping against hope that Sophia had calmed down enough to speak to him again.

He was contemplating hitting the gym to work out his frustration when he heard the text alert on his phone go off. Snatching it up, he quickly scanned through Sophia's message.

*Gio, I'm sorry things got so heated last night. If it makes you feel any better Richard IS a piece of shit! You'll never believe what he did. He stole my father's research! I have to go read him the riot act but after, I'm going to come over so we can talk. I'll call you as soon as I'm done.*

*Oddio.* He sat there staring at his phone for a long moment, letting the implications of her message sink in. For a second, he was elated. There was no way Richard was going to be able to win Sophia back now. That English idiot had just hit the last nail on his own coffin. However, his relief was short-lived.

The man had committed academic fraud. Was that illegal? Even if it wasn't, it was unethical. The University would have no choice but to fire him if it got out. And Sophia was going over to confront him on her own.

If Richard had stolen Jorge Márquez's research and passed it off as his own, what else was he capable of? Cornered rats could be dangerous. Especially now that his transgression had been uncovered.

On impulse, he called downstairs and told Enzo to get him a car, a dark nondescript one.

Sophia would be furious if he interfered with her handling Richard tonight, but what she didn't know wouldn't hurt her. He was only going to drive himself over to the Englishman's house and sit outside.

If all went well, she would never know that he was there. But if there was any sign she was having trouble, he would be close by to make sure she was all right.

---

*EIGHT, nine, ten...*

Counting wasn't working. Sophia was still so angry she couldn't see straight. It was a small miracle she'd been able to drive without getting into an accident.

She took the steps of her father's house two at a time and knocked on the door with a determined balled-up fist. Several minutes passed before she saw movement at the curtains.

"Richard! Open up!"

Still nothing. He was sitting behind the curtain, watching her like some sort of peeping Tom. Did he think she was going to give up and go home? The entire house was lit up. It was obvious he was home.

"I can see you behind the curtain damn it! Open the fucking door!"

That finally did it. The door swung open and Richard stood there, a sour expression on his face. "Darling, I know I'm in the wrong here, but that is no reason we can't have a civilized conversation like two decent people."

"Decent!" The man had some brass balls on him. "Are you fucking *kidding* me?"

A look of sheer panic crossed his face. Scanning over her head, he pulled her inside and shut the door.

"Are you seriously afraid of what the neighbors will say? After what you did?"

Richard stepped back and ushered her deeper inside the house. He had redecorated, replacing her father's Spanish-inspired decor with heavier furnishings. It looked like the inside of an English lodge.

Suddenly that made her furious. "What did you do—throw away all his things after you took his research and published it under your name?

"Sophia, will you stop please and listen? I didn't steal a single thing." He stood up straighter and stared down his long narrow nose at her. "Your father stole from me."

She shook her head. "Unbelievable! I never realized what a liar you are."

He threw up his hands. "I'm not lying, and I'm insulted that you would believe I would. I'm aware we've been having a hard time lately but you are still my best friend in the world and Jorge was like a father to me."

He stepped closer to her and put his hands on her shoulders. "I swear I'm telling you the truth. I helped your father out from time to time and he took the idea to study online trolling from me. I had no idea he had pursued *my* idea behind my back. When I found out, I was crushed. Completely disillusioned "

Her breath was trapped in her lungs. God, he was good.

Sophia exhaled slowly. "Nice try. But he didn't get the idea for the study from you. He got it from *me*."

She had never told anyone that, not even Kelly. It hadn't been a big deal at the time. One freezing Sunday morning, she had been sitting there in his garage while her father worked on his car. They had run out of topics of conversation so she brought up a blog post she'd read recently on the harassment of female bloggers in the gaming industry. The article discussed how the Internet allowed for the evolution of online trolls, people who hid behind the anonymity of their computers to say and act with impunity.

Since it was a question related to his field, her father's attention had been caught and he started talking to her about it—really talking and not lecturing. It was the most two-sided conversation they'd ever had. Instead of sermonizing, he listened and they'd debated pros and cons until he came up with a unique angle he wanted to pursue further.

Of course in time she regretted giving him the idea. Since she'd come up with the topic in the first place, her father assumed she would be eager to hear all the details. She had been privy to the evolution of his thoughts on the subject and then some. She knew way more about online trolls than she wanted to.

"From you?" Richard finally asked, his face was twisted in dismay.

"*Yes.* During one of our damn Sunday morning visits. So don't stand there lying to my face and say he stole it from you because I know better."

He paled, turning a pasty gray. Staggering to the new leather sofa, he threw himself down on it and buried his face in his hands.

In all her time with Richard, she'd never seen him display that kind of emotion. He was never at a disadvantage, and he never dropped that superior attitude of his. She almost felt sorry for him.

*Don't even think about letting him off the hook.* He had lied and until she called him on it, he'd expected to get away with it. She couldn't let that happen.

"You have to go to the dean of the University and tell him the truth."

He put his hands down and stared at her. "I can't do that Sophia. I'll lose my job! I was just tenured."

"You got tenure based on a lie. They gave it to you based on your amazing research paper, the one that you stole!"

Richard rose and came towards her, his hands up. "Only you know that. Jorge was so secretive about his work. The rest of our colleagues have no idea what he was doing towards the end. And I did help him with a lot of it. He didn't even finish. Once he was gone, it was only natural that I take over. My contribution was significant, too! He would have wanted me to have it."

Sophia laughed hoarsely. "You're kidding, right? He would never have wanted someone else to steal his thunder. And what happened to your own project? The one on *ethics?*" she asked, her voice dripping with sarcasm.

"I am still working on that," he said. "But it wasn't ready and the tenure issue came up quickly when your father passed away and Aaron Spitz took early retirement."

By now he was pacing around the room, wringing his hands and looking at her with a wild light in his eye. "The department wanted to keep me on, but there was another candidate with equal seniority—that obnoxious Leonard Cox. You remember him right? From the faculty dinner?"

Her answer wasn't important, and he kept right on going with his justification. "I needed an edge on Cox, and your father's research provided it. I never dreamed it would overshadow my own work the way it did, or that it would be the reason they gave me tenure. It just happened. But Sophia, darling, after all that I went through with your father, don't you think he would have wanted things to work out this way? I am his spiritual heir. He said as much several times."

"You're not listening," Sophia said with a slow shake of her head. She took a deep breath and tried to come up with a reason he would understand.

"You have to come clean about what you did now before you permanently damage your career. Sooner or later, someone is going to find out. You can't complete a study like my father's without leaving a paper trail. Somewhere out there is evidence that he did it, not you. You can't ignore that."

Richard seemed to crumble in front of her. His face fell, and he stared at her with bright wounded eyes. "No, believe me, I checked. But if somewhere down the road someone finds something suspicious, I can explain it away…as long as you back me up."

Her mouth dropped open in shock. "You expect me to lie for you?"

"What I want—no, what I need—is your loyalty, like when we were together. If you could just be like that again, when I had your unequivocal support, then everything would be fine."

The truth slammed into her like a brick. "Oh, my God! That's why you wanted to get back together. You knew I would eventually find out about this. It wasn't about your feelings for me. All that noise about that two of us belonging together, finally meeting your parents, it was bullshit. You just wanted was to make sure that I would keep my mouth shut!"

"No! That's not it! I sincerely believe we are meant to be together. It's what your father would have wanted," he said frantically putting his arms around her and trying to pull her to him.

Utterly disgusted, she pushed him away. Breathing heavily, she stared at him. "That is not going to happen."

"*Why not?*"

She laughed shortly. "Well, for one, I am in love with another man. But even if I wasn't, our relationship is over. It has been for a long time."

Richard made a face. "The Italian? Are you serious? He's nothing but a spoiled playboy! No, he's worse! Don't you know about all the terrible things that man has done to his wife? It's all over the Internet. All you have to do is Google him!"

She held up a hand. "Gio is a good person. The only thing wrong with him is his ex-wife. She's deranged and has been smearing him in the press for her own ends. Seriously, she's a mess. Although right now I'm not exactly in a position to throw stones when it comes to exes," she added pointedly before standing up straight. "I'm done arguing about this. You have until Monday to speak to the dean."

Richard's hands fell down to his sides. The manic look in his eyes dulled and his expression closed up. "If that's what you want," he said slowly.

"It is."

"All right then. But can I ask you for one favor?"

Sophia's head drew back. "What is it?" she asked suspiciously.

"I want you to take a few days to think about this—really think about it. Consider what I did for your father and what he wanted for me, for *us*. And then decide if asking me to sacrifice my career and reputation is what you want."

"I'm not going to change my mind."

"I understand. But please do it anyway."

Sophia wrapped her arms around herself. "I will, but I'm not making any promises."

He nodded. "Good, that's good. Um...do you want to stay for dinner?"

*Unbelievable.* "No, I can't," she said slowly. "Gio is waiting for me."

"Oh, of course."

Giving him a last look of frustration mingled with disgust, she started for the front door.

"Sophia, wait." He crossed in front of her, blocking her path. "I just remembered those things I found, the ones that belong to your mother. I put them in a box in the garage. Do you want them since you're here?"

*Crap.*

All she wanted was to walk out the front door and never come back. However, if there was anything of her mother's here, she couldn't leave without it.

"It's one box?" she asked, suppressing a sigh.

"Yes," he assured her, gesturing towards the kitchen.

Determined to grab the box and leave as quickly as possible, she hurried through the garage door, leading the way.

Behind her, Richard stopped at the threshold to flick on the light. Her father's vintage Chevette was right where he'd left it. It didn't appear as if Richard had moved it, supporting her theory that he bought the car out of guilt.

Nothing else looked different either. Walking around the front of the car, she peeked on the other side. No box.

"Richard, where is—"

A sudden rush of movement behind her was her only warning. She started to spin around, but she wasn't fast enough.

Something heavy crashed into her head. There was an explosion of light and pain that burned across her vision like a meteorite before everything went dark.

# CHAPTER 24

*G*io checked his watch for the fifth time. He was sitting in a car across the street from Richard Selwyn's house—Sophia's father's old place.

When he'd asked Enzo for the address, he was unsurprised to learn his security chief already had it. The address had been part of the background check he'd run on Richard, one he conveniently neglected to tell Sophia about. It would have only pissed her off knowing he'd invaded her ex's privacy that way. But again, what she didn't know wouldn't hurt her.

As soon as Sophia walked out the door, Gio was going to start the engine and drive back home. With luck, he would beat her there. She would never find out that he'd been here at all.

Except it had been almost a half-hour and she was still inside. Her car was across the street a little up from the house, so he knew he hadn't missed her leaving. How long did it take to tell someone off?

Another few minutes crawled by and his concern grew. What if something had happened? He knew his woman well enough to assume she had come here guns blazing. Richard had probably been on the defensive. As strong and capable as she was, Sophia was much smaller than him. What if he'd done something to her?

A rush of adrenaline nearly propelled him out of his seat and up the steps of the house. It was only Sophia's voice echoing in his head that stopped him. This was exactly the sort of thing they had been arguing about.

What if they were just talking, somehow managing to work the situation out on their own?

Drumming an indecisive beat on the steering wheel, he stared at the house. Minutes passed and he started to feel a little ridiculous. Everything was fine. Any minute now, Sophia was going to walk out that door and if she saw him out here, their relationship might be irreparably damaged.

He was fingering the key in the ignition, contemplating driving away, when the garage door opened. While he watched a dark blue Chevrolet pulled out into the street. Leaning forward, he scanned the interior as it turned in front of him.

The driver was Richard, but the passenger seat was empty. Peering closely, Gio caught a glimpse of something that turned his blood to ice. As the car was pulling away it passed under a streetlight—illuminating a bit of something dark pink sticking out from under the closed lid of the trunk.

Sophia had a dress that shade. It was one of the outfits he'd made Gavin, his English buyer, present to her. He loved the way the color complemented her caramel skin.

Panic flooded him. He needed to move. The car started to disappear down the street. With hands that trembled, he turned the key and started the car. Gunning the engine, he made the same left turn the Chevy had. He exhaled when he spotted Richard a bit ahead.

He fumbled for for his phone and hit one on the speed dial just as the car pulled out onto the highway.

The phone rang and rang, ratcheting up his tension. He could barely breathe when it connected and went to voicemail. "You've reached Sophia Márquez. I can't come to the phone right now. Leave a message at the beep."

Crap, he'd forgotten he swapped out the number one position on his speed dial. Hitting two, he waited impatiently for Enzo to answer.

"Yes, Gio?"

"Enzo! I'm following Richard Selwyn. He's driving a blue Chevrolet, and I think he has Sophia in the trunk!"

"Holy shit, are you sure?"

Doubt assailed him. What if he was wrong and it was something totally innocent, like a rag?

"Oh, God, I don't know, but I see something sticking out of the trunk. I think it's her pink dress, but I could be wrong. Am I being crazy?"

There was a beat of silence and Enzo inhaled. "Doesn't matter. We can't take the chance that you're right. Follow him. Make sure you stay at least three car lengths behind. Try to keep some cars between you, but not at the cost of losing him. *Don't lose him.*"

"I won't," Gio said, pressing hard on the accelerator and slipping into the same lane.

If Richard looked behind him, it would be harder to identify the car with the lights blinding him. At least he hoped that was the case.

"Okay," Enzo said. "I'm calling the police now. Better safe than sorry. Can you tell me where you are?"

"Um, we're near the Banbury exit on highway M40."

"Can you see the license plate? Is it still BG38 RSL or did he change it after he bought the car from Sophia?"

"I didn't see it," he said, swallowing in dismay. "I was too busy staring at the trunk, and I'm too far now."

"It's all right. He probably didn't change it. I'm going to call the police now from the house phone. I'm staying on the line. I'll be with you the whole time."

Gripping the steering wheel, Gio nodded stupidly before remembering Enzo couldn't see him. "What else should I do?"

"Exactly what you're doing. I'm tracking you on your cell by the way in case you need to leave the car. If you do, though, see if there's anything in the car you can use as a weapon."

Gio twisted around quickly. "It looks pretty bare."

"I know," Enzo said, exhaling quickly. "It's a company car. Do your best. I'm gathering the rest of the team and they're meeting me downstairs. We'll get to you as soon as we can."

Gio swallowed hard, checking manically for the vehicle ahead. Sweat was trickling into his eyes. Hastily, he wiped at them. His worst fears were rising up, threatening to choke him.

"Enzo, what if she's already dead?"

His heart was already hammering in his chest, but when Enzo didn't answer it almost stopped.

"She's fine. It might not even be her in there. It might be some random cloth he slammed in the trunk link and this guy is going to be slapping you with a lawsuit for stalking or something."

"It's fucked up that that's the best case scenario, but I don't care. If I'm wrong, let him sue."

"That's it. Just think about your lawyers tearing him up...Have you tried calling her?"

"No answer."

"Well, that doesn't mean anything. She might be driving or her phone ran out of battery. I'll leave instructions with the doorman to call me if she arrives here." In the background, Gio could hear talking and hurried footsteps. "We're leaving now."

Ahead of him, the Chevrolet changed lanes and drove toward an exit. No one else followed suit so Gio waited till the last minute and then pulled behind him. "He's getting off. There's no one between us now."

"Stay far enough away from him so he can't make you out. Do you recognize where you are?"

"No. The exit said something quarry and it's pretty isolated."

The area was disturbingly deserted. It was almost rural with a few buildings thinly spread out in the dark countryside. Praying that he was wrong, he continued to follow the car ahead, grateful that it was distinctive enough to see by moonlight alone because the street lights were sparse out here.

Long minutes passed and the fear clawing at his stomach worsened. The buildings had disappeared, and he was the only other car on this road. There was no way Richard could have failed to spot him following.

"Enzo, he has to know I'm behind him. What should I do?"

He could try and run the car off the road, but he might end up hurting Sophia.

There was no answer. "Enzo?"

Snatching the phone up, he was dismayed to see the phone had dropped the call. He tried to redial, but there were no bars.

"Shit!" He looked up and his blood ran cold.

The car was gone. He was alone on the road.

"No, no, no!"

Breathing in and out slowly, he hit the gas. Richard must have accelerated and possibly made a turn somewhere up ahead.

Please, oh please, he thought. There was no way that stuffed shirt Richard was driving in these backwoods for pleasure. He had Sophia in that trunk. Gio knew it in his heart. He had to find them.

He almost missed the turnoff. It was hidden by a tree. Hitting the brake, he stopped and made sure there wasn't another exit up ahead.

If there was, he couldn't see it. Turning the wheel sharply, he shot down the street.

The dark road flew past him. It seemed endless and he was about to start howling in rage when the road suddenly forked. He slammed on the brakes.

Oh fuck, which way had they gone?

# CHAPTER 25

Sophia groaned and tried to open her eyes. Something was wrong with them. She blinked but it was still dark, and her head was killing her. Her brain wasn't working. Thoughts skittered in and out of her head with little connecting them.

She took several deep fortifying breaths, fighting the confusion of her muddled mind. What the hell had happened? And where was she?

The space was dark and the air had an oily metallic smell. Reaching around her fingers grazed rough carpet underneath her.

Her dizziness was swiftly replaced by fear. Reaching up she felt cold metal as her body finally registered the sensation of movement.

She was in the trunk of a car. Oh, holy hell. She was in her father's Chevette. Richard had hit her—he'd tried to kill her.

Bile rose up in her throat as she frantically scrabbled at the trunk lid above her. Little broken sobs escaped her while she pushed futilely at the barrier. It didn't give a millimeter, and furthermore her dress appeared to be trapped in the catch of the lock. She tugged at the skirt until it ripped free.

"Let me out! Somebody help me!" she yelled, banging on the lid.

There was no answer and no sounds of traffic. Where was Richard taking her?

Dread pooled in her stomach, but she kept yelling, trying to make as much of a racket as possible. In the front of the car, music started to play loudly.

He was trying to drown her out. Knocking even louder, she screamed at him. "Richard! Let me out!"

The music turned up again and she swore violently. Her fear turned to anger. That shit! How could he do this to her after all she had done for him?

For two years, she had swallowed her pride and done her best to support him and his career. And in return she'd been taken for granted, denigrated, and most likely cheated on. By rights, she should have kicked his teeth in. Instead, she had made a clean break and tried to be civil whenever she had to deal with him afterward. If he hadn't kept hounding her, she might have been able to stay on that high road.

*Okay, think, think.* He was going to have to stop the car somewhere. She would have to reason with him, promise to lie and back up his story about her father's research.

*He will never buy it!*

But she didn't have a choice. She had to make him believe it.

GIO TRIPPED CLIMBING out of the car. Pain shot up his knee as he fell hard, but he ignored it and scrambled up. Breathing hard, he stood and ran in front of the hood to where the headlights lit the forked dirt road.

There has to be something here, he thought, running around looking for a sign of which path the car had gone. He pulled out his phone. There were still no bars, but he turned on the bright flashlight and used it to scan for evidence.

Was that a tire track?

The hard packed road didn't reveal much, but the dirt on the shoulder did have a tire impression and it appeared to be a recent one. Running across the grass to the other side, he looked for more tracks. There were some but they were all on top of each other, and they weren't as defined as the set on the left side of the fork.

But what if he was wrong? *Fuck, fuck, fuck. Breathe.*

He had to calm down and act rationally. Bringing up his phone, he texted Enzo, telling him to send people down the right path as soon as they caught up. He needed a plan B in case he was making a mistake. The phone still had no bars, but he might drive close enough to a cell tower long enough for the message to go through.

Sprinting back to the car, he climbed behind the wheel and sped down the left road.

*Please, God, don't let me be too late.*

# CHAPTER 26

They had stopped. Outside, a car door slammed and Sophia heard Richard climb out and start walking around.

"Richard, please! Think about what you're doing. You have to let me out of here!"

Except for footsteps, there was silence.

"I won't tell anyone what you did, I promise! Just let me out of here."

That finally caught his attention. "I don't believe you." His voice was low, a little above a whisper and it was coming from right above her.

"I swear on my father's grave," she said, flinching at the lie. "No one has to know."

He didn't answer for a long time. "You should have taken me back. Everything would have been fine. You would have done what I said. You always did what I said."

His voice was monotonic and distant. She could picture him standing out there with his hands on the lid, looking down on her the way he always had.

"You have to let me out of here. People know I went to see you and why."

"By that I guess you mean the Italian. Kelly, too. Doesn't matter," he said in the same remote tone. "I have a plan."

This was bad. He was starting to disassociate, justifying his actions and planning his next steps after he got rid of her.

"Whatever it is, it won't work," she said, raising her voice, refusing to accept that her situation was going from bad to worse.

"It will work!" Richard yelled, hitting the lid for emphasis. "I'm going away for a while. I'll tell the University someone died. When I come back, I'll have a paper trail proving that research is mine. If anyone comes looking for you, I'll show them my evidence and tell them you saw it. You even apologized for suspecting me of doing anything wrong. And then you drove off to meet your billionaire boyfriend. I have no idea what happened to you after that. Maybe his crazy ex-wife did something to you. You were complaining about her to me while we shared a convivial cup of tea."

*Holy fuck.* That sounded totally plausible. "No one will believe that, least of all Gio. He'll never stop looking for me. He's probably searching for me right now."

The words were out before she could think about them, but she instantly knew they were true. Gio loved her and he would move heaven and earth to find her.

There was no response. More footsteps sounded and the car door creaked. Then there was movement and a splash.

"What are you doing, Richard?" she asked in a panic.

The only noise was the sound of water. In less than a minute it was seeping in from underneath her. *Oh, God.* He was dumping the car in a lake or something, letting her drown. This trunk was going to be her coffin.

"Richard! Richard! Please, I won't tell!" she screamed.

But he didn't answer. She could hear more splashing, but the noise grew progressively fainter as Richard abandoned her. Water continued to pour inside. It was half-way up her torso and seemed to be coming in faster now.

*Shit. I'm going to die in here.*

# CHAPTER 27

*N*othing. There was nothing. Just more road and a bunch of fucking trees. *I've gone the wrong way,* Gio thought with a sickening pang. Should he turn around?

Indecision kept him going until he spotted a sign up ahead. He floored the car, shooting towards the sign and then slowing down to read it.

*Old Anderson Quarry 1.2 km ahead.* Could that be it? Nothing else was near.

Driving faster than he ever had in his life, he raced the remaining distance to the quarry entrance.

There was a gate, but it looked old and was standing open. At first, he couldn't see anything else. Slowing down so he could maneuver the tight turns of the path, he rounded a curve. Moonlight reflected off something shining up ahead. Was this one of those unused quarries that had been filled in with water? Why had Richard driven here?

The realization that he came here to dump the body followed instantly. *Don't think about it.* Find them, he ordered himself.

His blood was throbbing in his ears. Reaching inside for the control his friends teased him about, he forced his chest to pump up and down evenly until the panic dissipated enough for him to think. They had to be along the water. If Richard was trying to get rid of the car he'd want to be as isolated as possible. Which meant he would drive to the other side of the quarry.

Gio topped a rise in the road and saw something that would give him nightmares for the rest of his life.

The Chevrolet was half-submerged. Richard was at the open passenger door pushing it deeper into the water. Throwing his own car in park, Gio leaped out and ran into the lake. He barely registered its freezing cold temperature as he splashed toward them.

Richard saw him right away. Desperate panic twisted his face. He lifted something and there was a popping sound. Gio's left arm stung, but he ignored it, putting his head down and charging like a bull at his enemy. The coward broke away from the car, streaking to the right away from him.

But the skinny Englishman was no match for the rage powering him. His opponent may have been a little taller, but Gio outweighed him with an additional twenty pounds of sheer muscle.

Using a move he'd only seen on television, he clotheslined the asshole, wrapping his right arm around Richard's scrawny neck.

They fell in the shallow water near the shore. The rat underneath him twisted viciously, breaking his hold and scrambling away. Throwing himself forward, Gio leaped on him, punching and trying to shove his head under the surface of the water. Richard put up his hands to protect his face, using his legs to push him away.

In the distance, Sophia screamed, sending a shaft of pain down his chest. Roaring, he slammed his fist down onto Richard's head with all his weight behind it. The force knocked the taller man backward toward the shore. Gio didn't wait to see if he got back up again. He spun around and waded to the car.

# CHAPTER 28

*I*n the distance, Sophia could hear Richard shouting something and the distant sounds of splashing. Was there someone else out there?

"Help! Help me!" she screamed, craning to keep her head above the freezing water. The level had risen to cover most of her torso, but it wasn't rising as fast anymore.

*Wait, wait.* This was her father's car. It had some kind of pass-through, where the backseat folded down, allowing access to the trunk. Sophia stopped beating the lid and started pushing at the back panel.

It gave very slightly. Scrabbling at the edges of the seat, she searched for the catch mechanism, praying she would be able to reach it from the wrong side of the seat. In the darkness she couldn't find it, but her movements rocked the seat back and forth. Twisting around and curling up her upper body to give her legs as much room as possible, she started kicking as hard as she could.

Years of soccer had made her legs powerful, but the mechanism on the other side must have been stuck. The thick muscles on her thighs strained and the car rocked with her effort. The creaking metal finally gave, but not all the way. A gap the width of her hand opened. Searching by touch, she felt around for the catch to release the seat.

*Fuck!* The thing that held the seat up had wires wrapped around it. Her father had never fixed it. Instead, he'd wired it shut. Sticking her face at the opening she'd made, she took a deep breath and began to search for the end of the tangled knot. She needed to unwind it.

Wouldn't her father have put the twisted ends in the front? Where were they? *Shit.* Had her kicking moved the ends?

Sobbing now, she started pulling, straining against the wire until her fingers bled.

"Sophia!"

"*Gio?*"

Oh, thank God! "Gio, I'm in here!" she called out, sticking her hand out of the gap and waving.

There was a lot of splashing and then the whole car rocked as Gio opened the back door and climbed inside. He reached for her hand and she took hold of his gratefully, gripping tightly.

His face filled the gap. "*Porca vacca!* I don't have the key. Does this thing come down?"

"Yes, but it's wired shut."

"Fuck, I'm going after the trunk key!"

He climbed out of the car and ran off. An excruciatingly long minute later, he was back.

"Sophia, he doesn't have the key on him."

"Richard's still out there?"

"Yes, but he's unconscious. Where is this wire? We have to undo it."

She stuck her hand out and put it over the catch. Gio reached back behind him to the roof and flicked on the overhead light. Able to see his outline more clearly, she cried out in relief.

"This thing is too taut. I need to put the seat up a little to give it some slack."

"Okay," she said, drawing back her hand and pushing away.

The trunk grew darker as the gap narrowed, but she could hear splashing as his hands loosened the restraint.

"I got it! I got it!" he yelled, pulling the seat towards him.

Her relief was short-lived. The seat didn't go down all the way. But the gap was bigger, and Gio's strong arms reached inside to wrap around her head before he retreated and took hold of the top of the seat.

Metal creaked as he pushed and pulled at the seat to try and free it. His movements rocked the entire car and then she felt something else.

"It's moving!" The car slid forward, as if it was resting on an incline.

It was sinking deeper into the water, taking the both of them with it.

# CHAPTER 29

*G*io froze as the car began to slide farther into the lake. His effort to pry the seat open wider had started a slow glide down the slope the vehicle was resting on.

Gasping, he jumped out and braced against the doorframe, using all his strength to stop its momentum. His feet slipped in the mud. Desperately, he pushed while the distant sound of another car registered.

Had Richard regained consciousness? Was he escaping?

"Hold on, Sophia," he called to her when he heard Enzo shouting. "I'm over here!"

Flashlight beams swept over him, and multiple male voices called out as they ran into the water. "They're coming, *mi amore*."

"Hurry!" she cried, but it sounded garbled.

Despite his best efforts, the car had sunk more and the water level nearly covered the gap. Sophia had her face stuck in the opening, but there were little waves lapping up higher, and she was swallowing some water.

"Help me!" he cried when Enzo reached him. "He locked her in and threw away the key."

Enzo ran to the other side and opened the door while two other men moved to the front of the car to try and stop it from submerging further.

A shout went up and one of the men, Linetti, splashed into view.

"We're on a drop-off and the front wheels are over the edge!" he reported. "I almost fell in. If the car goes any farther, we won't be able to stop it. It's deep. Too deep."

*Fuck!*

"Brace it!" Enzo snapped.

Behind them, Linetti called the police and updated them on their situation.

"It's going to be okay, Sophia," Gio said, reaching into the gap to grab her hands.

He prayed he wasn't lying. Beside him, Enzo moved up and down, looking for the obstruction that was keeping the seat up.

"There's nothing blocking it," he said. "It's just stuck. We have to work it back and forth."

"*Cazzo.* Sophia! Can you hear me?"

By now, the water had risen above her ears. He could still see her mouth at the gap, desperately spitting out water. Her face was almost completely covered. She didn't answer them.

Gio sucked in a big gulp of air and stuck his face into the gap. Covering her lips with his own, he breathed into her, holding her hand the whole time.

"Gio, you have to move her back or we'll slam this thing into her face. There must be an air pocket at the other side. That back edge is still above the surface."

*Madre di Dio.* He broke off and moved back

"Sophia, baby, we need you to move!" he shouted, but with her ears submerged he couldn't be sure she heard them.

"Gio, we have to do this!" Enzo ordered.

"Fuck, fuck, fuck!" He squeezed Sophia's hand hard, and she squeezed it back.

His heart was threatening to burst open in his chest. Shaking, he took another breath and bent to give it to Sophia, expelling everything he had in his lungs before reaching into the trunk and taking hold of her shoulders.

Roaring in pain, he pushed her hard towards the back of the trunk.

He was almost blind with fear and rage, but he did what Enzo was yelling at him to do. Together, they rocked the seat back and forth while the other two men braced the car as best they could.

It was inevitable that the car slid farther down the slope. The water rose and submerged the opening. Every second that passed was like a dagger to his heart.

And then it got worse.

Ominous bubbles rose up in front of him from the gap. It was taking too long. Sophia was losing air. She was drowning.

"Pull, pull harder!" Enzo was yelling himself hoarse, but there was no point.

Gio was already at his limit, the muscles in his arms tearing as they pried the seat wider. It gave suddenly, sending his head slamming into the back of the front seat. Ignoring the flash of pain, he lunged forward, reaching into the water-filled space.

He caught hold of something and pulled Sophia out by the leg. He gathered her to him, positioning her head above the water, but she didn't move.

"Gio, let's go! Give her to me," Enzo shouted at him.

Twisting around, he held her out, forcing himself to let her go. Enzo picked up Sophia's limp body, moving away so he could climb out of the back seat. Behind them, the two other guys let go and the car slid deep into the water.

The front end went over the hidden edge below, upending the back like the Titanic before the whole thing slid down with a huge gurgle of escaping air.

The four of them turned and started for the shore. The freezing air filled Gio's burning lungs as he struggled to reach the water's edge.

Enzo laid Sophia down on the gravel bank, and Gio fell down next to her, working off his sodden coat so he could move better. Bending, he opened her mouth and breathed into it, but the cold had weakened him and he started coughing.

"Let me," Enzo said, gently pushing him aside.

Nodding, Gio let the more experienced man work while he took Sophia's cold still hand in his.

"Please, baby, please wake up," he whispered.

Linetti and the other junior security guy crowded around them. He sat helplessly, watching another man try to save the love of his life.

*Please, God, please let him save her!*

If he lost Sophia, he couldn't go on. He'd spend the rest of his days reliving the moment where he pushed her away, drowning her in that water-filled trunk.

Sophia hadn't moved in all this time. She lay there unconscious, her caramel skin pale yellow in the moonlight. Enzo continued chest compressions, periodically breaking off to administer air. Long minutes passed with no change.

There was no hint of movement, no rise and fall of her chest outside of what Enzo was forcing her body to do.

She was dead. Sophia was dead.

# CHAPTER 30

Gio sat on the rocky shore. Numbly, he stared down at Sophia's hand in his. He tried to squeeze it, but he could barely feel it. Distantly he could make out the sounds of sirens and shouting, but it was a world away, one where there was still warmth and sunshine.

This place was cold and empty. Nothing mattered, not even when the paramedics ran up and took over chest compressions from Enzo.

It was too late.

"Gio!"

It was Enzo, waving in his face. He was saying something about not watching, but Gio ignored him. All that mattered was holding her hand and not letting go.

They had thrown a blanket over Sophia and another over him, but one of the EMTs was still pushing on her chest. Another had one of those plastic things they fit over her mouth with a bulb attached. The EMT kept squeezing it, forcing air in and out of Sophia's lungs like a bellows.

He should tell them it was too late. He had pushed her into the water-filled trunk and she had drowned.

In the end, it hadn't been Richard. *He* had killed her.

But Gio didn't say anything, and he didn't move. He was made of stone, up until the moment Sophia turned and coughed, spitting out water. Then he was shouting—or it should have been. His voice came out thin and half-strangled.

"Sophia!"

She was alive. The relief would have knocked him to his knees if he hadn't already been sitting.

"Baby, look at me," he said, his grip tightening on her hand as he brought it to his lips.

"What happened?" she whispered. Her voice was raspy, damaged from nearly drowning.

"You're fine now," Gio said, his head swimming. "Don't try to talk."

She grimaced and tried to sit up, but stopped short and put a hand on her chest as if it hurt.

"Stay down, miss," one of the EMTs ordered. "We're bringing a stretcher."

Sophia gave him a tiny nod, but her attention was diverted to something behind them. Gio turned around to see Richard being walked to a police cruiser. The Englishman was on his feet with his hands cuffed behind his back, weeping openly.

"I'm sorry!" he kept crying. "I'm sorry!"

*You haven't begun to be sorry*, Gio vowed to himself.

He turned back to Sophia and tried to stand as the EMTs transferred her to a stretcher, but he must have moved too quickly because he staggered. Despite being fitted with an oxygen tank, Sophia reached out to him, touching his left arm.

"Gio, you're bleeding!"

Glancing down at his arm, he was surprised to see a stream of bright red blood flowing down to his elbow.

Everything grew very bright for an instant. The glare of the headlights from so many emergency vehicles temporarily blinded him.

*Wait.* The popping sound. Richard had pointed something at him. There had been a noise and then his arm had stung.

"Oh," he said slowly. His voice sounded as if it was coming from a million miles away.

"I've been shot."

Then everything went dark.

# CHAPTER 31

*S*ophia grimaced and cracked one eye open. Bright fluorescents stung her sensitive retinas. With a little groan, she lifted her head and looked around.

Oh, yeah.

She was in a hospital room, hooked up to wires and tubes. The EMTs had saved her life last night, but her ribs were bruised and one of them was cracked. Breathing was painful. She reminded herself that it was a small price to pay for being alive—repeatedly.

The clock on the wall read two PM. Barely five hours had passed since she'd finally gone to sleep, but she'd refused to rest until she knew Gio was out of danger.

He'd had emergency surgery when they had arrived at the hospital. The bullet hadn't been in a dangerous place, but he had lost a lot of blood. Enzo had told her that Gio hadn't even noticed, and none of his security team knew he had been shot.

He could have died. It had been so close, but the cold water of the quarry slowed the bleeding down, enough to allow the doctors to save his life with multiple transfusions.

It was ironic that she'd been in better shape than Gio in the end. In fact, the hospital staff had to negotiate with her to stay in bed while he was under. The surgeon assured her he was just sleeping off the anesthetic, but he still hadn't woken when she finally collapsed.

In the meantime, Gio's best friend Alex had blown in, throwing his weight around and shouting at people. Most of the doctors and nurses scrambled to carry out his orders. The rest ran around trying to escape. She was grateful for Alex's presence. He had made sure the staff would wake her if there was any change with Gio. There was also the added benefit of him interceding between her and the police.

Detectives had come to interview to find out what had happened. She quickly understood that their primary concern was the Italian billionaire's life, but since it was also her chief concern she didn't begrudge them their questions.

However, they grilled her relentlessly, making her repeat over and over again what Richard had done. They wanted to know every detail of her history with him. And all she wanted to do was find out how Gio was.

Alex had come in during the middle of all that. He'd shut the detectives down with a brusque commanding presence she'd occasionally glimpsed Gio use when he was talking business. The questions had stopped immediately, the officers cowed by that dominance that must have been innate to the rich and powerful.

Right before the detectives had left, Alex had taken them aside and hissed something with a ferocious expression. It had taken her a minute to realize he was calling for Richard's head. Alex had looked so intimidating that she'd blurted out an apology to him for putting Gio in danger, stunning him into silence.

"Never apologize for something like that," he said, his brow creased. "Gio loves you, and he wouldn't want you to feel guilty for some psycho's actions."

"It wasn't psychotic," she said, explaining about the stolen research and how Richard would get fired once the truth was out.

"He did this for a *job?*" Alex asked in disbelief.

She shrugged. "You'd be surprised what people will do for tenure."

The handsome Greek man had shaken his head and promised to follow up with the police and Gio's family so she could rest. But that had been hours ago and she had slept enough. Gio should be awake now and she wanted to see him.

With slow painful movements, she rolled to the side and pushed herself up to a sitting position. She wasn't hooked up to an IV, but she did have a monitor taped to her finger. Taking it off, she braced herself on the bed, hoping the oversized hospital gown wouldn't fly open in the back while she hunted down Gio.

Sophia stopped short in the doorway. Alex hadn't left. He was pacing in the hallway and, for a second, the expression of dismay on his face terrified her until she heard what he was saying.

"No, no. Stay put, Calen, Gio's going to be fine. Him and Sophia both. You have enough to deal with. How is Maia taking it?" Alex paused and grimaced. "How much blood? Fuck," he said. "And you said you think her family is involved?" He broke off and saw Sophia standing there. "Listen, I've got to go. Sophia woke up. Okay, I will."

He hung up the phone and gave her a reassuring smile, waving away a nurse who hurried in her direction.

"What's going on?"

"Nothing for you to worry about," he said, coming closer. "You should be in bed."

She narrowed her eyes and stared him down—or up. He was a head taller than she was. There was a bit of a standoff for a minute, but Alex soon caved in to her stubbornness.

"Okay, something is going on with one of Maia's friends," he explained. "She's gone missing. Calen wanted to come when he heard Gio is in the hospital, but Maia is frantic and they can't fly over here."

"Because they found blood. A lot of it," she supplied, nodding sickly.

Alex inhaled deeply and held out his hands in a gesture oddly reminiscent of Gio. "I don't want you to worry about this. You don't even know the girl. I haven't even met her. Just focus on getting well again and go lie down."

Struggling against a surreal sense of detachment, she agreed— but not about lying down. "I want to see Gio."

"He's fine—"

"*Now*, Alex."

She could tell he wanted to argue with her, but after a slight hesitation his expression softened. "Follow me."

Gio's room was two floors up. Judging by its size, he'd been given the presidential suite of hospital rooms. He was lying on the bed asleep, a little pale, but nowhere near as bad as she'd imagined. But she didn't relax until his broad chest moved up and down in deep even breaths.

Without waiting for help, she went to the side of the bed and climbed in. Luckily, it didn't seem to be a standard size. Apparently, the presidential suite meant bigger hospital beds too.

Alex made an approving little noise as she arranged herself to cuddle up on Gio's right, avoiding the bandage on his left side. Once his good arm was touching hers, she fell asleep instantly.

When she woke, she was staring into bright gold eyes.

"I'm so sorry, *mi amore*," Gio whispered.

Raising a brow, she gave him a mock scowl. "You better not be apologizing for saving my life."

He didn't smile. In fact, it looked like she'd broken his heart.

"I'm sorry for killing you."

"*What?*"

His amazing eyes grew red and he blinked rapidly. "In the car, when you were trapped. We had to shut you in the trunk to work the seat loose. We hoped there was air at the other end, but it had sunk too far." He raised his hands and gave them a damning glance. "I pushed you away, and you drowned. You were dead."

Sophia's mouth dropped open. She didn't remember that, but her memory was still pretty fuzzy about last night. Inhaling deeply, she moved until she was burrowing into Gio's arms.

"I was dead the minute Richard locked me in the trunk. The only reason I'm still alive is because you saved me." She tilted her head to meet his eyes. "What were you doing there, anyway?"

He bit his upper lip and sucked in a breath. "Um, after I received your text I decided to wait for you outside of Richard's."

Her eyes widened.

"Don't get mad," he said quickly. "I was simply concerned for you. It turns out I had good reason to be."

Sophia buried her face in his chest. "Man, you're never going to let me live that down, are you?"

His good arm came up from underneath her to pass over her back before stopping at her butt. Pushing her tighter against him, he lowered his head to kiss her forehead. "I'm not going to say I told you so—after today. I told you so," he added playfully.

She wrinkled her nose at him and reached over to twist one of his nipples through his hospital gown.

"Ow!" he said, laughing. "All right, I'm sorry. I won't say it again."

Mollified she gave him a quick kiss. "You weren't right about everything. Richard didn't attack me because he was obsessed with me. He believed I'd be easier to control if we were still together. He knew I'd find out about the stolen research sooner or later. And I was sort of a pushover back when we were a couple."

Gio snorted. "Well, you're not one now. In fact you're the strongest, most fierce woman I know. Enzo said if you hadn't kicked the seat open as far as you did we might not have been able to free you in time."

He paused to run a finger down her cheek. "I can't believe

Richard thought he was going to get away with it. He should have known I would turn the world over if you disappeared."

Hugging him tighter, Sophia rubbed her cheek against him. "Have I told you I love you lately?"

He smiled down at her, a soft hot grin lighting up his face. "No, but you did yell it not so long ago."

She giggled. "Now you can hear it at a normal volume. I love you."

Gingerly, he moved his bad arm so he could trace her lower lip with his fingers. "And I love you, *mi amore*. More than anything."

# EPILOGUE

Sophia spun in her office chair while she tried to find the right words to say to Maia over the phone. She knew Calen wanted everyone to be as honest as they could about the possibility of a happy ending when it came to the disappearance of her friend, Tahlia. But she couldn't dash all of her new friend's hopes, either.

"Maia, I think you're right. Until they find a body, you have to keep looking—as long as you're not knocking down doors yourself. You're a mother, right? You have a little girl, and she has to be your priority."

"I know that," Maia said with a sigh. "And there's no way in hell Calen would let me search myself. He has three guys on it. But I can tell he thinks it's pointless."

"Don't give up," Sophia said in a low voice. Where would she be if Gio had given up on her?

"I won't," Maia said after a pause. "Listen, I have to go. The baby's crying."

"Okay. We'll see you next week," Sophia promised.

Gio was flying them to New York for the opening of a new

five-star hotel. He was an investor in the Caislean chain, and they were both invited to stay at the hotel that first week. So were Gio's other University friends, so it would be a reunion of sorts.

"See you then," Maia said before hanging up.

Sophia put down the receiver of her phone and stared at it for a while. With all the good in her life now, there was also some bad. She felt terrible for Maia, but there was little she could do except support her.

The recent events had taught her some valuable lessons, however. Chief among them was the realization that she should embrace Gio and everything that came with him. She wouldn't look back. Life was too short. Any second things could change and the people you loved might be gone, so you had to appreciate them now while you had them.

Kelly had gotten a little sick of hearing Sophia tell her she loved her. Gio hadn't. He never would. She was sure about that.

Glancing at the clock, she counted down the minutes till she could go home—the penthouse Gio had bought off Alex. She had given her landlord notice and they had moved the last of her belongings a few days ago.

For the foreseeable future, Gio was going to be working out of the London office, commuting there when he had meetings and working from home when he didn't.

His father hadn't been thrilled to hear that because it meant that Gio was effectively stepping back from many of his duties at the bank. But Salvatore didn't fight him on it—not since they had announced their engagement. As long as he finally got his grandchild somewhere down the line, Salvatore would deal with it.

Exactly when the latter was going to happen was something she'd been thinking about a lot recently. Elynn and Eva had been right. Gio longed for a family.

Of course, he hadn't said that. The one time she'd brought up children, Gio had told her it was enough to be married to her. He didn't want to pressure her into compromising her timeline or her professional goals. Babies could wait.

But with her new *carpe diem* attitude, she wasn't sure she wanted to wait anymore. Work shouldn't supersede what she wanted in her personal life, and she did want children. Why put them off? Especially since she had a partner who was going to be one hundred percent invested in them now.

At five o'clock sharp, Sophia was out the door, hurrying home to Gio. He'd been in London that morning for a meeting, but returned in plenty of time to make dinner tonight.

He loved to cook, and she loved letting him.

She burst through the door of the penthouse fifteen minutes later. Gio was already busy in the kitchen, sleeves rolled up, his hands covered with flour. He was making pasta from scratch. Ravioli from the looks of it.

"Hi baby," she said, kicking off her heels and running over to the kitchen to give him a proper greeting.

His gold eyes glowed warmly as he bent to return her kiss. He held up his floured hands regretfully. "I would hug you, *mi amore*, but I'd ruin that dress."

Glancing down at the deep purple number she was wearing, she nodded. "Let me change, and I'll come and help in a minute."

She ran to the bedroom, glorying in the domesticity of their relationship. Feeling a little wicked, she changed into her pajamas. They were staying in to watch the original Star Wars trilogy together for the first time, and she wanted to be comfortable. Of course, the fact that her new sleepwear consisted of sexy little silk negligees, instead of old flannel, would ensure they didn't finish their marathon tonight.

Throwing a robe over the brief little gown, she stepped into the bathroom. She washed up and then studied her reflection in the mirror.

A newer, more confident woman was staring back at her. Things had changed quite a bit since meeting Gio, including her self-image. She was proud of her curves and would never hide them again.

*Speaking of...*

Sophia put a hand on her belly, passing it over the softly rounded surface. She would never have one of those flat washboards you saw on magazines, but she no longer looked at it and despaired. It was healthy—no matter how big it got.

*Okay, here goes nothing.*

Reaching up she swung open the mirrored door to the medicine cabinet, taking out her birth control pills. She tossed them in the trash and went back out to the kitchen.

Pausing in the threshold, she took a minute to watch her man work. His tanned and very talented hands were busy shaping and assembling the pasta in neat little rows. He managed to keep the kitchen immaculate while he cooked, a feat she had never been capable of.

"Our kids are going to clean their own rooms without being asked, aren't they?" she asked with some amusement.

She waited for him for him to turn to her before pulling the sides of her robe apart to flash him, giving him an eyeful of her silk-bound body.

Gio dropped the piece of pasta he was holding on the floor. The next thing she knew, she was sitting on top of a pile of perfectly assembled little rows of ravioli.

"Gio, the dinner!"

"We can order in," he growled, his face buried in her neck.

Giggling, she wrapped her arms around his head, guiding it into her full breasts. Gio sighed like he was coming home. He tugged the thin straps of her gown down, leaving her naked from the waist up. Tugging his head closer, she guided his mouth to her dusky brown nipple.

He took one with a groan that reverberated down her body. Between her legs, her pussy contracted, sending little sparks of pleasure radiating out like fireworks.

She must have murmured that last part about fireworks out loud because Gio laughed before lifting his head. "You haven't seen anything yet."

His hands went for her gown, and she helped him by wiggling enough so he could pull it off. Completely naked, she wrapped her legs around his waist, enjoying the way the rough cloth of his pants and shirt felt against her bare skin. Shameless in her hunger, she rubbed up and down, abrading her nipples and wet pussy against him.

Gio said something in Italian she couldn't understand and his hands moved faster and harder in his eagerness. She loved being touched by him, the no-holds-barred way he handled her body—a little rough but always reverent. It was a heady combination of love and lust that never failed to arouse her.

Reclining on one arm, she scooted backward when he pushed her, bracing her leg on the edge on the counter. Gio's head moved between her legs, his tongue snaking out to lick and probe her. Moaning aloud, she threw her head back and shifted to brace herself with both arms.

She felt like a goddess being worshiped. Images of fertility idols danced behind her closed lids and she laughed aloud, something Gio apparently took personally. He sucked her clit into his mouth hard, nipping it with his teeth. His fingers circled her entrance and pushed inside, making her gasp.

"Not laughing now, are we?" he teased, making her giggle. He huffed against her wet lips and reached out to nip her again.

"*Oh, God*," she cried as his fingers worked inside her tight channel rhythmically, teasing her G-spot with determined strokes.

That was part of what she loved about him—he never wasted any time.

Her pussy had started to flutter and spasm around his fingers when he reached up to pull her hips to the edge of the counter. With one hand, he tore open his pants and then he was there, thick and strong, parting her folds with a long smooth push.

His size made it a little hard to take him easily, but that was why he was always careful to make sure she was burning to a fever pitch before he fucked her.

There was a little burn, but it dissipated quickly, transmuting into pleasure like quicksilver. Clamping down on him, she rocked when he moved, matching him thrust for thrust. He took a fistful of her hair and tugged her head to one side, exposing the length of her neck. His mouth moved up and down the sensitive skin there, leaving her weak and boneless in his arms.

He pulled her off the counter and onto the floor, a little rain of abused ravioli falling down on them. She was too out of breath to laugh. All she could do was hang on, grabbing his hips and ass while his cock drove deep. Each stroke caressed her sensitized nerves, sending little ripples of ecstasy throughout her body.

Her control started to splinter. Putting her lips to his ear, she urged him to go faster and harder with desperate little whispers. He slammed into her again and again, driving down in a counterpoint to the upward pitch of her hips. The friction grew like a sunburst filling the sky until she couldn't focus anymore. Vision blurred, she convulsed around him, fighting to hold the pulsing head of his cock tight against that magical little spot that made her shiver and writhe helplessly on the floor.

"*Madonna mia.*" Above her, Gio's head moved back, his neck corded with tension.

His cock jerked repeatedly, and she was filled with heat as he spilled his seed deep into her waiting womb. She cried out and wrapped her legs around his waist, taking all of him. Endless moments later he finally collapsed over her with a guttural groan.

Neither of them was capable of speech for a long time. They lay there on the floor until their bodies cooled and their breathing returned to normal. Eventually, Gio lifted his head to smile and kiss her softly.

She burst out laughing and reached up to pick off the stray

ravioli that had gotten stuck to his shoulder. "It's a pity, 'cause this looked delicious."

He grinned down at her wickedly. "I can make more."

Gio helped her to her feet and they took in the disaster that was now the kitchen. He couldn't hide his expression of dismay. Peeking at him from behind her lashes, she smiled and elbowed him in the ribs.

"You're dying to clean this all up, aren't you?"

He wrinkled his nose and threw an arm around her. "It can wait until after we shower."

Taking her hand, he led her to the massive master bedroom, a space bigger than her old apartment. He stood in front of her, pulling off his shirt and revealing that glorious six-pack. She wiped her mouth surreptitiously, in case she was drooling, and started to slip off her robe absently.

Damn, the man was gorgeous.

He was peeling off his pants when he turned to her with a contemplative expression. He said something she didn't catch. She was too busy staring at him. He possessed such masculine beauty, it was easy to forget that the best thing about him was his kindness and generous loving heart. Such a man shouldn't exist—let alone be hers.

"I'm sorry, what was that?" she asked, struggling to focus on his words.

He smiled. "I said I know you were joking about kids earlier. But I meant what I said when I proposed. I'm not in a rush to have a baby, no matter what my friends might have told you."

Reaching over, he tugged off her robe, which was trailing off one arm like a long forgotten streamer. He pressed a kiss to the sensitive spot behind her ear before taking the length of silk and folding it neatly on a chair.

He was perfect. Absolutely perfect. How could she not want to have a baby with this man?

"Yeah, about that…"

The End

---

Continue the Singular Obsession Series with Patrick Tyler and Tahlia's story, Trick's Trap, A Readers' Favorite Romance Sizzle Finalist!

*"She's a gamble he's willing to take."*

*"Trick's Trap by Lucy Leroux is a mesmerizing contemporary romance with a twist; it is sizzling and engrossing." - Romuald Dzemo for Readers' Favorite*

Thank you for reading the Roman's Woman! Reviews are an author's bread and butter. If you liked the story please consider leaving one.

Subscribe to the Lucy Leroux Newsletter for a *free* full-length novel!
www.authorlucyleroux.com/newsletter
or keep up with her L.B. Gilbert releases
www.elementalauthor.com/newsletter

# ABOUT THE AUTHOR

Lucy Leroux is another name for USA Today Bestselling Author L.B. Gilbert.

Seven years ago Lucy moved to France for a one-year research contract. Six months later she was living with a handsome Frenchman and is now married with an adorable half-french toddler.

When her last contract ended Lucy turned to writing. Frustrated by the lack of quality romance erotica she created her own.

Cursed is the first of many regency novels. Additionally, she writes a bestselling contemporary series. The 'Singular Obsession' books are a combination of steamy romance and suspense that feature intertwining characters in their own stand-alone stories. Follow her on twitter or facebook, or check our her website for more news!

www.authorlucyleroux.com

# BOOKS BY LUCY LEROUX

# TRICK'S TRAP

## A SINGULAR OBSESSION, BOOK FIVE

*She's a gamble he's willing to take.*

When world-class poker player Patrick Tyler meets his match, Tahlia, in an underground game, he's immediately drawn to her swift talent and striking beauty. But it's not long after their meeting that she mysteriously disappears. With nothing but a bloody crime scene as a clue to her whereabouts, she's presumed dead.

Or so he thought...

A chance encounter changes everything.

Alone, afraid, and homeless, Tahlia needs Patrick now more than ever.

Feeling compelled to help, he throws her a much-needed lifeline--a lady's choice card game. When Tahlia's family finds out Patrick's plans, they will stop at nothing to get their hands on her. Will Tahlia be able to protect him from her family or will this game of high stakes end in the most devastating loss?

Available Now on Select Vendors

# CURSED

## A SPELLBOUND REGENCY NOVEL

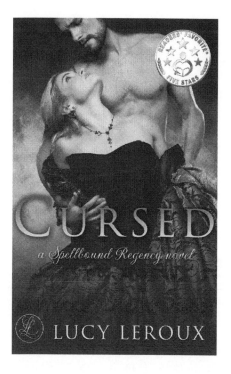

**Isobel Sterling is a governess with a lot of secrets—including an uncanny ability she's been hiding her whole life. Until the day arrives when she has to use it to save herself from a madman. But first she has to master it. *Fast*.**

Governess Isobel Sterling feels fortunate to have found a safe haven in the Montgomery household. The children are kind and The Lord and Lady of the house leave her alone. Her life is as good as it can get, until the day mysterious visitors arrive from abroad.

At first Isobel is flattered by the single-minded attention she receives from their handsome young guest, Matteo Garibaldi. At least she is until girls in the village begin to disappear. Isobel has a terrible suspicion that the disappearances are linked to the darkness she can see growing behind

Matteo's eyes. Filled with dread she does everything possible to avoid his company—until she is locked in with him for the night.

Available Now on All Vendors

# WRITING AS L.B. GILBERT

# DISCORDIA

## AN ELEMENTALS PREQUEL SHORT

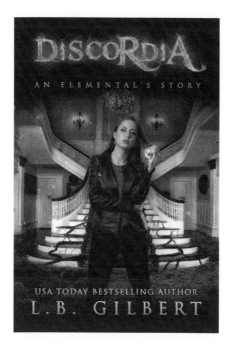

Fire Elemental Diana's first solo mission is a disappointing one—stop a pack of carrion-eating fae from eating tourists in the Everglades. But then a Greek God's relic complicates her simple case.

Free Everywhere

# KIN SELECTION

## A SHIFTER'S CLAIM NOVELLA

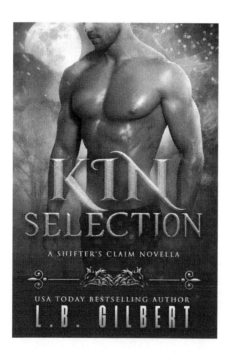

**Animal activist Deena Hammond had no idea the wolf cub she just rescued is a shifter—not until the Werewolf sent to recover him kidnaps her.**

Saving a wolf cub from an animal testing facility changes everything for Deena Hammond, a feisty and dedicated animal activist. Determined to protect the innocent animal, Deena's shocked when the cub shifts into a small toddler right before her eyes.

Bound by honor to keep their existence a secret, Yogi, a wolf shifter, kidnaps Deena and brings her back to the cub's family. Knowing a hellion with curves likes hers is the ultimate temptation for the other males in his pack, Yogi stays close to Deena, fighting to keep his desire for her under control. But she just might ignite the animal within him.

Available Now on All Vendors

# FIRE

## THE ELEMENTALS BOOK ONE, A READERS' FAVORITE SILVER MEDAL WINNER!

**A kick-ass heroine with pyrokinetic abilities and a license to kill. Enter Alec...vampire, scholar, and worst of all—*fan*. What could possibly go wrong?**

Diana, the fire Elemental, is nearly burned out. Tired of traveling the world and losing innocent lives, she's slowly slipping into a depression that may consume her. But when she discovers that a child's life is in danger, she feels compelled to help. However, teaming up with one of the most powerful vampires in North America is the last thing she wants to do.

Academic scion, Alec Broussard prefers his studies over the opulent and vicious lifestyles of vampires. And when he learns of another missing child, Alec can't shake the suspicion that his coven may be to blame. Joining forces with an Elemental may be his only hope to save the child and clear his coven's name.

As Diana and Alec work together to save the children, they must relinquish their prejudices and trust one another. In time, Alec is wearing down the walls around her. But just when their friendship intensifies, Alec's future is threatened. Now, it's up to Diana to save him before it's too late. Can this Elemental find the fire within her to protect him once and for all?

Available Now on Select Vendors

# FORSAKEN

## A STANDALONE, PART OF THE CURSED ANGEL COLLECTION

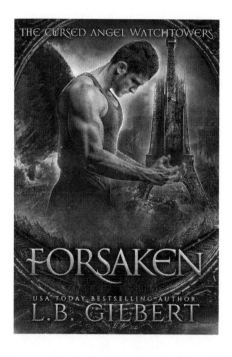

**Years ago, he left her to die in the wastelands. Now his fate rests in her hands.**

Cast out of Heaven thousands of years ago, Ash is given a chance to redeem himself. If he defeats the demon king and delivers the city from the curse plaguing it, his long exile will end.

But raising an army and killing the king is only the beginning. Now, in the ruins of post-apocalyptic Paris, this fallen angel is struggling to keep Bastille afloat amidst a never-ending series of disasters.

His only hope in stopping the relentless cycle of destruction rests in Kara, a woman he'd betrayed years before and leader of a mysterious band of scavengers who have somehow escaped the curse's influence.

Available Now on Select Vendors

Printed in Great Britain
by Amazon

87694081R00149